Kalki's

PONNIYIN SELVAN

Dr M. Rajaram is an exceptional IAS Officer with balanced views on administration. His efficiency in administration has brought him many prestigious awards, notably the Best Collector Award, Malcolm Award, Anna Award, etc., from the government. He has authored more than 40 books: *Quality Educational Administration: Who Will Bell the Cat?, Thirukkural: Pearls of Inspiration, The Elemental Warriors, Food for Thought, Passport for Success, Blossoms in English, The Yellow Line, Glory of Thirukkural, Higher Education for Better Tomorrow, Better English, Glory of Tamil, The Success Mantra in Bhagavad Gita, Tic-Toc-Tic, Bosses: The Good, the Bad and the Ugly, Corporate Wisdom in Thirukkural, Oriental Wisdom,* etc. His English translation of *Thirukkural* earned him a well-deserved tribute from Dr Abdul Kalam, the late President of India. His book is so popular that it has been added to the White House Library.

Praise for the book

'*Ponniyin Selvan*, a popular Tamil novel unfolds an epic story based on historical facts and characters with lot of twists and turns keeping the readers spellbound reflecting the glory of Indian literature.'

—Sri M. Venkaiah Naidu
Hon'ble Vice President of India

'*Ponniyin Selvan* is an outstanding historical Tamil novel rendered in simple and elegant style by Dr M. Rajaram.'

—Ki Rajanarayanan
Sahitya Akademi Award Winning Tamil Writer

'*Ponniyin Selvan* is a story of plots within plots highlighting the greatness of the Chola Empire rendered in elegant style without losing its original flavour.'

—Dr Avvai Natarajan
Former Vice Chancellor, Tamil University, Tanjore

Kalki's

PONNIYIN SELVAN

Volume 3

Translated by M. Rajaram

RUPA

Published by
Rupa Publications India Pvt. Ltd. 2022
7/16, Ansari Road, Daryaganj
New Delhi 110002

Sales centres:

Allahabad Bengaluru Chennai
Hyderabad Jaipur Kathmandu
Kolkata Mumbai

ISBN: 978-93-91256-18-0

Tenth impression 2022

15 14 13 12 11 10

Printed in India

Contents

I

Ferocious Boar

Vandiyathevan sensed the danger to the crown prince and attacked the boar with his spear, but in vain. The prince, caught under his horse, was struggling to get out. The boar started attacking Vandiyathevan's horse. But he caught hold of the branch of a tree and let go of the horse. Now the boar turned towards the prince. Just then, the branch which Vandiyathevan was holding on to broke, and he fell down and became unconscious.

When he opened his eyes, Aditya Karikalan was sprinkling water on his face. Vandiyathevan sat up.

'My God! Prince, you are alive!'

'Yes, thanks to you…'

'What happened to the boar?'

'It's there.' Aditya Karikalan pointed at something a little way away.

Vandiyathevan looked in that direction. The boar was dead.

'Prince, such a small animal gave us so much trouble! But tell me how you managed to kill the beast.'

'I didn't kill it. It was you and your spear.'

Vandiyathevan was puzzled.

'Prince! But I didn't do anything, I am ashamed that I could not help you in danger.'

'I came out from under my horse and took your spear and threw it on the beast with all my force. It fell with a deafening noise. At the same time, you landed right on the boar from the tree. It did not die of the spear alone. The beast died of shock.'

Aditya Karikalan laughed. Vandiyathevan joined him.

'Oh my God! What a ferocious beast!' remarked Vandiyathevan

'I really thought that the lord of death had come in the form of a boar!'

'Prince! That's a good sign. Death that followed you is dead. All our worries are gone. And we have won in our challenge with Kandamaran. Let us drag this boar along. Shall we leave now?'

'I'm tired. Why don't we relax here for a while?'

'This is the first time I've heard that you are tired. Yes, you were caught under the horse for a long time.'

'That's nothing. My mind is also tired. Vandiyatheva, didn't we see a boat a little while ago? It must be somewhere near this bank. Why don't we go and look for it?'

Vandiyathevan was startled.

'Oh my god! Where is the leopard?'

'It should be hiding somewhere.'

The two looked around.

Vandiyathevan shouted, 'There!'

There was a canal feeding water into the lake. A fallen tree in the canal was acting as a bridge between the banks. The leopard was walking over it.

'My God! The women in the boat!'

The two men shouted simultaneously, concerned for the women.

'Wounded leopards are dangerous.'

'Vandiyatheva, let's kill the leopard and take it along with the boar.'

'How can we cross this canal? We can walk over the fallen tree, but our horses cannot.'

'There is not much water flowing in the canal. We can get down and walk through the canal along with the horses.'

Both the horses stood together, like their masters. They appeared to be exchanging notes in their own language about the dangers they faced. The men mounted their horses and led them to the canal. The water level was low but muddy. The horses had a hard time crossing the canal.

The two looked in all the directions before riding on. Karikalan was ready with his bow and arrows. Vandiyathevan was ready to throw the spear at the leopard.

Suddenly a woman's shrill cry was heard over the usual sounds of the forest: 'Leopard! Leopard! Danger! Danger!

When Manimekalai spotted the leopard on the tree branch, one of the maids in the kitchen in the resthouse also saw the animal and screamed. The two men heard the noise. They rode fast in the direction of the voice. They were shocked by what they saw.

Nandini and Manimekalai were climbing down the steps to bathe in the lake. At the same time, the leopard was slowly climbing up the branches of the tree. The leopard had been badly hurt in its fight with the wild boar. Survival instinct was topmost on its mind. It was ready to pounce on the two women. Karikalan and Vandiyathevan sensed the danger. Vandiyathevan was hesitant to use the spear. If it missed the mark and fell on the ladies, it might kill them. But Karikalan, without hesitation, aimed his arrow. The arrow landed on the leopard's stomach. The leopard roared and pounced on the two women. Nobody knew what happened. The leopard and the two women could not be seen. A few minutes later, all three appeared in different places in the lake. A part of the lake turned red, mixed with blood.

2

Love and Revenge

The two friends came running to the bank of the lake. The leopard was floating on the surface of the lake. The two men jumped into the water in search of the women.

Vandiyathevan swam towards Manimekalai who had fallen into the water because of shock. When she saw Vandiyathevan swimming to her, she closed her eyes, unable to control her joy.

But she did not realize that Karikalan had stopped him and sent him towards Nandini. Karikalan now went to Manimekalai who did not open her eyes till Karikalan lifted her to the shore and gently placed her down. Only when the crown prince placed his fingers near her nose to check her breathing did she slowly open her eyes. She thought that her saviour was her beloved Vandiyathevan. She wanted to express all her love and gratitude through her glance. The moment she saw the crown prince, she got up and moved away in shock.

The prince laughed.

'Manimekalai, you don't like me?'

'Prince, how can a girl not feel shy when some stranger touches her?'

'Silly girl, you have made me a stranger. Don't you know that your people are planning to get us married?'

'Till their plans materialise, you are a stranger to me.'

'But at least tell me whether you like this alliance or not.'

The Princess of Kadamboor thought for a while.

'Prince, why don't you talk to my father?'

'Girl, if your father agrees, will you…?'

'If my father agrees to the match, accordingly, I'll give a suitable reply to him.'

Karikalan laughed again.

'Manimekalai, I know the cause of your disappointment. Had Vandiyathevan carried you ashore, you would have been happy.'

Manimekalai was embarrassed.

'Prince, you know my mind.'

'Yes, I know your mind. Look there. See the joy on Nandini's face in the company of Vandiyathevan.'

Manimekalai looked in the direction pointed out by the crown prince and felt envious.

The leopard's claws had hurt Nandini's shoulders. After saving Nandini, fear gripped Vandiyathevan. Nandini smiled.

'Why are you trembling in fear? Am I a leopard?'

'Queen, I am shaken because I had to touch you and carry you.'

'Guilty minds are always shaken.'

'I am innocent, Queen.'

'Are you innocent? You sought my help to get into Tanjore Fort. You promised to come to me after meeting the princess at Palayarai. But you didn't keep up the promise and yet you consider yourself innocent?'

'Queen, pardon me for my lapses. I'm bound by the orders of my boss.'

'Yes. Even to save a woman from the mouth of a leopard, you need the orders of your boss. I was watching. The prince showed an unusual interest in rescuing Manimekalai. I think he would have been glad if I had drowned. And without knowing the mind of your boss, you have saved me.'

'Queen, it's not like that. The crown prince has come all the way from Kanchi to meet you.'

'But you came running to stop him from coming here and failed in your mission. Remember whenever you interfere with my work, you will fail.'

Nandini continued.

'Your guilt is evident from your face. On that fateful night, at the memorial in Thirupurambiyam, you were caught by my men. If I had winked my eyes, you would have been killed in no time. But I saved you. You remain ungrateful.'

'Not at all, Queen. My heart is full of gratitude for you.'

'I've been here for several days. And not once did you come to meet me to express that gratitude.'

'You are the queen and the wife of the finance minister of the Chola Kingdom.'

'You are insinuating that I am married to an old man! Don't mention that I am the wife of Paluvettarayar. I am not his wife.'

'Oh my God! What are you saying?'

'Nothing but the truth. If a girl is forcibly abducted and brought home, will she become the abductor's wife by default? A forced marriage will never bind her.'

'But... but... you...'

'I know what you are coming to. I consented to a forced marriage for a specific reason. There is a special trait for all women. They will never rest till they avenge the injustice meted out to them. You never helped me to find my love; please help me now at least to seek revenge.'

Vandiyathevan felt as if he had been struck by lightning and he remained in a state of shock.

'Queen! What do you mean? What is the connection between me and your love? What is the connection between love and revenge?'

'There is a connection. But right now, I have no time to explain. Look there. The prince and Manimekalai are coming towards us. If you come to my room by midnight tomorrow, I'll tell you everything.'

'Queen, how is it possible to come at midnight. Your chamber is highly guarded.'

'You escaped from the same ladies' chambers once, didn't you? Why can't you use the same way? Where there is a will, there is a way.'

Vandiyathevan was shocked. But Nandini remained silent with a seductive smile playing on her lips.

3

You Are My Sister

Karikalan and Manimekalai reached Vandiyathevan and Nandini. The prince noticed the blood on Nandini's cheeks and shoulders.

'Oh my God! You were hurt by the leopard!' exclaimed the Prince.

'Yes, Your Highness. But the animal could hurt only my body, not my mind,' Nandini replied with sarcasm.

These words hit him hard. Before the crown prince could respond, Manimekalai spoke anxiously.

'Yes, sister! The wound is deep. Fortunately, I have some ointment.'

'Dear sister, do you have any ointment to heal the wounds in my heart?'

'Yes, I have. Come with me.'

Manimekalai dragged Nandini to the resthouse. The two friends followed them and sat on a marble bench under a huge mango tree near the resthouse.

Soon Nandini and Manimekalai returned. Nandini's wounds were covered by a dark paste.

'We are waiting to take leave of you.'

'Prince, it is already lunch-time. Having come this far and saving us from danger, it is but proper that you stay and have lunch with us.'

'We'll stay, provided Manimekalai reveals that magical ointment that heals the wounded heart.'

'Prince, perhaps she refers to time, the healer,' remarked Vandiyathevan.

'There are some wounds which even time can't heal,' said Nandini.

'Tears are the best healing medicine for women.'

'You are wrong. Tears don't heal all wounds.'

'Well, Queen, if we are not right, tell us what you think is right.'

'Music and song are the best remedies.'

'Yes, Kandamaran also said that his sister Manimekalai is good at music and singing.'

'Gentlemen, stay with us for lunch and Princess Manimekalai's musical performance.'

'We'll stay,' agreed the crown prince enthusiastically.

Vandiyathevan stood up and looked around.

'Vandiyatheva, what are you looking for?'

'Prince! I am thinking of the leopard and these two women. I wonder how this leopard managed to live after being caught by them.'

'Didn't we see the dead leopard floating in the water?' quizzed the prince.

The crown prince too stood up.

'Look there. The leopard is trying to get into the boat.'

Karikalan smiled.

'Aha! The leopard is strong-willed. Looks like it is not destined to die.'

'Come, Prince, let's go and kill the leopard. A wounded leopard is most dangerous.'

'Does a wounded leopard require two great warriors? Manimekalai can easily kill the beast with her knife.'

'Vandiyatheva! The Queen of Paluvoor has high regard for our valour. Can't you manage it alone?'

'Shall I send Manimekalai?' asked Nandini.

Vandiyathevan murmured,

'Yes, but the problem is that she might apply some ointment and revive the animal.'

'What are you looking at?' asked the crown prince.

'I will bring the head of the wounded leopard and place it at the feet of the Paluvoor Queen and make her happy.'

With these words, Vandiyathevan walked away. Manimekalai had already gone to supervise the cooking preparations.

'Nandini, I came here only because of your invitation. With tears in your eyes, you begged for the life of Veerapandiya. In a state of frenzy, I brutally beheaded him. Of course, you won't forget the past. Can't you at least forgive me? Why did you ask me to come here?'

'My Lord, you are the first born of the emperor. I am after all an orphan. Who am I to forgive you?'

'No, Nandini! You are not an orphan. You are my sister, like Kundavai. I am your brother.'

'My Lord, since I have become somebody's wife you have been treating me like your sister. But how can I consider the emperor's son as my brother?'

'You have not understood me, Nandini. You are really my sister. You are the emperor's daughter.'

Nandini laughed as if she had heard a joke.

'Are you all right, Prince? Or have I gone insane?'

'I am sane. And so are you.'

'Prince! Why tease me? Do I look like the emperor's daughter? Do I have any royal signs on my face?'

'Nandini, I've been watching you since you were five. I have always been mesmerized by your radiant beauty. I understand the reason for it only now. Amongst the women married in the Chola clan, there is none equal to the beauty of my grandmother, Kalyani. Even at seventy, her beauty is still matchless. All her beauty has taken refuge in you. Even Princess Kundavai is no match for you. My grandmother's beauty has come to you through my father.'

'My Lord! What are you saying? I don't know if I have lost my mind or my hearing.'

'No, Nandini. You are all right. You are my father's daughter. That makes you, my sister. Before marrying my mother, the emperor fell in love with a fisherwoman of Lanka and married her. You are her daughter. And hence, my sister.'

Nandini appeared shocked. She was staring at the crown prince for a while. Then her face became calm again.

'My Lord, who told this to you? Was it, by any chance, the Vaanar Prince Vandiyathevan?'

'Yes, sister. Princess Kundavai conveyed this news through him.'

'Now I understand. People have been conspiring to keep us apart from the beginning. Looks like the conspirators are still busy in their avowed mission.'

'You are wrong, Nandini. There is no conspiracy here. When we were young, Queen Mother separated us. At that time, I didn't understand her actions. In fact, I was angry with her. Only now do I realize that she has saved us from a great disaster. They could have told us earlier. A great injustice was meted out to you and me by withholding the truth. Let the past be past. Let us forget it. Even if we cannot forget, let us at least forgive them.'

'Did Vandiyathevan tell you just this or is there something more to the story?'

'Why do you call it a story Nandini? Don't you believe it?'

'Prince, I don't believe it. If I were born as the emperor's daughter, why should I have to suffer so much? Ok, let's say it is true. I want to know whether he said something else.'

Karikalan hesitated and then poured out everything.

'Yes, he also told me that you are now conspiring with the bodyguards of the Pandiya King to destroy the Chola clan. You are worshipping a sword with the fish emblem belonging to the Pandyias. You also crowned a little boy as the Pandiya King at the war memorial in the forest near Thiruppurambiyam. Forget all that Nandini. You are the daughter of the Emperor Sundara Chola. You too have a right to share the glory of the Chola Kingdom. You are our dearest sister. It will be my first duty to set right all the wrongs done to you.'

'Lord, do you believe these stories? Then why did you wait for so many days? Why didn't you try to talk to me earlier?'

'I was confused, Nandini. I was also looking for the right time to explain everything to you. This is not something to be shared with you in the presence of others. Thanks to a wild boar and a leopard, I got the opportunity today.'

'The wild animals are dangerous but not as dangerous as human beings.'

'Sister, you said earlier that we cannot forget the past. I agreed. But I asked you to at least forgive me. You have not responded to my request till now.'

'My Lord, I'll forgive whatever you did to me in the past. Perhaps, I may forget them too. But I can never forgive what you did to me today.'

'Nandini, what did I do today?'

'I am coming to that. Look at that Vandiyathevan.

He saw me in Tanjore one day. He told me he would consider it a blessing if he were even by my feet. But I did not yield to his lust, therefore he has spun this yarn. He even promised to bring me your head if I wanted. He is afraid that I might share these things with you. That was why he tried to prevent your coming to Kadamboor. And that is why he never leaves your side. He is a treacherous fellow. I don't even want to touch him with my feet. And today you made him touch my body and carry me from the lake while you were a silent spectator. Now tell me, can I ever forget this? Or even forgive?'

Nandini's eyes went red. On hearing this, Karikalan was shocked.

'My dear sister, I don't know whom I should believe. Can Vandiyathevan be so cunning? I even thought of getting him married to Manimekalai.'

'My Lord, you need not believe my words. Just observe him for two days. You will know the truth.'

4

The Boat Moved Away

The Prince and Nandini continued their conversation.

'Nandini, it was not just Vandiyathevan who wanted to prevent me from coming to Kadamboor. Another fellow, who goes by the name Alvarkkadiyan too was against my visit. And to cap it all, the prime minister, the person whom I worship, also cautioned me.'

'The prime minister is your father's best friend and you also worship him. That's why he wants to be doubly sure that you don't get the crown.'

'What?'

'The prime minister thinks you are short-tempered and immature. He wants your brother to ascend the Chola throne. But when your brother went missing on the stormy seas, all his plans went amiss.'

'But why should all of them prevent our meeting?'

'I'm the only one who knows their minds. My Lord, many people think that I am Alvarkkadiyan's sister as I grew up in his father's house. But he had a secret love for me and wanted me to bear many children for him. Any man who comes near me comes only with a lustful motive.'

'Oh my God...'

'My Lord, that's my bad luck.'

'Why accuse everyone simply because of what that old man Paluvettarayar did to you?'

'Lord, I beg you, please don't speak ill of Paluvettarayar. He fell in love with me and married me. He made this orphan his queen.'

'Nandini! Have you really accepted him as your husband? Then... then...'

'No! But I'm indebted to him. It's just gratitude and nothing more. We are not living as husband and wife. I gave my heart only to one man. I will never take it back or give it to another.'

'Who is that lucky fellow, Nandini? No, you need not answer that question. But answer this: who are you? If you are not my father's daughter, if you are not my sister and if you are not Alvarkkadiyan's sister, then who are you?'

'Lord, I am dying to tell you. I'll tell you when we meet next.' Nandini broke off her conversation with the prince as she saw Vandiyathevan and Manimekalai approaching them.

Now Nandini spoke to Vandiyathevan.

'Your hands are empty. What happened to the leopard's head?'

'Queen, I'm not fortunate enough to place the head of the leopard at your feet.'

'Is this your valour? You used to boast about your clan. My Lord, you just beheaded the Pandiya King. But this man's ancestors plucked the heads of all the three emperors and planted them in their field as saplings.'

Nandini succeeded in poisoning the mind of the crown prince.

'Great planting! Great farming!' The prince laughed loudly to hide his disgust.

'You trumpet the glory of your ancestors but you can't even bring the head of a wounded leopard. Shame on you!'

'Queen, what could I do? The wounded leopard was dead. I didn't want to behead a dead leopard.'

'How did that happen? I saw the beast slowly climbing into the boat,' asked the Prince in surprise.

'It was I who pointed that out to you, My Lord. It got into the boat and then died. Perhaps, it felt guilty for hurting the junior Queen of Paluvoor.'

The crown prince cooled down.

'Vandiyathevan! It could have died in the water itself. Why did it get into the boat?'

'Prince, perhaps, it's like me, afraid of water. Of all the ways of dying, I dread dying in water.'

'But a short while ago you jumped, courageously into water. Perhaps, you have so much compassion for this naughty girl.' Nandini did not finish.

'Queen, honestly, I'm more afraid of women than water. I jumped in because the prince ordered me to. Only now do I realize that I shouldn't have done it.'

'Yes, yes. Now I remember. You are afraid of falling in water but you are never afraid of pushing somebody into water and drowning him.'

Nandini was cleverly alluding to the drowning of Prince Arulmoli in the stormy sea.

Manimekalai intuitively knew that Vandiyathevan was in trouble and the prince and Nandini were teasing him. She did not like the conversation.

'Sister, the food is getting cold. Let's go.'

Let the whole world oppose you. But I'll be on your side, my dear. Don't ever worry.

Manimekalai spoke to herself, pitiying Vandiyathevan.

She conveyed these words through her eyes to Vandiyathevan. But Vandiyathevan did not look at her even once. He was lost in his own world of grief.

Nandini's treacherous words, the great charge she had leveled against Vandiyathevan would shock any sensitive being. But if anyone were to study a little more about Nandini there wouldn't be anything shocking.

Nandini had been abandoned by her mother Mandakini and was brought up in a stranger's house. She was ridiculed and insulted by the children of the royal family. All her ill-feelings had crystallized into hatred. The only thought that filled her mind was a thirst for revenge. If only she had had a life of love and compassion, she would have been a normal person.

Whosoever loved her, either ignored and insulted her or died all of a sudden and vanished from her life.

Her life had been full of disappointments and grief, and her heart was now as hard as galvanized steel. What else is needed to make a girl's mind turn into poison?

The four were having their lunch in silence without the usual enthusiasm present at a picnic party. Nandini, Karikalan and Vandiyathevan were lost in their own personal grieving.

A few minutes after lunch, Manimekalai spoke to Nandini in a listless voice:

'Sister, shall we go back? Shall I ask the boat to be brought in? Are these people coming with us?'

Karikalan was shaken from his reverie.

'Aha! How can we go back without listening to this girl's music? Manimekalai, we are eager to hear your sweet voice. Please don't disappoint us.'

Nandini spoke for both.

'No, Prince, I have not forgotten that. Manimekalai, please bring your musical instrument.'

Manimekalai filled the place with melodious music. Everybody was mesmerized. A love song, in particular, filled the air with sweetness and aroma.

'Is that all a dream, my friend
The time we spent together
On the mountains
Beside the waterfalls
Beneath the fruit trees
Hand in hand lost in happiness
Defying all security
Like a thief you came in stealth
With boundless love hugged me tight
Smothered me with kisses....'

All were mesmerized...

Vandiyathevan looked at Manimekalai every now and then. And

every time he saw her, he found that she was looking at him with all the love in the world. Vandiyathevan was in for a greater shock. *Oh my God! I have wronged this angel in making her think that I am in love with her.*

In their devotion to music and song, they failed to notice the wind becoming stronger and stronger. Only when a huge tree was uprooted by the strong winds did they wake up to reality. They noticed all the signs of an imminent, big storm.

Nandini was the first to notice the storm.

'Oh my God! Where is our boat?'

The boat was moving deeper and deeper into the water.

'What can we do now? We are stranded,' screamed Nandini again.

'If you ladies know how to ride, please take our horses. We'll manage,' offered the Prince.

'No, we can't leave now. Let us stay here till the storm subsides. What are we going to do at the palace? See, we have enough food. Manimekalai is there to entertain us. I have never been this happy in the recent past.'

Vandiyathevan was worried.

'That's not proper, Prince.'

'I suspect this man must have let loose the boat under the pretext of looking for the leopard.'

'Sister, why do you blame him? Even when he came here, I saw the boat near the shore. Don't worry. My father will send a boat to rescue us,' said Manimekalai.

Soon her words came true. Two large boats came towards them with Sambuvarayar in it. He was happy to see all four of them safe. They all boarded the boat.

The lake resembled an ocean in turbulence. A greater storm was raging in the minds of all four who had been rescued. Sambuvarayar was the only one who remained calm.

5

Mob outside the Monastery

As Ponniyin Selvan had been charged with the offence of trying to usurp the Lankan throne from his own father, he was desperate to prove his innocence before his father in Tanjore. However, the Prince was waiting for a message from his sister Kundavai.

Meanwhile, he spent his time taking part in the daily rituals of the monastery, looking at the beautiful Buddhist paintings and speaking to the chief monk who had travelled far and wide.

One day there was commotion outside the monastery. The chief monk was agitated.

'I don't know who spread the rumour. They say you are now in our monastery and we are trying to make you a Buddhist monk. They want to see you as the emperor and not as a monk. Therefore, people have gathered in large numbers outside the monastery. I don't know how I'm going to manage this mob. May Lord Buddha show us the way,' he lamented.

'Master, I feel guilty for having caused this embarrassment,' answered the Prince.

'Don't worry, Prince. It's a pleasure to suffer even a hundred times more than this for your sake. Your enemies are desperate to know where you are. I'm sure that they propagated these rumours and have instigated the people.'

'Master, who are my enemies? I have no desire to rule this kingdom at all. Let me go out and tell this to the people. Then my enemies will become my friends. I don't want to be a nuisance to you any longer.'

'Prince, your sister Kundavai has asked me to keep you in hiding here and take care of you till further orders, for some reasons.'

Just then, a young monk came running in.

'The crowd is swelling each second. The situation is out of control. We have informed them several times that the Prince is not in our monastery. But they don't believe it. They want to come inside to find the truth.'

The Prince intervened.

'Master, your disciples have told the people that I'm not here. Now if I go out and appear before them, it won't be nice. Shall I leave the monastery through the canal at the back before the people come inside? There is a Chola Palace very close by in Anaimangalam I will stay there till the commotion dies down.'

The chief monk liked the idea but he had his reservations.

'Prince, that's a good idea. But there is a problem. There might be people near the canal.'

The young monk offered a suggestion, 'Master, let's tell them that only one person in the mob can come inside to look out for the Prince.'

The Prince agreed.

'If a single man comes in, I will talk to him and change his mind.'

'Prince, two days ago, a boatman and his wife from Kodikkarai came here to look for you. His name is Murugaiyyan, son of the lighthouse keeper. He is there in the crowd now.'

'I know him very well. He won't go against me. Please call him in.'

The monks silently walked away from the Prince to meet the restless mob.

The crowd surged on seeing the chief monk coming towards them.

'Gives us back our beloved prince, Ponniyin Selvan.'

People were furious. Behind them the sea too was in a state of eruption and a great storm was raging. It was moving fast towards the land.

The young monk silenced the crowd.

'Dear people, all of you cannot enter the monastery at the same time. Name one volunteer amongst you. Let him come into the monastery and search for the prince. Is this acceptable?'

The crowd roared in acceptance.

'Name somebody to come with me into the monastery.'

Hundreds of people volunteered. There was commotion again.

The young monk silenced them and spoke in a soft voice,

'Don't shout. Let us give preference to someone who has seen the prince recently. It will be easy for him to recognize the Prince.'

Rakkammal who stood in the front came forward.

'Yes, we have seen the prince.'

The young monk talked to her husband Murugaiyyan standing near her.

'Is she right?'

Murugaiyyan replied, 'She has not seen the prince recently. I saw him in Lanka last month.'

'Then you are the right person for the job. Women are not allowed inside the monastery. Murugaiyya, come forward.'

The young monk took him inside and the chief monk addressed the mob sensing their restlessness and lack of confidence.

The appearance of the chief monk was graceful and his face revealed love and compassion. Nobody dared to put an irrelevant question to him.

'My dear people, I'm moved by your love for the prince, Ponniyin Selvan. He is born to rule a great country and not to become a monk.'

Silence prevailed for a while.

The chief monk continued.

'I understand your concern for the safety of the Prince. But now it is time to worry about your safety. A storm of unprecedented ferocity is nearing the coast. Look at the sea.'

People were shocked when they turned towards the sea. The ferocious dance of nature frightened everyone. The waves went so high, touching the black clouds. Each wave appeared as a huge black mountain of water. Soon the sea entered the town of Nagapattinam.

Boats and ships were being tossed on top of the moving water. Houses were submerged. The mob started to scatter in all directions. Within a few minutes, the place was completely deserted.

The boatman's wife Rakkammal was standing alone.

'My husband! My husband!' she shouted.

'Your husband is safe. He will come back soon. Now you run for your life.'

The chief monk's admonition was soft.

Meanwhile, a stranger came near Rakkammal and whispered in her ears. She went off reluctantly with him.

Who is this man?

With this doubt in his mind, the chief monk went inside the monastery.

Inside, Murugaiyyan was in a state of surprise to see the prince. He was reverentially listening to every word coming from him.

Orders were given to bring a boat for the royal guest. The boat came. The prince took leave of the chief monk and got into the boat. Murugaiyyan too got in and started rowing. The chief monk watched the boat till it was completely out of sight and spoke to all the monks gathered.

'We all belong to Lord Buddha who is nothing but love. I saw the sea water coming in, submerging houses and tossing everything in its way. Go into town and help the people caught in the disaster.'

6

Tsunami

The boat started moving. The water level was rising fast in the canal. The storm had picked up momentum. Loud noises of falling trees were heard. The boat reached the Nandi resthouse on the way to Aanaimangalam palace. The prince saw the huge Nandi statue. Water was fiercely flowing above the head of the Nandi statue. He shuddered on seeing the velocity of the raging storm. He suddenly asked the boatman to stop.

The boatman could not immediately stop the small vessel which was being tossed up and down in the fast-flowing current. However, when the boat was close enough, the prince jumped onto the roof of the Nandi resthouse to look around. The sea had entered the canal and all the coconut trees in the surrounding groves had fallen.

The prince looked towards the monastery. The monastery was also getting submerged in water. A chill went through his spine. He jumped back into the boat and asked the boatman to steer the boat back to the monastery.

The boat reached the monastery with great difficulty. The prince jumped off the boat and landed on the terrace. There was water upto the second floor. He searched everywhere and finally found the chief monk in an unconscious state at the lotus feet of the Buddha statue which was submerged in water on the second floor. He dived into the water and rescued him and took him to the boat. The boatman started rowing again. The chief monk regained consciousness after sometime.

The prince and the chief monk were devastated by the destruction caused by the tsunami. Huge ships with broken sails and small fishing boats were piled up on the shore like mountains. The wind had ripped off the roof of many homes.

Massive trees had been violently uprooted. Some of the fallen trees floated on water and their branches served as lifeboats to people caught in the floods. The sight of cows and sheep and their frightened cries were heart rending. The chief monk and the prince were deeply upset.

They reached the Chola Palace in Aanaimangalam in utter darkness. The prince and the chief monk got down from the boat. There was a guard at the palace gates with a flaming torch, talking to some people.

When he saw the boat, he ran towards the prince. He recognized the prince and was about to fall at his feet. The prince stopped him.

'Your Majesty, I was worried about your safety. I'm relieved to see you here.'

'Oh! You knew I was in the monastery?'

'Yes, Your Majesty! Princess Kundavai informed me when she was here, with strict orders not to reveal this to anybody.'

'Who are these people?'

'Your Majesty, they are from the affected villages seeking shelter in the palace complex for the night. Let me drive them away.'

'Don't do that. Let them stay here for the night and use all the supplies in the palace to cook their food. Now you take us to the top floor of the palace without their knowledge.'

The chief monk and Prince Arulmoli were in the Chola Palace at Aanaimangalam. They were discussing the relief measures into the wee hours of the morning.

Prince Arulmoli summoned the palace caretaker to find out the available resources in the palace. It was reported that the granary was full and the palace had more than twelve copper pots full of gold coins. The gold coins were sent by the Queen Mother for temple renovation works.

The prince spoke to the chief monk:

'Master, you distribute the grains and gold coins to the affected people.'

'Prince! It's not fair to divert the gold coins meant for temple renovation.'

'Let's use the gold coins now. I'm sure the Queen Mother would agree. In future, we can build hundreds of big temples and also rebuild a much larger and stronger monastery in Nagapattinam. Master, God wants me to do many great things. That's why, he saved me from so many dangers. See what happened today. The boatman came at the right time to rescue us in his boat from the submerged monastery.'

'Prince, it's true. Disaster of this magnitude has not happened in the last five hundred years. I request you to distribute the relief materials with your own hands.'

'Master, if I reveal myself now, it may cause confusion in the minds of the people. Therefore, you distribute the grain and gold from this palace.'

'Ponniyin Selva, this is the right time to reveal yourself through your relief measures.'

Suddenly they heard the loud sobs of Murugaiyyan.

'What is this? Why are you crying?'

'My wife! My wife!'

Ponniyin Selvan spoke softly to him,

'We are sorry for you. We will trace your wife in the morning.'

'Your Majesty, I'm not worried about her. She'll be safe. She has seen hundreds of storms like this in our coastal area.'

'Then why are you crying?'

The boatman spoke in choked voice,

'I feel bad that I suspected her intentions. She was the one who told me that you were in the monastery. I came here only because of her. A few seconds ago, Your Majesty praised me and you said that god saved you through me. But I came here because of my wife.'

The prince consoled him

'Your wife is a noble lady. But how did she know that I was in the monastery?'

'My aunt and my sister Poonkulali left for Nagapattinam in a boat. That must have made her guess you are here.'

'Which aunt?' asked the prince with excitement.

'The mute lady, the one who saved you from many dangers in the Lankan island.'

'Oh my God! Where are they? What happened to your aunt and your sister?'

'Your Majesty, their journey to Nagapatinam was interrupted by some ruffians.'

The boatman started to cry again.

Ponniyin Selvan consoled the boatman and got all the details from him. When he learnt that somebody had forcibly kidnapped the mute queen, he became furious and upset and he decided to go to Tanjore.

'I will travel in the guise of a merchant tomorrow along with this boatman.'

The prince asked the chief monk to take charge of the flood relief work.

The chief monk agreed.

The prince, disguised as a merchant, was walking down the crowded street carrying a bag on his shoulders. Behind him was the boatman carrying a larger bag.

Rakkammal, Murugaiyyan's wife who was hiding behind the wall of one of the damaged houses saw them. She remained silent till they reached near her. She then ran out in the street and fell down at the feet of the prince. The boatman tried to caution her in sign language and then shouted at her to remain quiet. But nothing could stop her.

'Oh my God! Is it the emperor's son? The one and only Ponniyin Selvan? The darling of the Chola Kingdom? Today is the luckiest day for me to see you alive.'

Everybody's attention was now on the prince.

7

Epic Journey to Tanjore

The boatman was shocked by his wife's excitement.

'Idiot! Are you crazy?'

'I'm alright. I'm not crazy. You are crazy. Your father's crazy and so is your grandfather. Can't you recognise our hero, the emperor's son—the darling of the people?'

The prince spoke to her softly.

'You are mistaken. I'm a merchant from Lanka. I'm taking this man as my guide. If you don't want him to come with me that's alright. But please don't create a scene here.'

Soon, they were surrounded by curious onlookers. The crowd immediately swelled.

The boatman's wife Rakkammal raised her voice,

'Oh my God, what happened to our Ponniyin Selvan? Has he lost his mind in the sea? Your Majesty, you are not a trader. You are born a ruler. If you have any doubts, please see the conch and the disk lines in your palms.'

The prince covered his palms.

'Won't you shut up?'

The prince then turned to the boatman.

'What is this nuisance? Can't you stop her?'

He went near his wife and whispered in her ears.

'Rakkammal, be quiet. The prince wants to go to Tanjore in the guise of a merchant. Please understand.'

'Oh my God, you should have told me that before. Out of my love for the prince, I have blurted out the true identity of the prince.'

Soon the prince was surrounded by the cheering crowd.

'Hail Ponniyin Selvan!'

Amongst the crowd was the City Council chairman who came forward to greet the prince.

'We heard rumours that you were at the monastery in our city. Yesterday's storm has wrought havoc in the town and the monastery is submerged. We are grateful to the almighty for keeping you safe.'

The prince now knew that there was no point in hiding his identity any longer.

'I'm moved by your words. I have to go to Tanjore very urgently. But if I travel with my true identity, my journey will be delayed. Hence this guise. Please let me go.'

A voice was heard from the crowd.

'No! We won't leave you, Prince. You have to be our guest for at least today.'

The council chairman spoke again.

'I beg you to accept our hospitality. All the roads are badly damaged due to the storm. It may take several weeks for you to reach the capital if you walk the entire distance. You may travel on an elephant like a king. We will follow you to Tanjore.'

The prince accepted the proposal.

That boatman's foolish wife has unwittingly revealed my identity. She has messed up my plans.

Sensing the mood of the people, the prince made up his mind. He now addressed the council chairman,

'I'm moved by your love. I will stay with you for a day and leave in the evening.'

It was quite an ordeal for him to reach the Chola Palace which was in the heart of the town. A grand feast was arranged. The enthusiasm of the crowd crossed all bounds. Drums and pipes started playing. People started dancing. Swordsmen demonstrated their skills in mock fights.

The prince met the people and had a kind word for everyone. He promised storm relief measures. Though the prince posed an elegant smile, inwardly he was in great distress. He was anxious to know the fate of the mute queen who was like his own mother.

Now the chairman climbed up on the podium and spoke in a majestic voice.

'Ponniyin Selva, our beloved prince, the people of this city and the surrounding villages have a petition. We are all worried about the health of Emperor Sundara Chola. We learn that the Paluvettarayars are conspiring to crown your uncle, Madurandakan, after your father. Madurandakan has not seen a single battle till now. And if he is made the king, that will be a proxy rule by the Paluvettarayars.

Many say that the crown prince, Aditya Karkalan is not interested in ruling the country. If this is true, the one and only Ponniyin Selvan, our beloved Prince, can be our king and ruler.'

In chorus, the crowd shouted slogans in support of the prince. The roar of their voices was similar to that of a sea in turbulence.

And then the prince addressed the crowd. It was as though the prince had cast a spell over the raging crowd.

'My dear people, I respect your sentiments. But you have forgotten the fact that my father is still alive. And when he is alive, it is neither fair nor proper to discuss the issue of succession.'

Now the chairman responded to the prince.

'Beloved Prince, it has been a time-honoured tradition in our country to name the successor even while the king is alive.'

'The emperor alone has the prerogative to name his successor. It won't be proper to debate on this issue of succession.'

'Yes Prince, we agree. If the emperor can decide on his own, he can name the successor. We want to come with you to Tanjore and present our petition to name you as the successor to the throne. We will then leave the matter to him.'

He could not delay his journey to Tanjore any longer. He had no other alternative but to agree with the people and start the journey. Maybe on the way he could think of some way to escape from the people and travel alone to see his father.

'Let me leave immediately to see my father. If you want to see the emperor you may also accompany me. Let us accept the emperor's decision on the successor.' He mounted the elephant. The long procession comprising thousands of people started its epic journey towards Tanjore. Many people joined them on the way. The procession became longer and longer.

8

Storm in His Mind

Paluvettarayar left for Tanjore on the day of the storm. He traveled with minimum soldiers to avoid the attention of the people.

The river Kollidam was in spate and a storm was imminent. Leaving the horses on the bank, he along with his men got into a boat. When the boat was in the middle of the river, the storm started.

Soon it intensified and started rocking the boat. The boatman struggled hard to keep the boat on its course. Simultaneously a greater storm was raging in Paluvettarayar's mind. He was enraged at himself for giving in to whatever Nandini had wanted. In her presence, his brain would get disoriented. Even if Nandini said something displeasing he always agreed. He never had the heart to speak out against her. He was ashamed that he was henpecked and being manipulated by her. When Nandini asked him to bring Madurandakan from Tanjore, he agreed but doubts sprang in his mind now. Having left her in the company of three young men made him restless. He hated all the three young men—Crown Prince Aditya Karikalan, Vandiyathevan and Kandamaran.

Once in the underground passage, Kandamaran had unwittingly commented on the good looks of his young wife, Senior Paluvettarayar had become so furious that he had ordered his personal bodyguard to kill Kandamaran. Mysteriously Kandamaran survived and the bodyguard died. He could not also digest the fact that his young wife Nandini nursed him back to life. Nandini was now in the company of Kandamaran.

Paluvettarayar was aware that the arrogant Prince Aditya Karkalan had once wanted to marry Nandini. The marriage did not take place for some reason. Paluvettarayar wondered why he should want to meet Nandini now? The crown prince might be a ruffian but he was blemishless when it came to women. But still…

What about Nandini? To what extent could she be trusted? Why should he blindly obey her words? He married her right from the streets without even knowing her antecedents. He was unable to pay heed to his younger brother's warning who had, on many occasions, directly and indirectly indicated her mysterious nature.

These thoughts were haunting Paluvettarayar's mind. He was in the grip of two powerful emotions—anger and lust.

I will get to know the truth in a day or two.

Paluvettarayar's boat was nearing the bank after a great struggle. Suddenly a huge fallen tree floating on the river hit the boat and the boat turned turtle. Everyone in the boat jumped into the water as they were prepared for the eventuality.

But, unfortunately, Paluvettarayar was in a different world. He never expected this. The course of the river carried him far away from the others. Water entered his ears, nose and mouth. He could not trace the men from his boat. He was alone, struggling in the river ravaged by a sudden storm. The warrior in him helped. He held on to a wooden log floating nearby and reached the bank. The place looked like a dark forest with no human habitation. The storm was in full rage with heavy rainfall. He began looking for some shelter to spend the night.

Suddenly the ground under him caved in, as the bank had breached in the heavy rains. He was carried away by the strong currents once again.

My lust for a woman has brought me to this…

He felt bad about himself and became unconscious.

When he regained consciousness, his hands were holding on to a hard surface. Some force pushed him upward. The next second he was on a granite floor. When he opened his eyes, he saw the temple of Goddess Durga.

Oh! My Goddess! My savior!

The old warrior tried to stand up but his body was shivering in cold. He lay down before the goddess. He was tired and lapsed into sleep.

Goddess Durga appeared in his dream with fiery eyes.

You and your clan have always been dear to me. That's why I've come to warn you now. The young bride in your palace is a poisonous snake. Her mission in life is to destroy your clan and the clan of the Cholas. She is waiting for the right moment. Remove her from your palace and your mind as well. If you don't, you and your clan will face disgrace.

Paluvettarayar woke up with a shiver.

Another day dawned. The storm had died down and the rains had also stopped. He came out of the temple to take stock of the situation. There was water everywhere. Further down, there was a dense forest.

Must be the one near Thirupurambiam. I can walk to Kumbakonam from there and seek help.

The temple was surrounded by water. He had to wait for the water to recede. He spent two days in the temple eating the fruits offered to the goddess. Finally on the third day when the sun was about to set, a large neem tree near the temple fell across the river serving as a perfect bridge to cross the flooded river. Pauvettarayar was ready to leave. Suddenly he heard a strange voice which chilled his spine. The voice came from a little distance away from the temple.

'Sorcerer! Sorcerer! Ravidasa! Ravidasa!' a voice called.

Paluvettarayar vaguely remembered hearing this voice earlier. He stood up and walked towards the direction of the voice. Hiding behind the temple pillar, he noticed a figure on the top branch of the fallen tree on the other side of the river.

'Sorcerer! Sorcerer!' the voice called again.

The figure was walking on the tree towards the temple.

Paluvettarayar lay down on the temple floor to know more about the sorcerer, the one who frequented his palace to see Nandini.

What is his relationship with Nandini? What is he doing in this godforsaken place? If I know the answers to these questions, I can find out if my young wife is cheating me. If I catch hold of that sorcerer, I won't leave him till I extract a full confession from him.

The man came near Paluvettarayar who still pretended to be asleep.

'Ravidasa! Ravidasa!' the man called.

Oh! My God! This voice belongs to that man who performed the folk-dance giving predictions at Kadamboor palace. Yes, it is that Thevaralan.

Paluvettarayar whispered to himself.

Let me wait and trap Ravidasan through this man.

'Sorcerer what is this? You have gone to sleep even before sunset?' asked Thevaralan and then he came near Paluvettarayar and turned him to see his face. Even then Paluvettarayar did not move.

He was shocked to see the face of Paluvettarayar and started running away from the place. Before Paluvettarayar could open his eyes the man jumped over the makeshift neem tree bridge and reached the other bank quickly. Next moment, he disappeared into the dense forest. Paluvettarayar also quickly followed him and reached the other bank. He waded through the thick bushes in the darkness. After wandering pointlessly in the forest for more than an hour, he saw a flaming torch at a distance.

Paluvettarayar moved towards the torch. Soon he was very close to the light. The torch illuminated the war memorial. He hid behind a wall to observe the sounds coming from inside. He saw two men talking.

'Sorcerer, do you know how long I have been looking for you? I was afraid that you may not come. I even thought the Death God had taken you,' said Thevaralan.

'How could death come to me? He is aiming for the emperor and his two sons. By tomorrow, they will be dead.'

Suddenly there was a flash of lightning. The whole place was bathed in light for a few seconds.

9

A Volcano Erupted

Thanks to the flash of lightning, Paluvettarayar was able to see the conspirators and identified one of them as the sorcerer Ravidasa who often visited Nandini. His brother, Junior Paluvettarayar had warned him about that man. The other conspirator was the one who had performed the folk-dance in Kadamboor palace when the midnight meeting had taken place. Senior was keen to listen to their conversation.

'The day has come with death looming large for the members of the royal family.'

'You have been repeating this statement for a long time. The lord of death has claimed the lives of many healthy people in this world. But he is still afraid to come near Sundara Chola, who is on sick-bed. And that lord is even more scared of claiming the lives of his two sons. You know very well how many times we tried to kill Prince Arulmoli in Lanka.'

'Don't worry. He has been waiting so long only to claim the lives of all the three tomorrow.'

'Let us hope it happens. Do you know why I'm shaking in fear? I saw the mighty Senior Paluvettarayar face to face a while ago.'

'What the hell are you saying?'

Thevaralan continued.

'As per your instructions, I came here this morning but I didn't see you anywhere. I went to the Durga temple to wait for you. I saw somebody lying there. I thought it must be you. I went near and turned him around, it was Senior Paluvettarayar.'

'Did you really see that old bandicoot or his ghost?'

'No, it was not a ghost. I saw him with the same face, the same moustache and the same scars.'

'Idiot, what did you do? Did you leave him alone? You could have killed him by throwing a large stone on his head.'

'You don't know anything about him. If I had done that, the stone would have broken, not his head.'

'At least you could have dragged him to the river. You missed a golden opportunity.'

'Yes, I regret my lapse. I won't be at peace as long as he is alive.'

'In a way, it is better for us that he is alive. Once the emperor and his sons die tomorrow, the chieftains of the kingdom will be on two sides fighting with each other. We can use that time to gather our army.'

'That's all fantasy, Ravidasa. For that infighting to happen the emperor and his two sons should be killed tomorrow. What's the guarantee that all three will die tomorrow?'

'Prince Arulmoli will be travelling on an elephant. The lord of death will accompany him in the form of Rakkammal's father, who will be his mahout with a poison tipped elephant goad to claim his life at the right time. The mahout will carry out our murderous mission.'

'Ravidasa, who will deal with Sundara Chola?'

'I have left Soman Sambavan in the underground treasury of Paluvettarayar's palace. I have asked him to wait till tomorrow morning.'

'Why should he wait?'

'Fool, if the emperor is killed first, then his sons will become alert.'

'Any news from Kadamboor?'

'Kadamboor is in a festive mood. Love dramas are being enacted very well. Why do you trust the Junior Queen of Paluvoor, Nandini?'

'She is not the Junior Queen of Paluvoor. She is the queen of the Pandiyas. She has taken a vow to avenge the death of the Pandiya King.'

'But Nandini is rejoicing in the company of the crown prince and others.'

'She has to be like that. There is no other way. She is an expert at hiding her real intentions. She cleverly managed Senior Paluvettarayar for the last three years by putting on a show of being his faithful wife. Why did Senior Paluvettarayar leave Kadamboor?'

'He left Kadamboor yesterday morning to fetch Madurandakan from Tanjore. I still don't trust Nandini.'

'Never ever doubt her. She is a good strategist. She cleverly removed Paluvettarayar from the scene.'

'Nobody can study her mind. Perhaps she sent away the old warrior to avenge Pandiya's death or indulge in the game of love. Who knows?'

'Why babble? Nandini forgot her love long back. Now she is ready to kill Prince Karikalan any time.'

'Perhaps she loves the young warrior, Vandiyathevan. Otherwise, why should she let him free thrice, when she could have easily killed him?'

Ravidasa, the sorcerer, laughed.

'You will be surprised. Many will be surprised. But the emperor's darling daughter Kundavai won't be surprised. She will be shocked to know that her lover killed her own brother Karikalan. That's how the junior queen is going to settle her scores with her.'

'What the hell are you saying, Ravidasa? Do you mean to say that Vandiyathevan will kill Aditya Karikalan? Has he become our man?'

'No more questions. Why should you bother about the hand that kills Karikalan? The blame will be on Vandiyathevan. See our queen's intelligence!'

'I reserve my judgment on Nandini till the mission is accomplished.'

'Karikalan will be dead before tomorrow night. Nandini will fulfil her mission at any cost. We have to fulfil ours. We should be ready at the secret passage that goes out of the Kadamboor palace. Nandini will come out through that passage. We should take her with us to the Kolli Hills and watch the drama unfolding in the Chola Kingdom. We should also take away the gold from the underground treasury in Tanjore. It will be sweet revenge to use the Chola gold to destroy the Chola clan.'

Ravidasa laughed again.

But Thevaralan was skeptical.

'You are building castles in the air. Let's first proceed to Kadamboor before it gets dark and see if things go as planned.'

All their words fell on Paluvettarayar's ears like molten lead. His heart was like a volcano on the verge of eruption. The thought of his deceiving wife devastated him. He felt betrayed.

Paluvettarayar thought of the loyalty of his clan towards the Cholas for the past several generations.

Who was Sundara Chola after all? Who were his sons? Sundara Chola's grandmother was from the Paluvettarayar clan and his anger against the emperor's son, Aditya Karikalan was of recent origin for the simple reason that he was rude.

He felt guilty about having helped and paved the way for a dangerous conspiracy to overthrow the Chola rule.

Oh my God! The emperor and his two sons are facing danger. I won't let that happen. I have a full twenty-four hours before me. I can do so many things in that time. I should immediately alert them tonight. I should reach Kadamboor before these devils.

Why should I let them go to Kadamboor? Why not finish them here itself? My arms are mightier than a sword. I have got all the information I want. If that demoness Nandini, masquerading as my wife, kills Karikalan... Oh my God, can such a beautiful form hold so much of poison?

He wanted to save Nandini from the heinous crime. He could even change her mind and free her from the clutches of these conspirators. If he could kill these two men here itself, that might set Nandini free.

With these thoughts on his mind, Paluvettarayar cleared his throat loudly like a lion's roar. The conspirators were in utter shock.

'Who is that?' shouted Thevaralan.

Paluvettarayar came out of hiding.

The conspirators were aghast to see the tall mighty figure standing before them in darkness.

The conspirators tried to run away. But Paluvettarayar's long arms stopped them. His right hand was firmly on the shoulder of Ravidasa while his left was on Thevaralan.

Yes, Paluvettarayar was more powerful than either of them. But how long could he manage these two young men at his old age. He pushed one man down and placed a foot firmly on his back. Meanwhile, he started wringing Ravidasa's neck. Thevaralan was fighting for life. Knowing his intentions, Paluvettarayar delivered a strong blow to the wrist holding the knife. The knife fell from his grasp and skittered across the floor to a place beyond his reach and his hand became lifeless. At that moment Paluvettarayar's foot lost a little pressure. Thevaralan wriggled out from under it and with his other hand hit the old warrior but winced with pain. His hand was hurt and became lifeless.

Meanwhile Ravidasa was trying to remove Paluvettarayar's hands from around his neck with all his might. All his efforts failed. The old warrior had an iron grip on his neck which did not slack even a bit. Ravidasa's eyeballs were popping out and he was gasping for breath. If the grip continued on his neck for a few more seconds, he would die of suffocation. He thought fast and shouted.

'Thevaralan, climb on the memorial and pull down the roof.'

Thevaralan sprang on the roof of the memorial. Part of the roof had already given way and was about to fall at any time. Thevaralan used all his might to push the roof down. A tree growing on the top of the roof also came down along with the roof.

Paluvettarayar saw it and knew that it would fall on him any second. He took his hand off Ravidasa's neck and tried to shield himself from the falling structure. Ravidasa used that small gap to wriggle away from his grip. The roof and the tree fell on Paluvettarayar's head. He became unconscious.

10

The Illuminous Comet

Senior Paluvettarayar was slowly regaining his consciousness. His inner mind was working.

Your ancestors are hurling curses upon you for bringing disgrace to your clan.

Tears were streaming down his eyes. Slowly his eyelids opened. He returned to the world of reality.

He vaguely remembered the conversation he had heard before he became unconscious.

'The old man is dead,' said a voice.

'Be careful. The old man won't die so easily. Even the lord of death won't dare to come near him,' said another voice.

'The lord of death may spare him but not the howling foxes. At dawn tomorrow, the finance minister of the Chola Kingdom will be nothing but a heap of bones.'

'We have used a part of our enemies' memorial to raise another memorial for a new enemy,' laughed the sorcerer Ravidasa.

'Come, let's get out of this place before our boat is washed away by the river.'

Paluvettarayar recalled these words of the conspirators. A part of the collapsed roof and the tree were still on him pressing him hard, making him breathless. Even after bearing so much of weight, for such a long time, he was still alive. The old man was surprised at his own strength.

Now he heard the fox's howling at very close quarters. He pushed away the tree and the roof. Meanwhile the strange sounds made by him while lifting the weight over him kept the foxes away.

He looked at the sky. It was clear. It was scattered with many shining stars.

A strange star in the northern sky drew his attention.

Oh my God! Is this not the comet?

Paluvettarayar took his eyes off the sky and looked around. Suddenly the skies and the entire forest region were bathed in a glow of light. The light was so bright that it hurt his eyes. That was not a streak of lightning. Then what else could that be? Yes, the comet had fallen. A comet falling was a powerful astrological ill-omen.

Something terrible is going to happen. A catastrophe was going to hit. Members of the royal household may be at risk.

The old warrior tried to stand up, ignoring his pain. At first, he could not stand up. He used all his might and rose up. He looked around.

Senior Paluvettarayar made a wild guess about the direction in which the town of Kumbakonam lay and started walking fast. He reached Kumbakonam in the early hours.

He wanted to send a reliable messenger to Tanjore and Nagapattinam. He remembered the Kumbakonam astrologer.

When Paluvettarayar reached the astrologer's house, he saw a chariot with two horses parked near it. He also heard women's voices.

Oh my God! Princess Kundavai! Why has she come here and that too so early in the morning?

Then he heaved a sigh of relief.

In a way it is good. If I can share the secrets with the princess, I will feel relieved. If I can tell her that the life of her father and her brothers are at risk, that shrewd girl will do something to save them. Then I can peacefully leave for Kadamboor to avert the catastrophe there.

When Senior Paluvettarayar entered the astrologer's house at the outskirts of Kumbakonam town, Princess Kundavai and Vanathi were already there. She was narrating the dangers surrounding her father and her brothers.

While she was half-way through the woeful narration, she heard a ruckus at the door. Senior Paluvettarayar pushed aside the astrologer's assistant and was barging in.

Kundavai thought fast.

Why has he come here? Let me eavesdrop on his conversation with the astrologer to know what is on his mind. That will give me a solution to all the problems. It's a rare opportunity for me. Let us hide inside the house.

Kundavai communicated her plan to the astrologer using sign language. She then grabbed Vanathi's hand and rushed into the next room. Senior Paluvettarayar entered the main hall, and spoke in his usual majestic tone.

'Can't you recognize me, astrologer? I'm Senior Paluvettarayar. I need your help in a big way.'

The astrologer responded in a trembling voice.

'What can this poor astrologer do?'

'I need to send an urgent message to Tanjore. I will give my signet ring to your assistant at the entrance. Can you put him on the job?'

'I'm at your service, Your Highness. Were you caught in the floods? I'm shocked to see you in this condition. Hope the junior queen is safe.'

Paluvettarayar broke into a hysterical laugh.

'No, she did not die in the floods. She is happy at the Kadamboor Palace right now. But I can't guarantee if she will be alive tomorrow. I will kill her with my own hands.

A great danger awaits the emperor and his two sons today. Death for the emperor is hiding in the underground treasury of Tanjore. Death for Prince Arulmoli is hiding in the goad carried by his mahout. Now it is your responsibility to save the emperor and his sons. Let your disciple rush to meet the emperor with my signet ring. You meet Prince Arulmoli. Can you do it for me? Can you leave right now?'

The sound of anklets from inside the house was heard just then.

'The sound of anklets has come as a sign of approval from Goddess Durga. I will take the chariot near the temple outside.'

'Your Highness, that chariot... that chariot... Please I beg of you...'

'Astrologer, don't worry about it. I will use the chariot for a noble mission to save the life of our crown prince. Even Goddess Durga will not object to that. She will make a sound with anklets once again to signify her approval.'

Princess Kundavai rushed towards the two men with the sound of anklets. Senior Paluvettarayar was not surprised to see her.

'Princess, I guessed you were inside. I did not have the courage to talk to you face to face. I deliberately spoke loudly so that you could hear me. I'm sure you overheard whatever I said to the astrologer.'

'Please forgive me for eavesdropping.'

'I'm the one who should beg for your pardon. Princess, I'm not sure whether I'm good enough to seek your pardon. If I can run to Kadamboor before nightfall and save the life of the crown prince, well then perhaps I may be qualified to seek your forgiveness.

For three years, I have been blinded by lust. You gave me several hints. My younger brother also tried to alert me. But I ignored them. Only last night, thanks to the grace of Goddess Durga, I overheard the conversation between conspirators from the Pandiya Kingdom and now I know whole the truth. I have been harbouring an evil bitch in my palace all along. She made me betray the Chola clan. She used the gold from our Chola treasury for their evil designs. Unless I kill her before nightfall today, my mind won't rest in peace.'

Princess Kundavai did something completely unexpected. She fell at the feet of Senior Paluvettarayar.

He was in a state of shock. Kundavai got up and spoke to him in a choked voice seeking a boon from him.

'Princess, are you testing me?'

'No. You are my grandfather. I seek a boon from you. Please don't refuse it.'

'Ask Princess, make it fast.'

'Promise me that you won't hurt your junior queen, Nandini.'

'Princess! Are you jesting?'

'Grandfather, I want to save my sister. Do you know that Junior Queen Nandini is my own sister? If you hurt her, you will be hurting the Chola clan.'

Paluvettarayar was shocked.

'Let me recollect some incidents for you. The mute lady who saved my brother Arulmoli from the river Cauvery is Nandini's mother. On the day you married Nandini and brought her home, my father fainted on seeing her. Do you remember that? My father thought he was seeing Nandini's mother, his first love. My father believed that his first wife was dead. He mistook Nandini for the mute lady Mandakini as their resemblance was uncanny. Thinking her to be a ghost of the mute lady, he swooned.'

Paluvettarayar recalled a few other incidents. At Nandini's insistence, he had taken her to visit the emperor at midnight. The emperor screamed on seeing her.

'Now I understand everything. Destiny is very cruel. If Nandini is your sister, then she becomes a sister to Aditya Karikalan too. Does he know about it?'

'He should have, by now. I had sent the warrior of the Vaanar clan to convey this message to my brother.'

'I don't think Karikalan would believe him. Nandini also won't know about it. Even if she knows, it is of no use. Somehow the conspirators will accomplish their mission. Princess, this news has increased my responsibility. I'm leaving for Kadamboor right now. I'm taking your chariot. It is your responsibility to save the emperor and Ponniyin Selvan.'

'Do not worry. I'm leaving for Tanjore right now. I will get another chariot for my journey. You need not worry about Ponniyin Selvan. The stars are on his side.'

Paluvettarayar was gone. A few seconds later, Nambi entered the house.

11

A Terrible Vow

Kundavai was surprised to see Nambi at the astrologer's house.

'Nambi, how did you suddenly spring up here?'

'Princess, all because of the false words of this astrologer. This morning I posed a simple question to this man, "Will I succeed in my mission today?" He said, "yes you will" but I could not move even an inch from this place, let alone succeed in my task.'

'Any news, Nambi?'

'Yes, Princess, the first bit of news is that Prince Arulmoli has left Nagapattinam followed by a cheering crowd.'

'I also heard that news. I came here only to stop my brother on the way. What is the other news?'

'Princess, the second message concerns this princess. The general of the Chola armies (South), Bhoothi Vikrama Kesari is marching towards Tanjore Fort along with a huge army. That is the news the prime minister got last night. In his message to the prime minister, the general accuses the Paluvettarayars guilty of holding the emperor a hostage in Tanjore and Prince Arulmoli as a prisoner in some undisclosed location. The general also demands that the Paluvettarayars should resign their posts and leave the city immediately. They should entrust Prince Arulmoli to the emperor and if they fail to do any of these, the general will lay siege on Tanjore Fort this evening.'

'But the prime minister did not even breathe a word about this development to me.'

'All with the good intention of evacuating this Kodumbalur Princess, Vanathi from the fort.'

'What…?'

'Junior Paluvettarayar might imprison her had she remained there.'

'Is that really so?'

'Yes, Princess. If you know the full message of the general…'

'What else is there in his message?'

'The wedding of Prince Arulmoli and the Kodumbalur Princess, Vanathi, should take place right way. Since the Crown Prince Aditya Karikalan does not want to rule, Prince Arulmoli should be made the crown prince and the general has warned that if all his demands are not met, he will raze Tanjore Fort to the ground within three days. He has also written that the people of the Chola Kingdom support him in this mission.'

Vanathi was listening to every word spoken by Nambi and finally responded.

'I wonder if my uncle has gone mad.'

'No Vanathi, he hasn't. Your uncle is just saying what is already there in the minds of people. But I'm afraid that any civil war amongst the clans will destroy the mighty Chola Empire.'

'Sister, I don't care about the impending war. But why the hell would my father's brother—the general, drag my name into the controversy. I want to meet my uncle right now and convey my displeasure.'

'What is the use? Your uncle will never listen to you. The only way to stop the civil war is through my brother Arulmoli. Nambi, where is Arulmoli now?'

'He was in Thiruvarur last night. As all the roads are flooded, he could not travel further.'

'The waters will soon recede. He has to cross this way. We will stop him here. Nambi, you go to Tanjore right now and give my request to the general to defer his plans to lay siege on Tanjore Fort till Arulmoli returns.'

'Let me also go to Tanjore and plead with my uncle not to drag my name into this affair,' said Vanathi.

'In which way are you involved, Vanathi? Nambi, did you say anything about this girl?'

'One of the demands of the general is to marry off this girl to Ponniyin Selvan. Princess, perhaps this girl is referring to that.'

'That is not the issue. Why should he talk about my marriage now? My uncle is trying to link my marriage with the issue of succession. I object to that. For the world it might appear that my uncle has started this work only to make me the Chola Queen.'

At that moment, a woman's voice was heard.

'So, the Kodumbalur Princess won't sit on the throne! Great!'

Everybody looked in the direction of the voice.

Poonkulali came in.

Kundavai was surprised

'Hi girl, how did you come here? We have been searching for you and your aunt since morning. Where is she?'

'Please forgive me, Princess. My aunt forced me out of the palace through the underground passage. She didn't like me staying in the palace even for a day. I also don't like the palace life. When Vanathi can hate the throne, why can't somebody like me hate living in the palace?'

'Sister, Poonkulali is trying to insult me. She thinks that I'm yearning for the Chola throne and she thinks that's the reason I want to marry your brother, Ponniyin Selvan.'

'I know how her mind works. Only a snake knows the ways of another snake,' Poonkulali was at her sarcastic best.

'Stop it girls. Why fight with each other? Poonkulali, where is your aunt?'

'She is in the underground treasury in Tanjore.'

'Oh my God! Why?'

'An assassin is hiding there. You won't believe how we tormented him in the early hours of this morning. He was running around thinking we were ghosts. Even now I can't control my laughter.'

'Crazy girl, tell me who is that assassin?' asked Princess Kundavai.

'Princess, I don't know. Somehow my aunt sensed that an assassin is hiding there to kill somebody in the palace. When my aunt tried to break the hands of the Ravana statue at the palace, all of you suspected her to be mad. But my aunt is not mad. She is very shrewd. The secret entrance to the treasury is between the hands of the Ravana statue.'

'Oh my God! We have been living in the palace all our lives. And yet we didn't know about the existence of that passage. Ok, let it be. Why did you leave your aunt alone?'

'All because of my aunt's obstinacy. She told me that she would take care of the assassin and wanted me to leave the palace and warn Ponniyin Selvan about the impending danger.'

'Then why have you come here?'

'I saw Nambi on the way and he brought me here. I would not have come here had I known that you were here.'

'Why do you hate the palace so much?'

Kundavai asked in a concerned voice.

'Some hate the throne. I hate the palace and it's people.'

Poonkulali looked at Vanathi with a sarcastic smile.

Princess Vanathi reacted with anger.

'Sister! She is targeting me. Let the whole world hear me. If Ponniyin Selvan marries me, I'm blessed to be his wife. But I won't sit on the throne. That is a promise.'

12

Floating Roof

Nobody expected that Vanathi would vow that she would not sit on the throne.

Kundavai was enraged by her vow.

'These two girls are sure to drive me mad. Nambi, why did you bring this boatgirl here?'

'Princess, the prime minister ordered me to go to Thiruvarur and bring back Ponniyin Selvan. All the roads are flooded. Then I saw this girl stranded. She told me that if I got her a boat, she would row me to Thiruvarur. I saw your chariot along with the attached boat. I thought I could borrow it. But Senior Paluvettarayar had taken the boat and the chariot. So, I came here to seek the astrologer's help.'

'Nambi, did you hear the words of Paluvettarayar?'

'Yes Princess, after hearing him I feel that every second here is like a hundred years. Even our emperor is in danger. I request you go to Tanjore right now. I have already sent the astrologer's disciple to find a boat for us.'

Vanathi stood up and screamed.

'No. I don't want to go to Tanjore. I will go only to see Ponniyin Selvan. Even if I were to die, I'd rather die at his feet.'

Poonkulalai was disturbed.

'Nambi, I can't come with you. I want to go to Kodikarai,' screamed Poonkulali.

The astrologer who had not taken part in their conversation till then also screamed.

'All of you, please keep quiet!'

Everything stopped. Nobody said anything. Suddenly they heard the sound of a storm.

'Ladies, you came to this poor man's house at the wrong time. I have been predicting the future for the entire nation. But I could not predict the floods and warn you in advance,' lamented the astrologer.

'What danger can come to us here?' asked Princess Kundavai.

'Princess, all the rivers are overflowing. My house will be marooned very soon. Let us leave this place quickly.'

All of them rushed out of the house. Waters from the nearby river Cauvery were breaching its banks and boundaries, gushing from all directions.

'Princess, let's move to the resthouse nearby.'

The astrologer guided them to the resthouse in the temple. They all went in.

Poonkulali was the first to reach the resthouse and climbed onto it quickly.

By that time, water had surrounded the resthouse on all the four sides. The water was rising fast. The astrologer and Nambi managed to climb up with great difficulty. Kundavai and Vanathi were still in the water. They tried to climb up. Poonkulali extended her hand to Kundavai and lifted her up. Vanathi was left alone. She tried to climb up twice and failed. Kundavai and Poonkulali tried to help her. While Kundavai was holding one hand, Poonkulali was holding the other. Vanathi looked up. When she saw Poonkulali holding her, she forcibly freed herself from her grip. The jerk caused by her action made her other hand slip from Kundavai's hold. Vanathi fell into the water with a terrible splash and began to float.

All this happened in a fraction of a second. Those standing on the resthouse screamed. The water took her to the roof of the astrologer's house.

'Thank god, I'm out of danger,' thought Vanathi.

The others saw her and felt relieved.

Let her be there for sometime. As soon as the boat comes, we can rescue her.

Vanathi's safety didn't last for long. The roof started floating in water. Vanathi was also floating along, maintaining a tight grip on the detached roof.

'Sister, I'm going to see Ponniyin Selvan. Mother Cauvery is taking me to him,' shouted Vanathi.

Vanathi was sure that the others, particularly Poonkulali, would have heard her.

13

My Astrology Won't Fail

The Chola Kingdom was known for its fertile soil and abundant water thanks to the rivers flowing through the kingdom. The Chola kings used even the war prisoners to build lakes and river banks.

The Grand Anicut (*Kallanai*) built with sand, stone and mud is a standing heritage monument trumpeting the architectural glory of the Chola kings. The Chola Kingdom had excellent water management system by harvesting the excess waters. The people of the Chola Kingdom were also used to the fury of floods and cyclones and knew how to manage them.

Princess Kundavai was deeply upset about Princess Vanathi being carried away by the floods.

'My God, the roof is floating. Vanathi is also floating!'

'Astrologer! When will your disciple return with a boat?' shouted Nambi.

'No point in believing this astrologer any longer. Nambi, can you save Vanathi? Or shall I jump into the water to rescue her?' asked Princess Kundavai.

Just then they saw the astrologer's disciple bringing the rescue boat. But Vanathi was moving away very fast on the roof. It might be too late if they waited for the boat to reach her.

Poonkulali spoke to Princess Kundavai.

'Princess, let me go. I will swim across and bring her here.'

Kundavai hesitated. She remembered that Vanathi had fallen back into the water because Poonkulali had offered her a helping hand.

'Please believe me, Princess. I have a moral obligation to save her.'

'I trust you. But I don't trust Vanathi.'

'Princess, she may refuse to get into the boat if I'm there. But I will pull her into the boat and jump out. I can swim back.'

Without waiting for a response, Poonkulali jumped into the water.

'Astrologer, till now I believed in astrology. But today I have lost my faith in that pseudoscience.'

'Princess, my faith in astrology has become stronger today. I knew about this impending danger for Vanathi but I didn't tell you. She will come out of it. And all my predictions about her will also come true.'

'Even if Vanathi is saved, your predictions will fail. Didn't you hear her terrible vow?'

'Princess, if my predictions don't come true, I will throw all my palm leaves of astrology in the river Cauvery.'

Nambi was at his sarcastic best.

'The river Cauvery did not even wait for you to throw your palm leaves. She has already entered your house on her own and swallowed all your palm leaves. What do you say now?'

The astrologer yet commented, 'My predictions will never fail!'

14

The Elephant Goes Wild

Prince Arulmoli was the royal guest of the people of Nagapattinam. A grand feast was given in his honour. After the celebrations were over, the prince left Nagapattinam on a decorated elephant and was followed by a massive, enthusiastic crowd. The prince and the people reached the town of Thiruvarur by night.

A grand reception was accorded there as well, with special poojas and a grand feast followed by a variety entertainment programme much against his wishes.

When the prince returned to the palace by midnight, disturbing news awaited him. All the roads to Tanjore were flooded. He was advised to postpone his journey for two days. But he was anxious to reach Tanjore at the earliest. Floods and breaches could never hold him back. He wanted to avoid the crowd to speed up his journey.

After deep thought the prince asked the palace employee to summon the palace mahout. The mahout was missing. But someone was at the gates insisting to see the prince.

'Your Majesty, a boatman by the name of Murugaiyyan wants to see you urgently.'

'Bring him in,' said the Prince.

Murugaiyyan came running in and fell at the prince's feet. He started wailing and narrated a woeful story.

'Prince, I found my wife in the company of some sorcerers in a graveyard. They were threatening the royal mahout about an impending danger. They also predicted that the royal elephant which was to carry you will become mad and push him down. The elephant will carry away the prince. People would kill the royal mahout thinking that the elephant went mad because of him.'

The prince consoled him

'Don't worry. I will manage.'

'Your Majesty, I'm ashamed of my wife.'

'Don't worry. I'll refine her,' comforted the Prince.

'Bring the royal mahout in the morning. Let us leave early.'

After Murugaiyyan went away, the Prince was in deep thought. It was evident that the conspirators were up to something. He worked out a strategy before going to bed.

The next morning, Prince Arulmoli approached the elephant and gently stroked the beast, whispering something in its ear. Murugaiyyan turned up to report that he could not find the royal mahout anywhere.

'Never mind, remove the chains from the elephant's feet.'

The chains were removed.

Now a mahout came running in with a goad in his hands. When he came nearer, the elephant lifted him in its trunk and tossed him far away. The goad in his hand also fell further away.

'The elephant has gone mad!'

People panicked and started running away.

They were running helter-skelter in fear. The prince recalled the words of Murugaiyyan about the conspirators. He knew now that the mahout who had approached the elephant was not the original royal mahout. He was a conspirator. The elephant also knew this instinctively and had thrown him away.

Prince Arulmoli whispered something in Murugaiyyan's ears. He then mounted the elephant. The elephant started running terribly fast.

'Oh my God, the elephant has gone mad!' Murugaiyyan shouted.

This frightened the people all the more. The elephant crossed the city limits of Thiruvarur and the prince chose an unused route to Tanjore to avoid the attention of the people.

The elephant ran. Unmindful of obstacles and rough terrains, the elephant ran fast through open fields, the canals and the breached rivers towards Palayarai. The prince was quite thrilled.

Murugaiyyan ran on the streets shouting

'The elephant has gone mad.'

He ran towards the pond where the fake mahout had been thrown by the elephant. He saw him struggling in the water. He was the sorcerer whom he had seen with his wife, Rakkammal, and the original royal mahout the previous day in the graveyard.

Murugaiyyan went near that man and enquired.

'Tell me where is the actual royal mahout?'

The fake mahout was shocked

'How do I know? Why ask me?'

'You cannot deceive me. Didn't you take the royal mahout to the graveyard and frighten him yesterday? Where is he and my wife Rakkammal?'

'Mahout? Rakkammal? What happened to you?'

In a trice, he played a trick and diverted the attention of Murugaiyyan and escaped.

Murugayiyan went in search of the original royal mahout. After great difficulty, he found him in an abandoned house bound by ropes. He had been kidnapped by the conspirators with the promise that they would give him an amulet to protect him from dangers.

People were worried about the whereabouts of the prince and assembled at the Chola Palace gates. They were debating amongst themselves whether the prince had ridden off on the mad elephant to control the beast or to prevent the people from getting hurt. They were all aware that the prince was a good mahout.

Murugaiyyan and the real palace mahout reached the Chola Palace. People came to know about the conspiracy to kill the prince and were shocked.

Some enquired about the elephant and went in the direction taken by the beast while others started walking on the highway to Tanjore. The crowd gained momentum with more and more people joining in at every village.

15

Love at First Sight

Vanathi was floating along with the detached roof. She was moving at the speed of the flowing water. Vanathi was in no mood to get down from the floating roof. She recalled the words of Senior Paluvettarayar. He had hinted that the prince's life was in danger. The girl naively believed that the river Cauvery was taking her to her beloved Ponniyin Selvan.

Then she remembered Poonkulali.

Oh! My God, why is she so interested in the prince? Why is she taking so much liberty with Prince Arulmoli?

Then another part of her mind admonished her.

She has every right to. Prince Arulmoli is alive today only because of her.

But the rest of her mind did not accept that logic.

No, it is not true. He is alive today thanks to his stars. She was lucky enough to be there with him when the prince was saved and shared the limelight. That does not entitle her to take liberties with the prince.

In the midst of her turmoil, Vanathi also longed for a similar chance. She wanted to save the prince at least once and score against that boatgirl.

As Vanathi was being dragged along by the force of the flowing water, she spotted a boat following her. She saw a man and Poonkulali in that boat.

Perhaps Poonkulali has been sent by Princess Kundavai to save me. Enough is enough. Already the prince is indebted to Poonkulali for saving his life. Let me not be beholden to her too. I would rather be drowned in floods than be saved by that headstrong girl.

Vanathi floated a long distance. She saw a riverbank full of dense trees on it. She remembered her earlier visit to this pilgrim centre known as Thirunallam.

The Queen Mother had once taken Princess Kundavai and Princess Vanathi there.

I remember an incident which happened at that time in the garden near the palace. I will never forget it in my life.

Princess Vanathi had come to the Chola Kingdom from her native Kodumbalur for the first time. She was amazed by the perennial rivers and fertile lands. There were no rivers in her hometown except for some lakes and ponds which would be half-full during winter and dry in summer.

Vanathi rejoiced at the sight of big lotus leaves which appeared like black umbrellas to the fishes in the pond. The dancing beetles around the lotus and lily flowers were a visual treat.

During her visit to Thirunallam along with Queen Mother and Princess Kundavai, they had stayed at the Chola Palace. Princess Kundavai and Queen Mother would be engrossed in endless discussions on spiritualism. But Vanathi's mind was attracted to the songs of the birds, the dance of the peacocks and the varied colours of the fragrant flowers.

Vanathi had never dreamt of such a joyous life. And she recalled her encounter with a stunningly handsome youth swimming in the river. The water was almost red in colour and the man's complexion was a kind of golden hue. She had been mesmerized by his handsomeness.

Vanathi had been covered in shame.

Oh! My God! How could I have lost my mind in the physical beauty of a stranger?

But her heart had not listened to her head. In spite of the repeated warnings, her eyes had moved in the direction of the handsome young man. It was love at first sight.

She had been ashamed of herself. When she had been about to

leave, she was distracted by the sound of nestlings from a nest on a tree. Pity and horror filled her mind. A few nestlings popped up their heads from the nest and screeched softly. Vanathi was touched by the panic in their voices. A wild cat was climbing up the tree very close to the bird's nest.

Vanathi screamed for help.

The young man bathing in the river came running towards her.

'What happened?'

The restless parent birds came near the nest and parentless Vanathi was moved by the scene. When the cat was about to extend its front paw towards the nest, Vanathi screamed again.

Meanwhile, the young man had come near her thinking she was in danger. He looked at her with a smile. Vanathi's heart melted.

For a while, she even forgot the plight of the birds. The young man tried to shoo away the wild cat. But the cat was unfazed.

'That cat is a real devil.'

He picked up a stone and threw it at the cat. The frightened cat jumped to another branch and went away.

But the nest was now hanging precariously ready to fall anytime. The young man thought fast. At first, he thought of climbing the tree to save the nest. Then he changed his mind and brought his elephant.

Vanathi was watching the young man saving the birds from the steps of the pond.

The young man got down from the elephant and looked around for her. He heard her laugh and came to the pond.

'Girl, why are you laughing?'

'I thought of your valour and I could not help laughing. You brought an elephant to fight with the cat. Great!'

The young man too laughed.

'Is that just a cat? Judging from the way you screamed, I thought it was a tiger.'

Vanathi became her normal self. She was no longer shy. She was confident as well.

'Why should one fear a tiger in the Chola Kingdom? The tiger is after all our symbol.'

The young man's face blossomed into a smile.

'You chatterbox, I'm not an alien. I belong to the Chola Kingdom. I have been on elephants to many a battlefield. Tell me, who are you?'

'Mahout, you ask too many questions.'

'Sorry girl, I won't ask. Looks like you hail from a royal family. I will be on my way now.'

The young man climbed the steps of the pond.

Vanathi was still in a teasing mood.

'Hey, mahout, will you take me for a ride on your elephant?'

'Sure! What will you give me?'

'You want wages? Ok listen. I'll recommend you to my uncle, chieftain of Kodumbalur. I will get you a job in our palace there. Or else, I will make you the head of the elephant battalion of our Kodumbalur army.'

'Oh my God, are you the Kodumbalur Princess?'

The smile vanished from the young man's face.

'Do you think that the Kodumbalur Princess is not worthy enough to ride your elephant?'

'There are hundreds of elephants in the Kodumbalur stable and there are hundreds of mahouts too. I won't be needed there.'

The young man walked briskly away from her. She was looking in the direction for a long time. She expected the young man to turn at least once to look at her but it didn't happen. He rode away on the elephant.

Meanwhile there was news of Prince Arulmoli visiting Thirunallam to see his elder sister Kundavai. All the girls in the palace were dying to have a glimpse of the handsome prince.

Vanathi was on the terrace. The prince was riding on an elephant. Vanathi could not believe her eyes. It was only at that moment she realised that the mahout whom she had ridiculed earlier was none other than Prince Arulmoli.

But was this man our prince? Oh my God! What have I done? I offered the King of Kings the post of a mahout at Kodumbalur!

She felt embarrassed.

He must have thought that I'm a shameless country brute.

She wanted to confess her blunder to Princess Kundavai. Many a time she tried to speak. But words never came out of her mouth.

She thought she could meet Prince Arulmoli and seek his forgiveness. But she had no courage to do so.

Vanathi recollected the events of that fateful day as she was floating on the roof in the flooded river. She knew Prince Arulmoli had a soft corner for her. He had conveyed that through Princess Kundavai.

But something was blocking the soft corner from blossoming into love. Vanathi knew what 'that something' was. Prince Arulmoli was aware of the factions among the Chola chieftains—one faction headed by the Kodumbalur Chieftain and the other faction headed by the Paluvettarayars. He thought that the Kodumbalur Chieftain, Vanathi's uncle was forcing the marriage on him because one day he might ascend the Chola throne. Vanathi's uncle had hinted at the marriage alliance several times. The prince was very careful in balancing the factions.

Now Vanathi recalled her vow never to ascend the throne.

If the prince comes to know about my vow never to sit on the Chola throne as a queen, perhaps his mind will change. But how do I communicate this to him? I want nothing but his love. If I happen to see the prince again, I should not miss the opportunity to express my love.

Suddenly, she saw an elephant and a mahout crossing the flooded river.

Who is the mahout? Is it the prince? But how can it be? Once I mistook the prince for a mahout. That does not mean that every mahout is the prince. Ok, let him be just a mahout. Let him save me from the floods.

Vanathi shouted,

'Mahout! Mahout!! Help me I'm drowning.'

But the mahout did not hear. The elephant did not stop and soon the elephant and mahout disappeared from view.

The roof picked up momentum. It was rotating as it moved fast. The huge trees and their gigantic roots started floating close to her. If the floating roof hit one of those mighty roots, it would break and sink in the water. Suddenly she sighted a huge crocodile with its mouth wide open.

The floating roof came near the bank. It was a matter of seconds before it would hit the strong roots of the trees.

Vanathi closed her eyes and prayed.

Oh Goddess Durga! Take this orphan girl to your lotus feet and give me peace forever.

16

Life and Death

It appeared as if there was no end to Vanathi's floating on the waters. When she realized that she was facing danger, she closed her eyes and started to pray. Suddenly she experienced a jolt caused by the roof hitting the roots of a tree on the river bank.

The roof crumbled. Sensing danger, Vanathi clung to the branches for her life. The force of the water was so strong it felt as if it would rip her legs from her body.

However, she climbed up the branch using all her strength and sat on it. When she looked down, she saw the crocodile with its jaws wide open as if to swallow her.

Suddenly, she saw an elephant walking towards her. It was the same elephant that had crossed the river a little while ago. Vanathi also saw a boat coming towards her.

Oh my God! Poonkulali is coming.

Vanathi was cursing her fate as she didn't like the idea of being rescued by Poonkulali.

The boat came very close to her. Poonkulali smiled at her.

'Princess, you have chosen a good place to hide! Come down fast. Do you know who is coming, there riding on the elephant?'

Vanathi knew the person on the elephant. However, she wanted a confirmation.

'I don't know. Who is he?'

'Well, he is the person whom you were searching for. The prince.'

She didn't want the prince to see her like this, sitting on a tree. She was eager to get into Poonkulali's boat. But the boat drifted away.

Poonkulali jumped into the water to rescue Vanathi without being aware of the presence of a hungry crocodile.

'Oh my God! Crocodile! Crocodile!' screamed Vanathi.

Poonkulali was shocked to see a huge crocodile very near her. Poonkulali was no coward. And yet there was nothing she could do to escape from that hungry reptile. One wrong move and she would be finished. The only way to escape was to get back into the boat. But the boat was beyond her reach. And the crocodile was advancing towards her. Her situation was even more perilous now.

Vanathi recalled how Poonkulali had saved the prince and moreover, Poonkulali had come here, just to rescue her.

So, her first duty was to save Poonkulali. Vanathi extended her hand and pulled Poonkulali up but the branch could not bear their weight. If both were to fall, they would fall right into the big mouth of the crocodile. Meanwhile, the elephant came very close to them and trumpeted. The crocodile was distracted by the sound and moved away.

Poonkulali and Vanathi screamed in fear. The elephant lifted Poonkulali and Vanathi to safety one after another. When they opened their eyes, they were on the river bank.

Poonkulali was in tears.

'Princess, I came to save you but you saved me from the crocodile.'

'No, not at all, we both were saved by that mahout.'

'Princess, I'm not very keen to live, but my aunt has given me a secret message to be passed on to her son. I don't want to die before delivering that message.'

Now Vanathi mischievously looked at the prince. 'Mahout, will you please take us with you for a ride on your elephant?'

Vanathi laughed at her own joke.

17

Pain and Pleasure

Prince Arulmoli enjoyed Vanathi's sense of humour.

'Hi girl, getting up on an elephant is not easy. It is as difficult as ascending the royal throne.'

'The beauty is that some undertake a difficult task even for petty reasons. I know a person who came riding on an elephant to save nestlings.'

'Oh Vanathi, you still remember that?'

'Warriors who go around the world busy doing heroic deeds might forget that. But a silly girl like me has nothing more worthwhile to do than remember such incidents.'

'Vanathi, this is not fair. I have to rush to Tanjore. How did you come here? Why are you alone? I heard that you were floating on the roof of a house. How did this girl come here?'

Poonkulali intervened.

'Prince, I'm happy you remembered me at least now. If you give me a few seconds, I will tell you what I have to, and go my way never to return.'

The two women were expressing their emotions powerfully for some reason.

'Ocean Princess, how could I ever forget you? I was calling you several times. You chose not to listen to me and you were furiously rowing your boat. I cannot forget how you both were hanging between the tree branches and the mouth of the crocodile.'

The prince laughed.

'I want to know how both of you came here. Can any one of you brief me?'

'Prince, your dear sister and I came only to meet you on the way to Tanjore. Princess Kundavai feels that if you enter Tanjore at this time, there will be a civil war. She wants to talk to you before you enter the city.'

'Where is she?'

'At Kumbakonam.'

'When we were in the Kumbakonam astrologer's house, the Cauvery breached and entered the astrologer's house. And I was washed away in the floods and now I'm here. Mother Cauvery saved you but she wants to drown me.'

'Vanathi please don't blame her. Mother Cauvery loves everyone. At times her love crosses all boundaries. People who don't know about her abundant love blame her.'

'Prince, I won't blame Mother Cauvery anymore. Your sister and the others ran to the temple near the astrologer's house and got onto the resthouse. I was foolish. I slipped down into the water while climbing up. I came floating along with the roof all the way up to here.'

'I think Poonkulali came to save you but my elephant saved both of you. It lifted both of you gently like a garland of flowers. Do you know what the same elephant did this morning? It threw away the mahout. I don't know whether he is alive or dead.'

'Oh my God, were you hurt by the mahout?'

'I was about to be. How did you know about it? Did the astrologer tell you?'

'No, the astrologer did not say anything. Senior Paluvettarayar told us.'

'What?'

'Yes, prince. Senior Paluvettarayar told us about the threats to your life.'

'I'm surprised. How did he know? Has he too become an astrologer? Did he say anything else?'

'Yes, but I shudder to repeat his words. The conspirators had planned to kill you, your brother and your father on the same day.

Paluvettarayar has rushed to Kadamboor to save the crown prince. He has requested the princess to warn you and the emperor.'

'Oh my God, since his warning has come true in my case, it ought to be true for the other two as well. Ocean Princess, you want to say anything?'

'Yes prince, the Lankan Queen wanted me to bring you to Tanjore Palace immediately.'

'I'm heading towards Tanjore only for her. I heard that somebody forcibly abducted her. Is it true?'

'Yes, prince. But it was done by our prime minister with good intentions.'

'Oh, that's his work. I'm sure he must have taken her to my father. Poonkulali, did the emperor meet the Lankan Queen?'

'Yes prince, they met.'

'My life's mission has been accomplished in that case. I can't think of anything happier than that. So long as my mother, the Lankan Queen is by my father's side, she will be safe.'

'Yes prince, I know. As long as she is there but...'

'What Poonkulali? What but...?'

'Prince, I don't know how to say this, I'm lost for words. The Lankan Queen believes that she is going to die soon. And she wants to see you before her death.'

'Oh my God! Just a few seconds ago, you gave me happy news. And now this devastating news. I can't delay even for a second. Vanathi, please ask the princess to forgive me. I'm proceeding to Tanjore straight away.'

18

Marching of Armies

It was a momentous day for the capital city of Tanjore. Forgetting the havoc wrought by the storm and the floods a few days ago, people were excited to see the most valiant warrior who won over Lanka and the hearts of the people—the one and only Ponniyin Selvan. News had reached the people of Tanjore that the prince had come out of hiding on the day of the storm and was marching towards the capital followed by thousands of people. They decided to give a rousing reception to the prince.

There were some unmistakable signs that something unprecedented was going to happen. The gates of the fort had been opened early in the morning as usual to let in the palace staff, vegetable and milk vendors.

But the massive gates of the fort were closed very soon and the people were wondering.

'What is happening here?'

'Perhaps all these steps are being taken only to prevent Ponniyin Selvan from entering the fort.'

'Must be so,' others confirmed.

When this rumour spread across the city, people became agitated. This caused a storm in the minds of the people, a storm whose intensity was no less than the storm that had raged across the kingdom a few days ago.

'Who the hell are these damned Paluvettarayars to prevent the Chola Prince, from entering the Chola Fort?'

Another terrible rumour was floating around that fateful day regarding the health of the emperor.

'Who will succeed in case of the emperor's death?' People raised the question with concern.

'Will the chieftains divide themselves into factions and fight against each other?'

As an animated discussion was going on, people were surprised to see armies marching on all the three roads leading to Tanjore. The armies were so huge that the people could only see the front portion of the army but not its tail end.

People heaved a sigh of relief to see the territorial insignia of the chieftains beside the larger tiger symbol.

The armies were led by the great general of the south command, Bhoothi Vikrama Kesari. Now everybody understood that the armies were coming to crown Ponniyin Selvan as the next emperor and get him married to Princess Vanathi, the general's niece. As that was what the people wanted, they became immensely excited on seeing the general and his massive army. People were eager to welcome them and host a grand feast in their honour.

19

The Crucial Meeting

All the chieftains loyal to the emperor had assembled outside the fort. The general of the southern command, Boothi Vikrama Kesari, the chieftain of Kodumbalur addressed them in a majestic voice.

'The whole world knows our loyalty to the Chola clan. But today our enemies have levelled a charge against us saying that we have gathered here to rebel against our emperor. That is not so. None can meet the emperor without the knowledge of the Paluvettarayars. The emperor is being held hostage by them.'

Several voices approved the words of the general. He then continued to speak.

'We have assembled here only to save the Chola clan and the mighty Chola Empire from disaster. The traitors have also poisoned the mind of our emperor to the extent of him losing his coherent thinking. Will any father abandon his two valiant sons and prefer coward Madurandakan for the throne?'

'We strongly doubt whether it is really the wish of the Emperor!'

Several voices rose in chorus.

'It is a story concocted by the treacherous Paluvettarayars.'

Somebody in the assembly shouted.

'Maybe. Today our mission is to know the truth. Suppose the emperor himself wants to crown Madurandakan as his successor, will you agree to it?'

'Not at all!'

'Never!'

The whole assembly shouted.

'I won't agree either. The issue of succession was settled during the lifetime of the late Emperor Paranthaka Chola. He proclaimed that after Emperor Sundar Chola, his heirs alone should ascend the Chola throne. Even Madurandakan's father late Emperor Kandarditya and the Queen Mother never wanted their son to ascend the throne. There has to be a very strong reason for the Queen Mother's stand. In these circumstances, why should our emperor want to crown Madurandakan?

There is another reason to prove that he has lost his mind. You all know that Senior Paluvettarayar never extended his cooperation for our soldiers in Lanka. But our warriors won the war under the dynamic leadership of our darling Prince Ponniyin Selvan. The emperor sent orders to arrest such a heroic son.

But the soldiers sent to arrest the prince refused to obey the orders. The prince offered himself to the hands of law and sailed to our country. They now tell us that the ship was caught in a storm and the prince was drowned. Once again, the Ocean King saved our prince and now, he has come out of his hiding in Nagapattinam. He is marching towards Tanjore followed by a huge crowd. We all have assembled here to show our solidarity to the people.

When our prince was about to leave Thiruvarur this morning, his elephant suddenly became mad and threw away the mahout. The mad elephant ran away. In the pandemonium, our prince has gone missing.'

Many people screamed but the general continued his speech.

'Initially, I too was shocked. But our Prince Arulmoli is as intelligent as he is valiant. He can't be so easily trapped by the traitors. Let us hope for good news about him very soon. In the meanwhile, I want to know your views on what we should do now.'

The assembly was unanimous that it's representatives should meet the emperor to reveal their strong views on succession. The Paluvettarayars should be removed from their powerful post and the emperor should relocate to Palayarai.

In case Karikalan did not want to be the king, then the throne should naturally be passed on to his brother Prince Arulmoli. No one else should be considered for that position.

If they were denied an audience and if the Paluvettarayars refused to open the gates of the fort, then they would have to lay siege to the fort.

Some thought it would be prudent to wait till they receive news of Prince Arulmoli.

Others had different views.

'What is the point in waiting? The army under the direct command of the Paluvettarayars is on the other side of river Kollidam. Presently the river is in spate. The army cannot come here now. This is the right time to knock down the fort and release our emperor from the clutches of the Paluvettarayars.'

When the meeting continued, a sentry approached the general and whispered in his ears

'Let the talks continue. I will be back in a minute.'

The general rushed out of the meeting.

20

At the Gates of the Fort

The general of the southern command mounted a horse and rode fast towards the northern gate of the fort. He saw an elephant coming towards the fort. On top of the elephant were a mahout and two women.

The mahout blew the pipe to announce the arrival of Princess Vanathi.

The general was surprised to see Vanathi's sudden arrival. He was equally surprised to hear the familiar voice of the mahout.

'Vanathi, my dear child...'

Before he could complete his statement, Vanathi interrupted him.

'Is that you uncle? Then, whatever I heard was true.'

'Yes, my child, it's me. But what is this? Do you have to carry the message in these circumstances?'

'Yes, uncle. Princes Kundavai sent me as the messenger precisely because of this risky situation. She got the news that you have surrounded the Tanjore Fort with a massive army. If somebody else had brought this message, the palace guards might block the messenger. She has also sent Poonkulali to help me to deliver this important message to the emperor.'

'Yes, this boatgirl is very smart. But what is this important message?'

'It is an urgent message for the emperor. It is about Ponniyin Selvan.'

'Oh, is it about him? Is he safe?'

'Uncle, he is safe. I also know where he is right now. But I cannot reveal that to you.'

'What? You can't tell that even to me? Is that you who is talking Vanathi?'

'Yes, uncle. I have promised not to disclose the whereabouts of the prince to anyone.'

The general was shocked.

'Girl, I'm totally disappointed. I thought if I send you to Princess Kundavai, she will mould you into a noble princess. But you have been groomed as an adamant brat. Enough is enough. You need not stay in Palayarai any longer. Get down from the elephant first. I shall pack you off to Kodumbalur right now.'

'Uncle, I'm aslo not keen to step on the soil of this capital city. That's why I'm still seated on the elephant. But the problem is this elephant becomes mad quite often. It was only this morning that this elephant was about to kill the mahout. Please don't come near the beast. I will deliver the messages and come to you. You can then pack me off to Kodumbalur or any other place on the earth. Uncle, but for heaven's sake, please let me go and do my duty now.'

The general thought for a while.

'Ok, my child. I'll let you go. What will you do if the doors of the fort do not open for you?'

'Uncle, use your military might to break open the gates.'

The general was proud of his niece.

'My dear child, only now you talk like the real princess. If the need arises, I won't mind breaking open the gates to let you in. But I don't think that is necessary. You have brought a message to the emperor from Princess Kundavai. Junior Paluvettarayar cannot stop you. When you deliver your messages, please deliver my message also to Junior Paluvettarayar. Tell him that my companions and I are waiting outside the fort to meet the emperor to know what is on his mind...'

'I will do that, uncle.'

Now the mahout blew his pipe to announce their arrival, the gates were opened and they entered.

21

The Prince's Royal Entry

The recent critical developments made Junior Paluvettarayar very agitated and he felt his brother Senior Paluvettarayar's absence.

The news of his brother missing in the floods, the presence of a huge army of the general of the southern command, Bhoothi Vikrama Kesari at the fort gates, missing Prince Arulmoli from Thiruvarur and news of the frenzied behaviour of Crown Prince Aditya Karkalan were all the causes of his mental turmoil.

Hence Junior ordered the gates of the fort to be closed with strict instructions to allow nobody to go in or come out. He wanted to update the emperor of all the developments in consultation with the prime minister. Another idea struck his mind. He wanted to take the prime minister along instead of meeting the emperor alone. His presence by his side might lend credibility to his words.

He met the prime minister and shared his concern. The prime minister was worried about the missing mute queen and Poonkulali. But he didn't like to share all these disturbing developments with the emperor.

'The emperor is already worried. Let us wait for some more time and try to find out what is on the mind of the general. Meanwhile I will get some definite news about the missing Prince Arulmoli and Senior Paluvettarayar.'

Junior accepted the sane counsel of the prime minister.

I will be happy if the prime minister takes the responsibility of informing the emperor at the right time. Let me focus on the security measures inside the fort.

He was also curious to know what was happening outside the fort. Meanwhile, a soldier came running to Junior to inform him about the arrival of an elephant carrying two young women. The mahout wanted the gates to be opened for them. Junior was surprised to know that one of the women was Princess Vanathi.

After all it is her uncle who has gathered a huge army outside the fort to invade it at any time. The girl has real courage to seek entry at this critical time. Why should I be bothered about this little girl?

He climbed up a flight of stairs to have a look. He overheard a part of the conversation between Princess Vanthi and her uncle. The general was requesting Vanathi not to go in. But Vanathi was adamant to deliver Princess Kundavai's message to the emperor and the Senior's message to Junior. She wanted to gain entry at any cost. At first, Junior wanted to deny entry to her. After overhearing their conversation, he changed his mind and wanted to open the gates.

It was strange that Senior Paluvettarayar had chosen Vanathi to send a message to him. The gates of the fort opened and the elephant entered. Junior welcomed Princess Vanathi.

'Princess, you ignored the words of your uncle and have chosen to come in as my guest. My child, please feel at home.'

Junior's voice was quite majestic.

'Thank you, Commander! Please let me do my duty first. I will deliver the messages. Then I won't care even if I'm thrown into your infamous underground dungeons.'

Vanathi's voice was equally majestic. The mention of underground dungeons reminded Junior of Princess Kundavai's visit to it along with this girl.

'I know you are familiar with our underground dungeons. But I don't have much time to speak to you about all that. Tell me about the message from my brother.'

'Your brother conveys that the personal bodyguards of the slain Pandiya King are involved in a terrible conspiracy. They have set a date to seek revenge. Your brother has asked you to be more careful with the security arrangements for the emperor.'

Junior laughed.

'Is that all? You needn't worry about the emperor's safety.'

'Commander, your brother thought that you might ignore and take his warning casually. That is why he wanted me to convey another important message. It seems you have been warning him of a sorcerer who was frequenting the palace of the junior queen. And your brother never heeded your warnings. He even chided you for poking your nose in his wife's affairs. I will repeat his words verbatim.

'Brother, I have erred. That sorcerer Ravidasa is the head of the personal bodyguards of the slain King Veerapandiya. He has taken a vow to destroy the entire Chola clan. One of his men might try to kill our emperor today. Don't be complacent. Tighten the security. Be extremely alert. Anything may happen anytime.'

This is the exact message of your older brother.'

Junior now realized that only Senior could have sent such a message.

'Why has he not come here? Why has he sent you?'

'He has not sent me. He conveyed the message to Princess Kundavai who has sent me here. The crown prince is also in danger. So, Senior has rushed to Kadamboor to save him.'

'Where did you meet him?'

'At the Kumbakonam astrologer's house. If you still doubt me, please listen to this. When your brother was crossing the river Kollidam in his boat, it capsized in the floods. He somehow managed to escape and reached the Thiruppurambiyam War Memorial in the forest. There he overheard the murderous plans of the conspirators. Are you convinced now? Shall we go to the palace?'

'Princess, I'm convinced. But no conspirator can enter the gates of the fort.'

'What if the conspirators are already inside the fort?'

'Impossible!'

'Well, that's your responsibility!'

'Your duty is over. You may go now.'

'No, Sir. I have finished just one half of my duties. I have to meet the emperor and deliver the message from Princess Kundavai.'

'You can deliver the message to me.'

'Impossible. Princess Kundavai has asked me to deliver the message personally to the emperor. Still, you don't trust me. Are you afraid?'

'The word fear is unknown to our clan.'

'Then let me go into the palace. After all, you are going to come with me.'

'But the emperor is not in good health today.'

'Don't worry. I have brought some good news for him. And if only you knew what the news is all about, you will feel bad about having delayed me for so long.'

Junior Paluvettarayar was surprised.

'Have you brought news about Prince Arulmoli?'

'Yes, Commander.'

'That's great. Where is he now? I'm sure the conspirators have not...'

'Yes, the conspirators made an attempt on his life. But by God's grace, the prince escaped unhurt. Are you happy now?'

'What a silly question girl! Let us not waste any further time. You may convey the happy news to the emperor in my presence.'

He ordered his men to search every square inch inside the fort and identify any suspicious persons.

He then turned around to see the mahout going into the palace along with the girls.

Is he the mahout? Why should he still be following the girls? His job is over. What business does he have with the Emperor?

A terrible thought entered his mind like a bolt of lightning.

Perhaps the mahout is an assassin from the Pandiya Kingdom? Or is he one of Commander Bhoothi's men?

He ran after the mahout.

'Stop here. You have no business inside the palace,' roared Junior.

Junior grabbed the mahout's hand with his iron grip.

The two women heard Junior's roar and turned around. There was fear and surprise on their faces. And then there was a smile.

Vanathi tried to speak.

'You know you... know... he... is... none other than...'

At the peak of anger, Junior did not listen to her. His fears were confirmed because the mahout stood transfixed in his place.

He tightened his grip on the mahout's hand.

'Who are you? Speak the truth!'

Without loosening his grip on the mahout, he used his other hand to turn his face towards him.

'Commander, I've come here to surrender. The emperor has issued orders to have me arrested.'

Light from the torches in the main hall showed the majestic face of the mahout. Junior recognized his face and his voice. Gradually and slowly his iron-like grip on Prince Arulmoli slackened.

Prince Arulmoli's golden face revealed mesmerizing powers. Despite provocation, there was not even mild irritation on his face.

Yet, the fearless Junior Paluvettarayar trembled and spoke in a choked voice.

'Ponniyin Selva, the darling of Chola kingdom. I beg your pardon for the grave offence of insulting you. My eyes were blinded. I long to hear the word "forgiven" from your lips.'

He was about to continue in the same strain when the prince stopped him.

'Commander, what are you talking about? How can this small boy forgive you? You only did your duty.'

'Even if my hand that blocked your entry into your palace was to be cut off, it wouldn't be an adequate punishment. Even if my tongue that uttered in dereliction was to be pulled out, it wouldn't be the right punishment for my crime.'

'Commander, the fault is mine. You were not expecting me to come as a mahout.'

'That's true. I never expected that. I have failed to give a royal welcome to the prince who has come home.'

'Commander, this is not the right time for formal protocol and royal paraphernalia. You just heard the evil plans of the conspirators. I'm afraid that they may be true. The Kodumbalur Chieftain has laid siege of the fort. That's why I came as a mahout and I brought his niece with me.'

Meanwhile all the guards came closer to him to pay their respects to the prince.

All started hailing the prince.

'Commander, should we stand here and talk?'

'No, your majesty, please get inside the palace.'

22

Trusting and Mistrusting

After Ponniyin Selvan went inside the palace, Junior Paluvettarayar ordered the guards to refrain from making noise as the ailing emperor was taking rest and the fort was under siege by enemies.

The leader of the personal bodyguards of the emperor asked,

'Who is our enemy? The Kodumbalur Chieftain is not our enemy. After all he wants to place Prince Arulmoli on the Chola throne.'

Junior's face turned red in ire.

'Who is he to decide on the issue of succession? Should we not hear what is on the emperor's mind?'

'Is the emperor really alright? There are all sorts of rumours going on. We, the emperor's personal bodyguards want to see him and confirm.'

'He is fine. Stick to your duty and don't poke your nose in these affairs,' said Junior, with fiery eyes and walked towards the palace.

He saw Poonkulali standing alone near the steps.

'Hi girl, why are you standing here? Did anybody refuse you entry into the palace?'

'No Commander, I don't want to go in as father and son are meeting after a long time. Why should I intrude?'

'I'm happy that at least you believe that the emperor is alive.'

'I not only believe it, Commander. I saw with my own eyes. He is doing well.'

'Tell that to these idiots. They don't believe that the emperor is alive.'

'Till this moment their suspicions are baseless. But what is the guarantee that their worst fears won't come true at any time?'

'You want to set a date for the emperor's end? Did you see some astrologer?'

'Apart from astrologers there are others who have set a date for the emperor. Didn't you hear what the Kodumbalur Princess said?'

'What is the guarantee that that is true?'

'But Commander, why should the Kodumbalur Princess lie in this matter?'

'Who knows? She might want to ascend the Chola throne as an empress? Maybe you too have such aspirations?'

'Commander, I should not have stopped to talk to you.' Poonkulali tried to walk away.

Junior's mind changed

'Girl, tell me all that you wanted to say.'

'Commander, I will. Otherwise, I will feel guilty. If something happens to the emperor, the entire country will blame only you.'

Junior's face fell.

Are you implying that I'm careless? See how many soldiers are guarding the palace round the clock?'

'I know, Commander. But danger can come from within the palace.'

'What...?'

'Commander, I saw a Pandiya conspirator with a sharp spear hiding in the underground passage in the palace.'

'Oh my God, what are you talking about girl? Do you know where the passage leads to?'

'It goes through the underground treasury.'

'Now I remember. It must be the work of that devil, Nandini, who has enslaved my brother. How many times I warned him! Do you know where the passage is?'

'My aunt took me through the passage this morning.'

'Who is your aunt?'

'The one who was dragged from Kodikarai in your palanquin.

Commander, I'm afraid...something may happen as we are discussing.'

'It's true.'

Junior went out and gave orders to his men to hunt for the conspirator. He then borrowed a torch from one of the guards and returned to Poonkulali.

'Girl, you show me the way. Let me see if you are telling the truth.'

Even at that time, Junior did not trust Poonkulali.

Perhaps she wants to know about the secret underground passage from me.

Junior followed Poonkulali with these thoughts storming in his mind. He was surprised at Poonkulali's speed.

Poonkulali had had the most hectic day. Even before daybreak, her aunt, the Lankan Queen, had dragged her into the underground passage near the Ravana statue. They had frightened the conspirator hiding there by making weird noises. The conspirator was so terrorized that he thought that there were ghosts inside the passage. He knocked on the other entrance of the secret passage towards Senior Paluvettarayar's palace. Junior Queen Nandini's maid opened the door and came in with a torch.

Poonkulali and the Lankan Queen slipped out of that passage. In a secluded place, the Lankan Queen conveyed to Poonkulali in sign language that she was going to die soon and would like to see Prince Arulmoli before that. Poonkulali did not like to leave her aunt alone. Yet, she wanted to fulfil her wish.

She scaled the walls of Senior Paluvettarayar's palace and reached the gates of the fort. She met Alvarkkadiyan there and joined him on the journey to find the prince. The Cauvery was flooded. They came to the Kumbakonam astrologer's house to find a boat to cross the river. They saw Princess Kundavai and Vanathi there. With these thoughts, Poonkulali was taking Junior to the underground passage.

Now Poonkulali wanted to find her aunt and also stop the assassin if he was still hiding in the underground passage. She was unable to do so by herself. So, she had sought the help of Junior Paluvettarayar.

As she was entering the art gallery, she saw a shadow from the terrace. She also saw a figure going along the wall. She wanted to check and hence stood there for some time.

'Why have you stopped girl? Are you afraid your lie is going to be exposed now?'

Hearing the stinging words of Junior she walked fast.

As soon as she entered the art gallery, she pointed out the entrance to the underground passage to Junior.

'You are right. You go down first.'

The commander ordered.

Poonkulali hesitated for a second. Her body trembled. Exactly at that time she heard a strange sound. It could come only from one person—her aunt Mandakini. It was more of a wail than a scream. She realized that the sound was coming from the emperor's bed chambers.

She ran towards the king's chambers. She was shocked to see a pointed spear coming towards the emperor from the terrace.

Prince Arulmoli, Vanathi and the empress were standing near the emperor's bed not knowing what was happening. Everyone was staring at Mandakini who was screaming like a crazy woman.

Poonkulali ran towards her aunt.

23

Our Goddess

Before she could reach the place, the pointed spear pierced her aunt. Mandakini screamed and fell down.

Everybody ran towards Mandakini. They all heard sounds coming from the palace terrace. A vessel was thrown on the lamp burning by the emperor's bed to put it out. The room was suddenly enveloped in darkness. For some time, pandemonium prevailed in the bedchamber. The sound of footsteps was heard.

'Bring a lamp immediately!' shouted Junior.

'Who is that?! Stop there! I'll finish you!'

Junior Paluvettarayar shouted at the unknown assasin.

Poonkulali guessed the identity of the person running away. Two maids brought lamps into the chamber.

Everybody was surprised to see the emperor sitting down on the floor near the dying Mandakini. Prince Arulmoli was by his side. Blood was dripping from the spear that had pierced the Lankan Queen. They were all shocked to see a knife stuck in the bed of the Emperor.

Prince Arulmoli gently placed Mandakini's head on the emperor's lap with teary eyes. The emperor was sobbing.

Poonkulali saw the scene unfolding before her; she rightly guessed what had happened a few seconds earlier. The assassin who threw the spear at the emperor knew that Mandakini bore it on herself and saved the emperor. Then the assassin must have tried to stab the emperor and escaped through the entrance.

Though Poonkulali wanted to run behind the assassin and kill him, she wanted to be with her dying aunt.

'Oh aunt! Whatever you predicted came true. I should not have left you alone.'

When Poonkulali began to wail, Prince Arulmoli consoled her. But Poonkulali's sobbing did not stop.

'Your Majesty, I don't have anybody in this world except my aunt.'

'Poonkulali, she is your aunt. But for me she is more than my mother. You have helped me many times in the past. But I could never forget what you have done today by uniting my father and my mother. Your aunt has proved her greatness by saving the emperor.

When my father saw the spear on this blessed lady, he, who has never moved out of his bed for the past three years, got up and ran to her. Knowing that his spear missed the mark, the assassin put off the lamps, ran down to the chamber and made a second attempt on the emperor. As the emperor had already gotten up from his bed, the assassin's mission was fruitless. His knife struck an empty bed.

If the emperor had been killed by the conspirator, there would have been chaos and civil war in the country. She deserves to be worshipped as the family deity by the Chola clan.'

His face was stricken with grief.

'Your Majesty, I have the Sea King. I will take refuge in him. I don't have anything to do here. I have nobody. If someday you and the Kodumbalur Princess come to Kodikarai...'

Poonkulali stopped mid sentence and walked fast towards the door after throwing a glance at Vanathi.

Vanathi tried to block Poonkulali. But Poonkulali pushed her away and walked faster. Junior Paluvettarayar blocked her again near the door.

'You saved our Paluvoor clan from disgrace. I'm indebted to you. I will give you whatever you want. I promise.'

Poonkulali responded with sadness.

'Commander, some of the people here are happy that the emperor is saved and he is able to walk again. Others are happy as the Paluvettarayar clan has been saved from disgrace. But nobody is worried about the death of my aunt. I'm now going to find the assassin who killed her. Please move aside.'

Junior was shocked by her words.

'I concede my failure. If I don't arrest him, I'll be disgraced. My disgrace will not simply go because the emperor is saved. I was stupid in doubting your words. I lost precious time there. The assassin must be hiding in the underground passage only. Come with me, let us catch him.'

Junior grabbed Poonkulali's hand and hurried towards the art gallery.

All the others in the room remained frozen in their places focusing their eyes on the emperor and the dying lady lying on his lap. It seemed as though they were alone and were living the life they had lost in those moments.

The emperor was sobbing.

'You have sacrificed your life for me today. I'm a stone-hearted sinner. Those who are born to rule have to harden their hearts. They do not have a choice.

The first sin I committed was to have deserted you leading to so many other sins. Ghost island in Lanka—I can't think of a happier heaven than that. What a great life we lived on Ghost island, my dearest. It was God's conspiracy that we were separated. My people conspired against you and me. Soon after my coronation, I came to Kodikarai in search of you. But I was informed that you had jumped into the sea and ended your life. Later I sent my Prime Minister but he too frustrated me. He knew that you were alive but he hid the fact from me. You had silenced him by taking a promise from him that I should not be informed you are alive. That resulted in all the disasters.'

Mandakini's face wore an indescribable expression of bliss and she spoke with her eyes.

I have nothing against you. I'm nobody in front of you. I have been avoiding you all these years. But once in a while I had the satisfaction of having a glimpse of you from afar.

Finally, the emperor said:

'Whenever I saw you, I showed nothing but disgust. You will have to forgive me my dearest. Today you came as our goddess to save me. Please forgive me for all my wrongs. You did not want my sons to succeed me to the throne. I have wronged you. You saved not only me but also my son. They say that you had a child. If it is true, please tell me now. I have to perform a father's duty for him.'

Mandakini understood the emperor's body language and consoled him using sign language. Then her eyes fell on Ponniyin Selvan; she touched the prince.

'You are my son.' Mandakini spoke through her eyes and closed them forever.

Mandakini's life left her body. Everyone was sobbing and wailing.

Prince Arulmoli was the only person who remained unruffled.

He spoke to the emperor.

'Father, let us not grieve the death of my mother. My mother is still alive. She has become our Goddess, the principal deity of the Chola clan.'

True to his words, he built a temple for the Lankan Queen when he ascended the throne as Raja Raja Chola.

24

The Opportune Time

Nandini was restless in the Kadamboor palace. Her lips kept murmuring the magic words,

'The time has come.'

She was staring at the sword lying on her bed. Nandini lifted the sword and held it close to her chest and spoke to it.

'Oh! Divine sword, the time has come for you to accomplish your mission. I've been waiting for long to reach my goal.'

Suddenly Nandini's body trembled in unbearable ecstasy.

'Oh, you have come? The spirit of Veerapandiya! Tonight, after avenging your death, I hope you will let me sleep peacefully. Just before your death you promised to make me sit on the Pandiya throne if we escaped from that danger. I don't want the throne or the crown. Your bodyguards brought a boy and claimed him to be your son. They even coronated him. I know you will leave me and go to heaven once I avenge your death.'

Now she heard footsteps very close to the entrance. As Nandini was trying to keep the sword back on the bed, Manimekalai entered the room.

Nandini who looked as if possessed a few minutes ago totally changed into the cool Nandini whom Manimekalai adored. She welcomed Manimekalai in a soft voice.

'Sister, I've come to share some sad news with you.'

Nandini was upset, wondering whether her plans of the last several years had been thwarted by some sudden unexpected development.

'Manimekalai, what is it?'

'Sister, Senior Paluvettarayar has not yet reached Tanjore. On the way...'

'What happened on the way? Is he coming back to Kadamboor?'

'Senior Paluvettarayar was caught in the floods. His boat capsized. He is missing now.'

Nandini remained unperturbed.

She asked in a voice devoid of any concern.

'How did you hear of this?'

'A person who went with Paluvettarayar has come back. He was sharing the news with my brother. Sister, my brother is hesitant to break this news to you. So, I came running.'

Manimekalai broke into a sob. Nandini hugged her.

'I know your love my dear, no need to grieve.'

Manimekalai was startled.

This lady's heart is made of solid rock.

Nandini understood her mind.

'Manimekalai, you broke the sad news to me and offered consolation. But I'm consoling you. You need not grieve. My husband won't be in danger. But I'm concerned about something else.'

'What is that sister?'

'Manimekalai, your brother and the Pallava Prince are lusting after me. I'm keeping this sword only to ward off such evil men. Aditya Karikalan loves you but you love Vandiyathevan. Your brother Kandamaran is against Vandiyathevan. He thinks that he was stabbed by him. Moreover, he wants to marry you to the crown prince so that you can become the empress and he can become the prime minister. So, they have poisoned the mind of the crown prince. Your brother has got the consent of the prince to finish off Vandiyathevan.'

'My beloved is a great warrior. Nothing can harm him sister.'

'So what? What if he is ambushed by armed killers all of a sudden? They will simply eliminate Vandiyathevan who blocks your marriage with the crown prince. They will slice him into pieces and feed it to the dogs and jackals.'

'Oh my God!'

'You can caution him. Didn't you say that he is a great warrior? Do you think he would run away if you warn him of the danger? No, he won't. He will be more stubborn. He would prefer to stay back and fight rather than run away.'

'Help me sister. I feel dizzy. I don't know what to do.'

'Yes, I have got an idea to save Vandiyathevan. Didn't you tell me that Senior Paluvettarayar's boat sank in the river and there has been no news about him?'

'Yes, I did.'

'Using that as a pretext, I will plead with Vandiyathevan to go to Kollidam to look for Senior Paluvettarayar. You too plead on my behalf. When two women plead for mercy, he won't refuse. The only way to save his life is to send him out of this palace as fast as possible. Once he is gone, let us speak to your father, your brother and even to the crown prince and convince them.'

'Even if he agrees to go, how will he go out of this place? My brother won't let him go.'

'Why should your brother know at all? Manimekalai, do you remember how he had given you a shock the first time when he came through this underground passage? Let us send him out through the same passage.'

'Yes sister, I'll leave now and I will come back only with him.'

Manimekalai left the chambers.

As soon as she left, Nandini heard a knock on the door that opened into the Hunters' Hall.

Nandini opened the secret door. She saw an ugly gory face.

'Sorcerer, have you come already?'

'Yes, Queen. And the time has come too.'

25

He Won't Die

Nandini turned around to bolt the main door and opened the secret door to the Hunters' Hall. Ravidasa stood there with a swollen face and wounded body.

'What is this? What happened to you sorcerer?' asked Nandini.

'Queen, why should you be surprised about the wounds? It is nothing new for me. Theveralan and I are alive today thanks to the spirit of our Emperor Pandiya.'

'Sorcerer, his spirit appeared before me also a few minutes ago. I told him that I would fulfil my vow today or else I will kill myself.'

'No Queen, you should live even after you fulfil your vow to witness the coronation ceremony of Veerapandiya's son. We also need your help to move the Chola treasury to our kingdom.'

'I don't like the idea of deceiving my husband once I have fulfilled the vow.'

'Queen, who is your husband?'

'The one who married me at his old age unmindful of public ridicule and the one who is helping me in fulfilling my vows. I am referring to *that* great warrior. Tell me how you got these wounds.'

'Yesternight an old tiger attacked me with its sharp claws and strong teeth.'

'Can't you face an old tiger?'

'Queen, that's why we rely on tricks and sorcery. If we miss our mark this night, we can never again make it. If news about Sundara Chola and Prince Arulmoli leak out, then Aditya Karikalan will become alert and will never fall into our hands again.'

'Sorcerer, what happened to the emperor and Arulmoli?'

'They should have been killed by now.'

'That's what you told me when you went to Lanka but nothing happened.'

'Queen, that crazy mute lady spoiled all our plans.'

'You said that Vandiyathevan had died at sea but he is still alive; guarding Aditya Karikalan night and day like an impenetrable iron armour.'

'Don't worry about it.

Queen, tell me about the arrangements you have made.'

'Better if you don't come here. Trust me, I will finish the job.'

'Queen, we are here because we trust you. Once the vow is fulfilled, we want to take you back to safety.'

'I'm sure my plan will work out without a hitch. Once the vow is fulfilled, I won't live in Paluvettarayar's palace even for a minute.'

'Queen, then we will take you with us.'

'How will that be possible?'

'Idumban Kari is waiting at the end of the underground passage with a palanquin to take you to Kolli Hills.'

'Sorcerer, any news about Senior Paluvettarayar?'

Ravidasa was shocked.

'He left for Tanjore. As he was crossing river Kollidam, his boat capsized and he is missing. But I don't believe it. Paluvettarayar won't die so easily. Will he come back here tonight? I'm worried,' said Nandini.

'Absolutely no chance of his coming here tonight. Now tell me what are your orders for me?'

'Sorcerer, you wait here. No matter what happens, don't enter my chambers. Come in only when I call you. If you come in before that, our plans will go up in smoke. In the event of any hitch in our plan, you will hear me cry and then you can come in immediately.'

'Queen, we abide by your instructions but we would never like to hear you cry.'

26

Hysterical Crown Prince

Vandiyathevan was restless in the place garden. He was exhausted. *I'm trapped in this Kadamboor palace, caught in the grip of a hysterical prince.*

He painfully recalled the venomous words of the crown prince.

'Don't ever come before me again. I will deal with you tomorrow morning.'

Why should the prince be furious? Oh well, no use in blaming him, as he is in a state of confusion.

Aditya Karikalan's frenzied behaviour touched new heights on that day. Unbridled enthusiasm, total exhaustion, uncontrollable anger, extreme hostility—he was a bundle of contradictions with unpredictable mood changes from moment to moment. In turn, Karikalan was torturing those around him.

Disturbing news from all quarters was fanning his fury. The first news brought by Sambuvarayar was about his grandfather. Malayaman was said to be gathering a huge army to invade Kadamboor. Sambuvarayar condemned the action of that old man.

'And yet, Malayaman is very old. Are you afraid of him?'

The crown prince taunted Sambuvarayar.

'Your Majesty, the word fear is unknown to our clan. Just give us a nod. We will show the old man...'

'It was I who asked my grandfather to come with an army as I'm caught here with you all alone, what if something were to happen to me...?'

Sambuvarayar was thunderstruck.

'Prince, if you have any doubt, you may at this very second...'

'Do you want me to leave your palace?'

'No no! This is your kingdom. This is your palace with the Chola tiger-flag flying here. Who am I to send you away? Give us permission. My family and I will vacate this palace.'

'So, you mean to say that you are fearless and I'm timid?'

'Prince, the whole world knows of your valour. When you were just twelve, you destroyed the enemy's army. When you were just eighteen, you beheaded the Pandiya King Veerapandiya and brought laurels.'

These words of praise touched a raw nerve in the crown prince.

'I know you are making fun of me because I was chasing a person who was running for his life and I cut the head of a defenseless man. I know that the Paluvoor devil is responsible for all this.'

The crown prince's laughter frightened Sambuvarayar. He regretted having initiated the conversation with the hysterical prince.

'Your Majesty, today is a bad day for me. Whatever I say seems to annoy you. Please let me go.'

'You may go now. But don't leave this palace. Nor will I leave the palace till I know the truth behind the conspirators' assembly held inside this palace four months ago.'

Sambuvarayar trembled.

Pitiying Sambuvarayar, Parthiban interceded on his behalf.

'Your Majesty, the Chola clan is known for its sense of justice as well as its valour. But you are not being fair to this elderly chieftain. You are hurting him with your stinging words. He has already given you an explanation and you have also accepted it.'

Aditya Karikalan laughed again.

'Yes, as long as I'm alive it is impossible for anyone to ascend the Chola throne. That's why they want to finish me off here.'

The crown prince laughed again before emitting fire on his close friend, Parthiban.

'Do you think I don't know that you too have joined these

conspirators? Do you think that I didn't know that you were aiming your spear at me when we went hunting? But for my friend, Vandhiyathevan, I would have been killed.'

Parthiban stared at Vandiyathevan.

'Your Majesty, this crook has poisoned your mind. If he proves that I have betrayed you, I will this very second...'

'Parthiban! You brought me here seduced by the words of that devil Nandini. Can you deny that?'

'Prince, I'm not refuting that. And there is no need for that also. Paluvoor Queen is good-hearted, her intention was to bring you here to marry you to Kandamaran's sister and bring peace in this empire. Nothing could make me happier than seeing the Chola crown on your most worthy head. I will tolerate Vandiyathevan's words as a former friend. But if he speaks ill of the Paluvoor Queen, I will kill him with this sword right now.'

Parthiban unsheathed his sword.

'Oh, my dear valiant friend, put the sword back in its case. Vandiyathevan never accused the Paluvoor Queen. He has come running all the way only to tell me that the Paluvoor Queen is my own sister. He never accused the Paluvoor Queen but he accuses you. You took my brother Arulmoli on your ship from Lanka. He says that on the way you pushed my brother into the sea and killed him. What is your reply?'

'Prince! Let me answer on behalf of Parthiban,' with these words, Kandamaran entered.

'Prince, I have happy news for you. Prince Arulmoli is alive. He is now heading to Tanjore accompanied by thousands of people.'

Kandamaran expected that the news would make him happy but he was disappointed to see Karikalan's anger which was now directed towards Vandiyathevan.

'What? Arulmoli is heading for Tanjore with thousands of people? What for? Vandiyatheva, what is happening now? Didn't you say that Arulmoli will be in Nagapattinam till I decide on the succession to the throne. Why the hell is he marching towards Tanjore now?'

Vandiyathevan responded in a soft voice.

'Your Majesty, I just repeated the words of Princess Kundavai. I don't know what has prompted the Prince to take this decision. Shall I go to Tanjore and find out?'

'So, you also want to leave me? You have all become my enemies. I know why Arulmoli is heading for Tanjore. It is the conspiracy of the Kodumbalur Chieftain. That old man wants to marry off his niece to my brother and make her the queen of Chola Empire. My sister, Princess Kundavai and you are all a part of this conspiracy.'

'Forgive me, Your Majesty. Neither your brother nor your sister have such thoughts. If you want, I will go there to find out.'

'You want to join them and take active part in their conspiracy? Kandamaran, arrest this crook and put him in the underground prison.'

Kandamaran approached Vandiyathevan with glee.

Before he could touch him, the crown prince changed his mind.

'No, don't do that. People of the Chola clan never falter in fairness and justice. They will never punish anybody till guilt is proven. Vandiyatheva, never see me again. I will decide tomorrow whether you will be sent to Tanjore or to jail. Don't stand before me even for a moment. Get lost.'

Vandiyathevan looked at the crown prince's face. There was a strange expression in the corner of his eyes.

This is part of the game I'm playing.

Yet, he decided to keep away from the hysterical prince.

'Your wish is my command, Your Majesty.'

Vandiyathevan hurried out.

Kandamaran and the crown prince remained, talking for a long time.

Vandiyathevan was upset and suspicion haunted his mind.

Suddenly his thoughts were interrupted by a girl's scream.

'Ghost! Ghost!'

27

He Is Our Common Enemy

It was pitch dark. Suddenly Vandiyathevan heard a girl screaming.

'Ghost! Ghost!'

His mind worked fast and he ran in the direction of the sound.

That is Manimekalai's voice. What is she doing here at this time? Why did she scream?

Vandiyathevan tripped on the roots of a tree as he ran with all these thoughts in his mind. Everything seemed to be appearing like a bad omen. Now Vandiyathevan heard the voice of Chandramathi, Manimekalai's personal maid.

'I'm here, near the lily pond. Come quickly.'

He heard Chandramathi running towards Manimekalai.

Vandiyathevan was listening in on their conversation unnoticed by them.

'Princess, why did you scream? What frightened you?'

'Chandramathi, I saw a figure with a thick beard, wearing a garland of human skulls over that wall. As soon as I screamed, the figure vanished.'

'Princess, it must have been a hallucination. There are no ghosts in this world. It is not possible for anyone to climb this high wall.'

'No. It was not a hallucination. I have never seen ghosts or spirits.'

'Princess, you only see the face of that handsome young man in your dreams as well as in reality.'

'Chandramathi, is this the time for teasing?'

'Then when can I tease you, Princess? You are waiting near a lily pond in a garden of flowers with fragrance all around, on an enchanting evening. When you were expecting the Prince of Vallam, a bearded figure appeared in his place.'

'And adding to my woes you too have come now.'

'Perhaps the ghost is scared of me.'

'Chandramathi, this is not the time for petty talk. I really saw a horrible figure over the wall. Have you finished that work assigned to you?'

'Princess, the mission failed.'

'Why?'

'I could see only the Chola Prince and the Kadamboor Prince talking to each other in hush-hush tones. I could not see the Vaanar Prince.'

'Perhaps he has been sent away on some work.'

'Not possible, Princess. I asked Idumban Kari. He told me that the crown prince was furious with the Vaanar Prince and told him to get lost. He must, probably, be here somewhere in the palace. Perhaps, dressed up as a ghost to scare you.'

'No Chandramathi, there are many people in this palace who camouflage their real self under a disguise. I'm sure that our warrior is not like that. You look out for him. Take the help of Idumban Kari if needed.'

'Princess, I hate this man, Idumban Kari, with his frightful eyes. I'm afraid of him.'

'You are not afraid of ghosts. But you are afraid of Idumban Kari. In a way it is better to avoid him. You yourself look for Vandiyatheven once again. I will be here till then...'

'What if the bearded ghost comes again?'

'Don't worry I will use your name and drive away the ghost.'

Vandiyathevan heard the clinking sound of anklets. He guessed that Chandramathi was going away.

Vandiyathevan was immersed in deep thoughts.

Who could have come as a ghost and frightened Manimekalai? Why is she eager to see me?

He knew Manimekalai loved him though he had never reciprocated. He always maintained a distance. He did not want to fan the fire of enmity with Kandamaran.

Manimekalai must have sensed some danger. Perhaps that is the reason she wants to see me.

Vandiyathevan was filled with gratitude while recalling her earlier help.

I should help her now. She is alone. I could avail her help to leave this deceitful palace. So, I must meet her.

Manimekalai was sitting near the lily pond in a romantic setting. When Vandiyathevan went closer to her, she was shocked to see a human shadow and lost her balance and was about to fall into the pond.

'Princess, it's me,' announced Vandiyathevan holding Manimakalai in his arms.

Manimekalai shivering in ecstasy and shyly tried to push his hands away. But Vandiyathevan brought her forward by tightening his grip on her.

'Don't touch me,' she whispered in excitement.

Vandiyathevan took away his hands.

'I'm sorry, Princess. Please forgive me.'

'Why should I forgive you?'

'I appeared suddenly and frightened you.'

'Yes, you did appear very suddenly. Agreed. But tell me, why did you hold me?'

Manimekalai was back to her usual mischievous self.

'I saved you from falling into the pond.'

'Wonderful. But on that day when I was drowning in the lake, you didn't bother. Now you have come to save me from falling into a pond which is only knee-deep. What irony!'

'The fault is mine. You saved my life once. I will never forget that help.'

'Nor can I forget the way you showed your gratitude. I have never seen anyone so ungrateful.'

'That's a grave charge, Princess.'

'Didn't you say that some killers were following you? I went into the Hunters' Hall to find out who they were. Before I returned, you had disappeared from the scene like a thief.'

'Princess, you don't know what kind of situation I was in on that day.'

'It has been ages since you came back to the palace. But till now you never tried to explain to me why you ran away on that day.'

'I've been waiting for the right opportunity, Princess.'

'Dumb words. Lame excuses. You don't even look at me.'

'Sister, pardon me.'

'I'm not your sister.'

'My friend's sister is my sister as well.'

'Kandamaran is not my brother. Nor is he your friend. He is our common enemy.'

'Princess, you know everything. Till a few months ago, Kandamaran was my best friend. He has now become my worst enemy. Parthiban is biding his time to finish me off. Aditya Karikalan's moods are also constantly changing. One moment he is full of love, the next second he is spitting venom. I spend my time wondering what danger lurks from where and when. Under these circumstances, if I try to talk to you to express my gratitude...'

'I'm happy that you are so keen on saving your life.'

'Princess, I'm not worried about my life. I'm worried that you should not be hurt because of me. I will never forget your help as long as I'm alive.'

'Please repeat that once again?'

'Why only once, I'll repeat it a thousand times. I will never forget you as long as I live.'

'You will be grateful as long as you live. So, the first priority is to save your life. If not for yourself, at least for me you have to save your life.'

'What is this about, Princess?'

'Please tell me the truth. Didn't you overhear the conversation I had with my maid a little while ago?'

'Yes, I did.'

'You know that I sent her to bring you to me, somehow.'

'I heard that, Princess. That's why I came to you.'

'Otherwise, you would not have come near me. Right? Oh my God! What concern! Your heart is made of stone. But I can't be like you. I can't bear to see you in danger.'

'Princess, I know I'm surrounded by danger. I'm used to it. Tell me, is there a new danger round the corner?'

'Get out of this palace as fast as you can.'

'You want me to run away like a coward?'

'You should not run away from a battlefield but nothing wrong in running away from conspirators.'

'Who are these conspirators?'

'Who else but Kandamaran and Parthiban.'

'They can't harm me. I won't run away from this palace because of them.'

'I can't bear to see my brother hurt you.'

'Princess, you are not responsible for your brother's acts.'

'Parthiban and Kandamaran want to kill you because of me.'

'If I'm hurt on your account, then I will consider it a great privilege conferred on me.'

'What Nandini said was right.'

'Oh, what did she tell you?'

'She told me that if I asked you to save yourself you wouldn't listen. She made it clear that we will have to work this a different strategy to save your life. Please come with me to see Nandini on a very urgent matter.'

'Princess, do you know what this "urgent matter" is?'

'I do. When Senior Paluvettarayar tried to cross river Kollidam, his boat capsized… You will have to go immediately and find what happened to him. Nandini wants to request you in person.'

Vandiyathevan thought for some time.

'She must have also warned you not to tell me this before she saw me.'

'Yes, she did.'

'Then why did you tell me, Princess?'

'Because I'm confused. Till a few days ago, I was quite innocent. I never suspected anybody. Now I have started suspecting everyone.'

'Perhaps you have changed after you met me, Princess.'

'Of course. Paluvoor Queen wanted you. When I was with her, I did not doubt her. But now when I'm talking to you, I doubt her intentions.'

'What kind of doubt, Princess?'

'She is also trying to hurt you.'

'Why should she hurt me?'

'I don't know. But her words and deeds create suspicion. She has a long sword and speaks to herself. Do you remember the time you entered into my room from the Hunters' hall?'

'How could I forget that, Princess?'

'Didn't you say that you were being chased by killers? At first, I didn't believe you. Then I went into the Hunters' Hall. There were several men hiding there. I didn't know whether they had come to kill you or they had come along with you. I was not sure at that time. I could not complain about them at that time because if I had mentioned about them I would have had to speak about you as well.'

'Princess, but now I realize how valuable your help was on that day.'

'A short while ago, Nandini sent me to bring you. Soon after I came out of her room, I went to her chamber again to clarify some doubts. The door was bolted from within. I heard voices from the Hunters' Hall. Some men were hiding in the Hunters' Hall. And there is some connection between those men and Nandini.'

Vandiyathevan realized the gravity of the situation. His intuition had been warning him of an imminent catastrophe. Now Manimekalai's words confirmed his intuition.

'Princess, you will have to help me now.'

'Tell me what I should do.'

'I know there are two secret passages to the Hunters' Hall from outside the palace. Apart from these two, is there a third way to reach the Hunters' Hall?'

'Yes, there is. There is a way for the workmen to enter the hall. My father used to take his guests only through that way.'

'Princess, please take me to the Hunters' Hall through that way now.'

'Why?'

'I want to know who's hiding there and what for.'

'I came here to save you from danger but now you want to see the very eye of danger.'

'I always carry a knife with me. It is better to meet danger half way rather than waiting for it to come to us.'

'I will take you there on one condition.'

'What is that, Princess?'

'I will come with you. I too have a knife with me.'

Manimekalai pulled out a knife and showed it to Vandiyathevan.

'Come, let us leave this place immediately before my maid returns.'

Manimekalai took Vandiyathevan out of the garden. Then she entered the palace and walked through the deserted corridor. Finally, she stopped before some steps leading to a door. The door was closed. She left Vandiyathevan to fetch a lamp.

She then walked up the steps and opened the door. Vandiyathevan followed her. She lifted her lamp to show him the way. They went down the narrow steps. After some time, Manimekalai whispered.

'Stop. I hear some footsteps...'

28

Monkey Grip

Vandiyathevan was listening to the sound of footsteps. It stopped. Then it was heard again.

'Should we go further?' whispered Manimekalai.

'Princess, once I decide I never go back. It is not my habit.'

'That shows your steadfastness. Like a monkey you never loosen your grip.'

Vandiyathevan was following Manimekalai. Suddenly he made an attempt to overtake her. Manimekalai tried to stop him. In the process, the lamp slipped from Manimekalai's hand and the light went out.

'Why did you try to overtake me?'

'When there is danger, I won't allow a woman to go before me. That is just my habit, Princess.'

'I will be grateful if you would give me a full list of your habits.'

'Princess, I will do that when time permits.'

'Let's go back to the garden.'

'Princess, if you are afraid of the dark, you may go back.'

'Why should I be afraid when a valiant warrior is by my side?'

'Then come with me.'

Vandiyathevan moved forward. When he was about to trip and fall, Manimekalai held him.

'This is not a regular passage. It is not even. You can't find your way in the dark. I have come through this passage several times. I know all the steps, twists and turns. You may be the most valiant warrior in the entire kingdom. But now you have to follow me, holding my hand. Or else, we won't reach the Hunters' Hall.'

'At your service, Your Majesty.'

It was pitch dark inside. Manimekalai grabbed his hand. She found that it was cold.

This fearless warrior doesn't fear even the vile conspirators. Why should he fear holding my hand now?

They walked in silence for some time. Vandiyathevan was about to fall many times. Every time Manimekalai tightened the grip on his hand to avert the fall.

'The way to hell will be dark like this,' whispered Vandiyathevan.

'Oh! Looks like you have been to hell.'

'I have never been to hell or heaven. But I have heard it from the elders.'

'They perhaps would have heard it from their elders.'

Vandiyathevan could not believe that a girl who was so shy could be so daring and talkative.

Manimekalai continued the argument.

'Agreed, the way to hell is dark. Tell me about the way to heaven.'

'It will be bathed in the light of a million suns.'

'In that case I'd rather prefer hell. I can't stand the glare of even a single sun. If I remain with a warrior like you, even hell will become heaven.'

'And if I hold the hand of a princess like you, hell itself will become heaven.'

Vandiyathevan bit his tongue.

I should not have spoken like that. I should not give her false hope.

'Your hand is cold. You look like a condemned prisoner going to his execution. Look, you are trembling.'

'Princess, your words may be true. Death may be waiting for me at the end of this journey.'

'But once you have decided, you won't go back. Neither of us knows how many killers are waiting for us at the Hunters' Hall.'

'Let there be a hundred. Who cares? I'm not bothered. But I'm worried about something else.'

'What is that?'

'If Kandamaran finds us walking in the dark holding each other's hands...'

'So long as I'm alive, you can't be hurt by my brother. Half of my dreams have come true. Who knows the other half may also come true soon?'

They heard the sound of a door being bolted. The sound shocked them.

'We are near the Hunters' Hall,' whispered Manimekalai.

They saw light at a distance. The light gradually grew brighter and brighter and it was coming closer and closer. Manimekalai left Vandiyatheven's hand and moved a little away from him.

The next second Idumban Kari appeared before them with a lamp in one hand and a sharp knife in the other.

He was startled to see them. But both Manimekalai and Vandiyathevan knew that he was putting up a show.

'Sir, Princess, what is this? Why have you come here in the dark? Had you ordered this slave, I would have guided you. Where are you going?'

'Idumban Kari, we received news that Malayaman is coming with a huge army. I wanted to double check whether the walls, the passages and entrances are secured. I sought the help of the Vaanar Prince.'

'Princess, that's quite surprising. I too was on a similar mission.'

'I thought so. The lamp we had brought with us fell down on the way. It went out. We saw some light here. We thought it could be you and hence we came here.'

'Princess, your brother wanted me to check the passages and walls. I did a thorough check and am returning now. Can we return?'

'You may go leaving the lamp with me. The Vaanar Prince lost his spear in the river Kollidam. So, he wants to pick up a spear from the Hunters' Hall for his use as a war may erupt at any time.'

'Princess you are right, a war may erupt any time. But it is better not to take strangers into the Hunters' Hall. You know better than that. I need to advise you.'

'That's true, Idumban Kari. But this man is not a stranger. He is our prince's best friend. Soon, he might become a member of our family. You may go leaving the lamp with me.'

Idumban Kari left after reluctantly giving the lamp to her. They now heard the hooting of an owl.

'How can an owl enter the palace?'

Manimekalai was surprised. But Vandiyathevan was not.

'Perhaps a dead owl in the Hunters' Hall has come back to life. Princess do you remember that once upon a time a dead monkey came alive on seeing you?'

The door to the Hunters' Hall was locked from outside. Manimekalai opened the door and they both went in.

At first, they saw nothing but stuffed carcasses of dead animals like elephants, tigers and bears.

When Manimekalai lifted the lamp, they both saw a bunch of human figures sitting in the midst of the animal figures. The human figures were half-covered by the stuffed animals. The door through which they had come in banged shut.

Vandiyathevan wanted to know who had closed the door with so much force. At the same time, he was pushed from behind. He hit the tailless monkey behind which he had taken shelter earlier.

Two powerful hands gripped him now. It was like a 'monkey' grip. Those hands then took away Vandiyathevan's knife and aimed it at Manimekalai who came running towards Vandiyathevan, screaming.

'Don't make noise. If you remain silent and do what we ask you to do, your lives won't be in danger. But if you try to shout, both of you will be killed. The first to fall will be this Vaanar Prince.'

A voice spoke in the dark.

Vandiyathevan recognized the voice of the sorcerer Ravidasan.

'Be quiet, Princess. Let us know why they have come here and what they want us to do.'

Vandiyathevan was unperturbed.

29

Pandiya Empress

Vandiyathevan was bound to the stuffed tailless monkey and Manimekalai to the horns of a deer.

'Sorcerer, I'm your enemy but she is not. Why bind her? Do with me whatever you want to. But let that innocent girl go.'

'Patience, brother, patience. You interfered with our work several times. We left you alive each time. Even then you keep following us.'

Vandiyathevan laughed

'Why laugh, my boy? Does hugging the tailless monkey give you so much joy?' Ravidasan was quite sarcastic.

'No. Your words tickle me. I can't help laughing.'

'What made you laugh, my boy?'

'Didn't you say that I have been following you wherever you go? I can say the same thing about you as well. Even now when I was headed for important work along with the Kadamboor Princess, you blocked me and bound me to this monkey.'

'Oh, is that what you think? But this is the last time we are interfering with your work. If you go back alive, you will never see me again.'

'Sorcerer, then I should struggle hard to be alive. Why don't you teach me some sorcery so that I can stay alive?'

'Oh sure, my boy. Whatever happens here, be a silent spectator and your life won't be in danger.'

'I think you love me a lot. That's why you let me go alive every time you capture me.'

'I do concede that it is sheer foolishness. We had to simply obey our queen.'

'Who is your queen?'

'Don't you know that? Our queen is the Pandiya Empress, the valiant wife of our King Veerapandiyan.'

'An ideal wife!'

'Scoundrel! If you malign our Pandiya Queen, I will kill you. This is my final warning.'

'You are the one who is maligning her. You call somebody else's wife as Veerapandiya's wife.'

'Our queen is here as somebody's wife for a purpose. Once our mission is over, we will take her to our kingdom.'

'What mission?'

'You will come to know soon.'

Ravidasan ended the conversation and tried to go near the wall.

'Sorcerer, I want one more piece of information.'

Ravidasan turned towards Vandiyathevan.

'Don't call me sorcerer hereafter.'

'What should I call you?'

'Call me "prime minister".'

'Your Highness, can you please tell me the name of the great kingdom of which you are the prime minister?'

'You don't know? I'm the prime minister of the great Pandiya Kingdom.'

'Sorcerer, your queen had asked the Kadamboor Princess to fetch me immediately. That is why we came together.'

'There are other ways to enter the queen's chambers. Why did you choose this way?'

'I don't have to tell you the reason and I will explain it to your queen.'

'Then wait for our queen.'

'Sorcerer, ask them to release me and Kadamboor Princess right now. Or else…'

'Or else…?'

'I will shout so loudly that the Hall will tremble.'

'If you do that, three spears will pierce your body simultaneously.'

Vandiyathevan looked around. There were three conspirators armed with spears ready to attack him any time.

'Brother, you are really bright. Once we had a plan to recruit you for our mission. But you were caught in the love-net of that Palayarai devil, Princess Kundavai. That's all right. Act smart at least now. If you shout, you will be killed.'

Ravidasan walked towards the face of the elephant fixed in the wall. He grabbed the tusks of the elephant and turned it around. A small hole appeared in the wall and light entered the dark hall. The Hunters' Hall was partially illuminated.

Meanwhile, Manimekalai released herself by cutting the ropes that bound her by using the knife from her waist.

The conspirators were focused only on Vandiyathevan. They didn't notice Manimekalai. Vandiyathevan noticed that Manimekalai was free now. Vandiyathevan hooted like an owl.

The conspirators were stunned. Ravidasan was peering through the hole in the wall. He was shocked and turned around.

'Oh, was that you?' Ravidasan rushed towards Vandiyathevan. The moment he lifted his hands off the elephant's tusks the hole in the wall disappeared. The Hall was enveloped in darkness once again. The three conspirators armed with spears ran towards Vandiyathevan. One of them was attacked by the stuffed deer with long horns. A gigantic stuffed bear fell on the second and made him fall on the floor. Another stuffed crocodile fell on the third. A huge stuffed bat fell on Ravidasan.

The conspirators were stunned by the sudden attack. They remained frozen for a few minutes. Manimekalai used that time to free Vandiyathevan. After being freed he threw the stuffed animal on the conspirators. It took some time for the conspirators to steady themselves. They pushed away the stuffed animals thrown on them and finally managed to stand. Meanwhile Vandiyathevan had armed himself with a spear.

At that moment, the door to Nandini's chambers opened. Hunters' Hall was now bathed in light.

30

An Iron Heart Melted

Nandini was shocked to see Vandiyathevan and Manimekalai in the Hunters' Hall.

'Oh my God! How did you get here?'

'Queen, Manimekalai told me that you wanted to see me. I simply obeyed your command. But now I realize the folly of listening to the advice of a woman.'

Nandini smiled.

Vandiyathevan continued.

'Manimekalai grabbed my hand and dragged me here to see you. Now I am trapped with these murderers.'

'I don't think they are murderers. If I had not come in here just now, you would have murdered them all.'

'Sister, these people are murderers. There is no doubt about it.'

Nandini smiled.

'This man was hiding behind the same tailless monkey some time ago. Perhaps that's why they have bound him to the same monkey.'

'These are the men who were chasing the Vaanar Prince earlier. He managed to escape from them.'

'Then why did you lead him to these people again? Why did you bring him through this underground passage?'

'Sister, a little while ago, my brother Kandamaran was saying that he was about to come meet you. I didn't want to be seen by him with this prince. That was why I chose this way. In a way it was a good thing. Otherwise, these murderers...'

'Manimekalai, they are not murderers. They have not come to

kill the Vaanar Prince. They set him free every time he was caught by them.'

'Sister, then who are these people?'

'Manimekalai, they have come to take me home. Both of you now come with me, I'll tell you my story. Let them be here.'

Nandini then spoke to Ravidasan.

'Sorcerer, if you harm them, it is like harming me. You should always treat them with utmost reverence.'

Ravidasan came forward.

'Queen, this man knows our secret signal. He was the one who hooted like an owl.'

'That is more than enough to show that he belongs to us. Sorcerer, you have lost your reason. I give you orders; no sound should come from inside the hall.'

Nandini took Manimekalai and Vandiyathevan to her chambers. The door was closed

'Manimekalai, you are brilliant. In a way it is better that you brought him through the Hunters' Hall. Your brother and Aditya Karikalan will be here in a few minutes. You must leave before that. And I also want to take leave of you.'

'What is this, sister? You wanted to send this prince to find about your husband. But now you say you want to take leave of us!'

'Manimekalai, after talking to your brother, I have changed my mind. I can't stay here any longer. This warrior also cannot stay here any longer. It will be really dangerous if he does. Vaanar Prince, please leave this place right now, at least, for the sake of this girl.'

'Sister, let him take me also with him. After both of you leave, I can't be here in this palace-prison.'

Vandiyathevan intervened.

'Paluvoor Queen, I'm ready to go. Before that I need something from you. If you yield to my request, I will go at once.'

'Warrior, tell me, what I should do.'

'Queen, I lost my sword in the floods. Give me your sword with the fish emblem. I will go away.'

'Warrior, there are hundreds of swords and spears in the Hunters' Hall. Why don't you take one from there? Why ask for mine? This is the only weapon I have to save my honour.'

'You have no other motive?'

'What…?'

'It could be to avenge the death of King Veerapandiya.'

'I thought you wouldn't bring up that subject in her presence. Now you have spoken, I don't want to hide anything. Manimekalai, you should know why I came to Kadamboor Palace.'

Nandini picked up her sword.

'I didn't come here to resolve the internal strife in the Chola Kingdom or to divide the kingdom. Neither did I come here to enjoy the pleasures of Kadamboor Palace life nor to get you married. I came here with the sole motive to avenge the death of Veerapandiya. I have vowed to kill the wicked man who beheaded my beloved King Veerapandiya. Either I will fulfil my vow or die.'

Nandini spoke as if possessed.

Vandiyathevan's voice was drained of all emotions.

'You want to drive me away because you think I will hinder your mission. That is why you have been bluffing that my life is in danger.'

'Oh, are you going to stand in my way? Why don't you reveal all this to your friend and stop him from coming here?'

'Queen, I can't do that. That's why I have come to you. I'm ready to even fall at your feet to prevent you from committing this heinous sin.'

'Heinous sin? Do you know the meaning of those words? Listen, Manimekalai. Let's say you have given your heart to a man. His enemy comes to kill your beloved as he lies on his sick-bed. You fall at his feet and beg for mercy. The enemy turns a deaf ear. He kills your beloved. Will your act of seeking revenge be called a heinous sin?'

'Never, sister.'

Vandiyathevan intervened:

'Even if the enemy is your own brother?'

'Why this silly question? I'm being nice to you only because you are my brother Nambi's friend.'

'Queen, why do you want to continue with your evil drama? Nambi is not your brother.'

'Then who is my brother?'

'Crown Prince Aditya Karikalan.'

'Did you share this imagined belief of yours with Karikalan? Did he believe you?' Nandini was sarcastic.

'Looks like he believed me. But I don't know what is on his mind.'

'He is fascinated with your imagination.'

'It's not my imagination. I saw it with my own eyes in Lanka. I saw a mute queen who saved Prince Arulmoli, Nambi and me from great dangers in Lanka. Prince Arulmoli worships her as his deity.'

'Why tell me all this?'

'Princess, there is a strong reason. When I saw that angel in the dim moonlight at Lanka, I was surprised. You resemble her very closely. You are almost her replica.'

'I don't believe you.'

'Queen, you know the truth very well. You have used that to your advantage. When I saw you in your Tanjore Palace, this sorcerer was also there. I went into the underground treasury while trying to escape. And there I happened to see some strange sights.'

'Strange sights? What were they?'

'Kandamaran was going away with Prince Madurandakan through the underground passage.'

'So what?'

'Senior Paluvettarayar and you also went through the same passage after a while. You were devoid of fine clothing and jewelry. At that time, I didn't know what was happening. Now I understand. You went there as your mother's ghost to torment the emperor.'

Nandini who had been unperturbed until then, broke down.

'What else did you find out?'

'You and your husband met Kandamaran in the underground passage. Kandamaran said something to your husband. Your husband gave a signal to his guard.'

'What was that signal for?'

'Queen, you know it. Senior Paluvettarayar ordered the man to kill Kandamaran. I saved Kandamaran's life. What did I get in return? Nothing but blame. Kandamaran thinks that it was I who stabbed him.'

Nandini spoke while she was looking at Manimekalai.

'Warrior, you are trying to confuse this sweet girl.'

'Queen, I never spoken about this to anybody and if you give me the sword in your hand, I won't open my mouth about it in the future.'

'I can't give you the sword. You can tell anybody you want. It would be better if you can stop Karikalan from coming here.'

Suddenly, Nandini began to sob.

'Queen, the crown prince won't listen. That's why I'm begging you.'

'The emperor has betrayed my mother. Why should I show compassion to him or his children? If whatever you said is true, I have stronger reasons for revenge.'

'Queen, do you think your mother will approve of your thirst for revenge? That angel considers the emperor and his children dearer than her own life. Do you think she could bear to see her own daughter killing one of the emperor's children? She won't. And if she comes to know of your act, she will hate you.'

Tears were rolling down her cheeks.

'Mother! My dear mother! I'm already tortured by the severed head of the slain King Veerapandiya. Why should you add to my agony?'

Manimekalai spoke after a long pause.

'Warrior, I never knew that you could be so cruel.'

'Manimekalai, he is blameless. What he says is for my own good. He wants to save me from a greater sin. Even then… you know… I'm deeply disturbed.'

She then looked at Vandiyathevan.

'Warrior, nobody could have done this. I concede. Here take this precious sword.'

When Vandiyathevan was about to reach for the sword, Nandini suddenly withdrew.

'Wait! You have to agree to do me a favour before accepting the sword. If I don't complete this mission, the Pandiya conspirators in the Hunters' Hall won't leave me. They will burn me alive. I'm not in the least bothered about that. Will you take me to my mother? I want to see her at least once before I die. I said that I don't believe you. It's a lie. I believe everything you said about my mother who is wandering in the Lankan forest. I have seen her too.'

'When? How?'

Nandini spoke amidst sobs.

'When I was a child, my mother used to fondly stare at me without even blinking her eyelids. When I woke up, that figure would go away. This was scaring me. When I saw my face in the mirror, I realized the striking resemblance between both of us.

When I grew up, I realized that whatever I had seen was real. When I saw the emperor's reaction everytime he saw me, I was sure I had a mother and there was a mysterious story behind it. Thanks to hints inadvertently dropped by Nambi and a few others, I learnt the truth in bits and pieces and used it to my advantage. Since then, I have been longing to see her and today after listening to what you said, I want to see her at once. If you promise to take me to my mother, I will at this moment abandon this mission of seeking revenge. And as a sign of having changed my mind, I will give this sword to you.'

Vandiyathevan was lost in thoughts.

Manimekalai joined in Nandini 's plea.

'Warrior, please promise to fulfil her desire to see her mother.'

Vandiyathevan spoke with hesitation, 'I will do my best.'

'Then we should leave at once. We should leave the place before Aditya Karikalan comes here. How can we go from here? We cannot use the passage through the Hunters' Hall. Ravidasan and the others won't let us go alive.'

'Queen, you give me the sword. I will take care of Ravidasan and the others.'

'No. That would complicate things. Manimekalai, is there any other way to get out from here?'

'Sister, I don't know. He managed to vanish from this place on an earlier occasion. Ask him how he did it.'

Nandini looked at Vandiyathevan.

'Yes Queen, there is another way. But it is not easy to go through that way. One has to jump from one terrace to another. I'm wondering whether you can do it. A better option will be to face the sorcerer and his men, defeat them and then use the underground passage through the Hunters' Hall.'

Manimekalai spoke in a shocked voice.

'Warrior, I can hear footsteps. They are coming.'

'Yes, there are sounds of footsteps in the ante-room.'

'Warrior, quickly go to the Hunters' Hall.'

'There is a better place to hide. Queen, give me that sword.'

Nandini tried to give the sword to Vandiyathevan. It slipped from her hand and fell down. The clanging sound of metal hitting the floor reverberated throughout the room.

31

Was It All a Drama?

The sound of the falling sword seamlessly merged with Nandini's tragic laugh.

'Warrior, I wanted to change my mind. But it looks as if fate has other plans. Let the sword remain here. You hide yourself.'

Ignoring her words, Vandiyathevan bent down to lift the sword. Nandini placed her foot on the sword's handle.

'Don't do that. The crown prince might have heard the sound of the falling sword. And if he does not see a sword here, he will be suspicious. He already doubts your intentions. So go away quickly.'

The sharp edge of the sword cut Vandiyathevan. He abandoned it. Nandini saw a speck of blood on his palm.

'I will honour my promise. I won't kill my brother. Leave immediately.'

'Go at once.'

Manimekalai also made a passionate appeal to Vandiyathevan to quickly quit the place.

Vandiyathevan reluctantly slipped into the storage room for musical instruments.

'Manimekalai, you hide behind the screen.'

No sooner had Manimekalai gotten behind the screen than Aditya Karikalan and Kandamaran entered the room.

Aditya Karikalan came near Nandini and looked around. He saw an unusual movement behind the screen. He pretended not to have noticed it.

He saw the beautiful sword on the floor and threw a questioning glance at Nandini. She could not withstand Karikalan's questioning glance. Unable to bear his penetrating glance she bent down to lift the sword but Karikalan grabbed the sword before she could. He noticed the blood stain on the sharp end of the sword.

'Queen, it looks like you are welcoming us armed with a sword.'

'That's the best way to welcome young tigers known for their valour.'

'Wicked tigers need sharp claws and sharp teeth. But the beautiful deer don't need them.'

'At times, even a deer may be forced to use its horns.'

'It does not suit a hand that plucks flowers and weaves them into garlands to hold a sword.'

'Prince, there was a time when this poor soul was waiting for her beloved with the woven garland but was disappointed. Now the hands of this orphan seek the company of a killer weapon.'

'Nandini, what is this? Many young warriors fall at your feet and even your slightest whim is a divine command for them.'

'That's why I need a sword like this to defend my honour.'

'Nandini, you are born to be a queen. Are you keeping this sword only to safeguard the honour of Paluvettarayar? Or just to keep away those lustful idiots from you?'

'What other motives could I have, Prince?'

'Why? There could be several other motives. You may want to avenge the death of your beloved.'

Nandini sighed.

'I don't deny that. Once I had such thoughts. I was biding my time. The time has come now. I have no strength. My heart also is weak. I will use this sword only to save my honour and that of my husband. So please give back my sword.'

'Nandini, let me take upon myself the responsibility of punishing the persons who try to hurt you or your husband?'

'Prince, how can you punish your dear friends?'

'Why not, Nandini? I didn't believe whatever you said about

Vandiyathevan the other day. But later Kandamaran confirmed what you said. You may forgive him. But I won't. Won't you tell me where he is now? No need. I can find out myself.'

Aditya Karikalan roared and started walking towards the screen.

Nandini fell at Karikalan's feet.

'Prince, please don't do that. I beseech you.'

'Nandini, reserve your compassion for something else. No mercy for a traitor who has been acting as my friend all these years.'

Karikalan brushed her aside and walked ahead.

Nandini was shocked and spoke to Kandamaran who remained frozen like a statue.

'Please stop the crown prince.'

Kandamaran gave a nasty smile.

Karikalan pulled away the screen wielding the Pandiya sword. He was surprised to see Manimekalai armed with a small knife.

'Oh my God! The Kadamboor tigress is here.'

Aditya Karikalan laughed and spoke to Kandamaran.

'Dear friend, take your sister to your mother.'

After the brother and sister left, Aditya Karikalan spoke to Nandini.

'Nandini, I enacted a drama to drive away those two so we could talk freely. Speak the truth now.'

Nandini was overawed by Karikalan's acting skills. 'My God! Prince, were you acting? It was one of the best performances I have ever seen.'

'You are the best actress in the whole world. I'm proud to receive your appreciation for my talent. Now tell me why did you invite me to Kadamboor Palace? Why did you send away Senior Paluvettarayar? Don't tell me that you came here only to divide the Chola Empire or to get Manimekalai married to me. I'm not in a mood to believe that.'

'Then why did you come here, Prince?'

'My mind was in turmoil. I wanted to leave this world but I also wanted to take leave of you before I go. Once you begged for a boon from me. But I cruelly refused. Every second I'm dying with guilt. Tell me if there is any way I can atone for my sins.'

'What atonement can there be, Prince? The dead won't come back.'

'Agreed. Hide not anything from me. I know why you asked me to come here. I know why you have sent away Senior Paluvettarayar. I also know why you married him. Just to torment me. I was living peacefully in Kancheepuram. You didn't like that. That was why you dragged me here to Kadamboor only to kill me with Pandiya's sword to avenge his death. If that were your wish, this is the best time to fulfil it. Come on. Kill me. That's why I sent Kandamaran and his sister away. Come on, Nandini. Take this sword. Kill me now.'

Nandini took the sword from the crown prince with trembling hands and broke into a heart-rending sob.

'You won't have another opportunity to avenge. You killing me is not a crime or a sin. On the other hand, it will be a great service for me.'

'Prince, I'm hiding nothing from you. Whatever you said about my motives is true. I made you come here just to take revenge. But now my mind has changed.'

'Why?'

'Because of a message brought by your friend Vandiyathevan.'

'Oh, you mean his latest discovery that you and I are siblings, right? When we were discussing that on the lake-front, you told me that you didn't believe that news. You thought that it was a conspiracy to keep us apart.'

'I tried hard not to believe that news, Prince. But the other message that he brought has killed my mission.'

'Oh! What is that?'

'He told me about my mother in Lanka. Prince, once I begged for a boon from you. You refused. Now I seek a boon from you once again.'

'First tell me what you want.'

'It is true that I had vowed to avenge the death of Veerapandiya. I also took a vow to kill myself if I fail to kill you. Now I want to kill myself in your presence. But alas, I have no strength in my hands. Please help me to fulfil my vow. Take back this sword and kill me with it.'

Nandini offered the sword to Aditya Karikalan.

The crown prince laughed out loud as he received the sword. The whole palace echoed with the sound of his laughter.

32

Mysterious Death

Vandiyathevan was listening in on the conversation between Crown Prince Aditya Karikalan and Junior Queen Nandini. His intution warned him of an impending danger through the lord of death. His mind was in a turmoil whether to enter and guard Karikalan from any danger or to wait for something good to happen as a result of the meeting. He decided to wait for an appropriate time to enter.

The conversation between the two continued.

'Nandini, I've done nothing to please you until now. Today is a happy day in my life. All my mental agonies will come to an end.'

'Prince, it's a happy day for me as well. Nothing could be sweeter for me than dying at your hands. There was a time when I longed for a garland from your hands. But now it has become a distant dream. At least let me have the good fortune of adorning my neck with a sword from your hand. Prince, come on. Kill me.'

'If it is true that you dreamt of marrying me in the past, why not make it happen now? Name the traitors who obstruct your dream. I will kill them first.'

'Prince, please don't do that. Let no one die on my account. Remember the message of your sister Kundavai—you and I, are brother and sister.'

'Nandini, you told me the other day that it was a concocted story of conspiracy to keep us apart.'

'Prince, we are blood relations. I've married Senior Paluvettarayar who is like your grandfather. That means I'm your grandmother.'

'Nandini, don't spin a story again. You may be his wife for the outside world. But I know you are staying in his palace for a specific reason.'

'Prince, that is your hallucination.'

Karikalan's voice got louder.

'Let us not waste our time in petty talk. Let us leave this place immediately. I will give up the great Chola Kingdom for you. I will give up my country, my parents, my brother and my sister, everything for your sake. Let us board a ship and go beyond the high seas. For me you are more precious than this kingdom.'

'Prince, you are ready to sacrifice the kingdom for my sake. But you won't let this orphan ascend the ancient Chola throne. Right?'

Nandini was spitting fire.

'Nandini, is the Chola throne more precious to you than I am?'

'Prince, of course I wanted royal pleasures. That's why I married Senior Paluvettarayar. That is why I tried to save Veerapandiya, for the same reasons.'

'Nandini you are an evil woman! Why irritate me? Now I understand your game. If you utter the name of Veerapandiya, I will lose my temper and try to kill you. And then, one of your love slaves, I mean the three young warriors who lust for you, will kill me. That is your hidden agenda. You heartless demon, where is Vandiyathevan? He should be hiding somewhere here. I now understand why you refuse to come with me. Yes, Vandiyathevan is the reason. You have planned to elope with him. That is the reason you sent Senior Paluvettarayar away on some lame excuse. Where is that crook, your new lover?'

Karikalan was running around madly, swirling the Pandiya sword.

Nandini fell at his feet.

'Prince, please listen to me and then do whatever you like. The charges you have leveled against Vandiyathevan are utterly false. You may cut open my heart and see. There is nobody but you in my heart. I promise. I promise.'

Nandini was sobbing violently.

Aditya Karikalan appeared to be a little pacified.

'Then why do you refuse to come with me? Why do you want me to kill you? Tell me the truth.'

'Alright, have it your way. My heart will hold no one but you. And yet, I can't come with you. There is a strong reason. I beg you to forget this orphan and marry someone suitable for the throne. If you promise to remain calm and control your emotions...'

'Nandini, tell me. However bitter it may be for me.'

'Prince, my whole life has been sort of an imagination. My birth is a work of fiction. Now I will tell you the truth. You can hear me out and then kill me with your own hands.'

'Nandini, tell me the real reason that prevents you from coming with me.'

'Prince, Vandiyathevan brought news about my mother is madly roaming the streets of Lanka. I also know why my mother became mad. I didn't tell this to anybody else. Now I'm sharing it with you. I will also reveal who my father is. Don't get annoyed.'

She came near Karikalan and whispered in his ear with a shiver and broke down into a sob.

Adithya Karikalan felt as if a thousand scorpions had stung him.

'No. No. It can't be. It's a lie!'

Karikalan shouted.

But the very next moment, he became calm.

'Yes, Nandini. Now I understand the turmoil in your heart. Everything is clear now. I now know the war which you fought in your heart. There is no way that we can be united. Oh my God! How did you bear this great weight in your heart for such a long time? There is only one way to resolve the conflicts of our lives. There is only one way for atonement. One salvation. One retribution. One punishment. Here it is.'

Vandiyathevan heard every word of the conversation. He could not hear Nandini when she revealed her father's identity but he could guess. It was the greatest shock he had ever had in his life.

Silence prevailed for some time. Vandiyathevan feared the worst.

So, he stuck his head out of his hiding place but could not see Karikalan and Nandini. He saw something else. He saw the ugly face of sorcerer Ravidasan peering out of Hunters' Hall. The next second, the secret door to Hunters' Hall opened. A tiger's head came out of the door followed by its body. Vandiyathevan was shocked and tried to spring out. An iron hand encircled his neck. He looked up to see a terrific figure towering over him.

Oh my God! Who is this wringing my neck? I'm gasping. My eyes will come out of their sockets.

Vandiyathevan managed to release himself from the grip, squeezed himself out and sprang out of his hiding place. He fell on the floor. He felt as if a rock had been thrown on his head. Then suddenly, the whole place was enveloped in darkness.

Vandiyathevan became unconscious.

The majestic figure dressed as a Kalamukha emerged. Nandini heard the sound of somebody falling and turned around. The Kalamukha figure was approaching her with a drawn sword. She looked at the figure with unbearable shock. Her intestines rose up to her throat. She was gasping for breath. She wiped her eyes and looked down. Karikalan was lying on the floor. Veerapandiyan's sword was stuck in his body.

Nandini screamed. The Kalamukha figure came closer to her.

'Evil woman! Traitor! At last, you have taken revenge!' Almost at the same time, Ravidasan entered the room, hiding behind a stuffed tiger. As soon as he saw the Kalamukha figure, he threw the stuffed tiger at the lamp. The lamp fell. A few seconds before the light went out, it showed the frightened face of Manimekalai. Manimekalai screamed and ran away.

The blinding darkness was accentuated by sorrowful sobs usually heard at the time of death. The sound of several footsteps was heard.

33

Who Killed the Prince?

Aditya Karikalan the great warrior and crown prince of the Chola Kingdom had died an untimely and unnatural death.

His body was lying in a dark room at Kadamboor Palace. Vandiyathevan was lying unconscious on the floor in the same room. Slowly, he regained consciousness and opened his eyes but he could see nothing. He felt severe pain on his head and neck. He struggled even to breathe.

Oh my God! But what happened to the crown prince? What happened to Nandini?

Vandiyathevan looked around to see nothing but a black mass of pure darkness. He tried to feel around with his hands. His hands got hold of something.

Yes, it is the knife with a twisted blade—much more powerful than a regular knife.

He recalled the chain of events.

How did this knife come here? Its blade is wet with blood. Whose blood? Who could have used it? Idumban Kari or Kalamukha?

He heard footsteps and he sat up and shouted.

'Who is there?'

His voice sounded coarse and strange. The Kalamukha's tight grip on his neck had damaged his vocal cords. He wanted to shout again, but his voice was feeble.

'Who is that?'

He stood up and walked a few steps with great difficulty. Suddenly, his foot hit something on the floor and he fell down on something soft.

He extended his hand and it touched something. His body started shivering. His hair stood on end. He was in panic. The faint light rays from the mirror illuminated the room. *Oh! My God! It is the Crown Prince Aditya Karikalan. It is his dead body.* Vandiyathevan's heart was in his his throat. Instinctively, tears trickled down from his eyes. He was trembling when he touched the lifeless body of the crown prince. His hands were drenched with the royal blood. He was ready to give his heart and soul to save Karikalan. But alas he had failed; destiny won.

He laid the lifeless body of the crown prince on his lap. He had lost his power of thought. He did not know what to do.

Now a group of men led by Kandamaran and his father entered the room with burning torches. He laid down the body of Karikalan and stood up.

Kandamaran became furious when he saw Vandiyathevan and charged him: 'Murderer! Betrayer! The worst enemy of the Chola clan! I thought you would have run away with your group.'

He then spoke to his father.

'Father, he is the killer in the guise of a friend. The traitor, who has brought indelible blame to our clan. See! Heinous crime is written all over his face.'

Ignoring his son, Sambuvarayar went near the body of the crown prince and was staring at the lifeless face of the prince for a while.

'What sin did I commit? Why should this happen in my palace? The world will blame me saying that I invited the prince as my guest only to kill him.'

Sambuvarayar hit his head and sobbed. Kandamaran tried to pacify him.

'Father, we are blameless. We have caught the assassin red-handed. Tell me father, what punishment can we give to this bloody traitor? No punishment will be adequate for this grave crime.'

Kandamaran's words baffled Vandiyathevan. He now realized that anyone could easily consider him as the prime suspect in the murder of the prince.

He blamed the cruel twist of destiny.

Paluvoor Queen, that venomous reptile saved my life twice, was that just for this? That devil has settled her score with Princess Kundavai. She will have escaped along with sorcerer Ravidasan and the others after accomplishing her mission. Who killed the crown prince? Nandini or Ravidasan? Or that Kalamukha? Or Idumban Kari who came in with that knife with the twisted blade? Or perhaps Kandamaran did, out of lust for Nandini? Or Karikalan himself?

Kandamaran shouted at his men. 'Arrest him now!' Only then did Vandiyathevan realize that he was trapped. With eyes that were full of love and grief, he looked at Kandamaran.

'What is this Kandamaran? Do you think I would do such a heinous crime? Why should I do that, my friend? What could I gain from this lowly act?'

'Don't call me your friend. I'm not your friend. I will cut out the tongue which calls me your friend. You ask what you will gain by this murder. You will gain Nandini's love. That's your greatest gain. You villain, where is that Paluvoor devil, Nandini?'

'Honestly Kandamaran, I don't know. I was lying here unconscious. I don't know what happened to Nandini. She could have left the palace through the underground passage along with the conspirators who are the former personal bodyguards of the slain King Veerapandiya.'

'Oh, you too have been deceived by her. But don't tell me you know nothing. No one will believe you.'

Vandiyathevan pleaded innocence.

'You need not believe me but you can ask your sister Manimekalai. She is the one who…'

'Don't talk about my sister! I will wring your neck and kill you.'

Kandamaran sprang on Vandiyathevan. Then he turned to his father.

'Tell me how we should punish this villain. If permitted, I will cut him to pieces right here.'

Sambuvarayar was startled by the words of his son Kandamaran. He looked up. Suddenly his darling daughter appeared from behind the screen in the chamber. Shock, disgust and grief gripped his face.

'Manimekalai, how did you come here?'

'Father, I was here only. Vandiyathevan is innocent.'

Kandamaran erupted.

'Father? Do you see how this evil fellow has corrupted the mind of my dear sister?'

'Brother, he is blameless.'

'Shut up, sister. Who asked you to come here? You have lost your mind. Go to the ladies' chambers.'

'Brother, you are wrong. I'm alert. I have not lost my mind. But you have lost yours. That is why you are charging this man with the crime of killing the prince.'

'Fool! Why are you supporting this murderer?'

'Because he is not a murderer.'

'Ok, if he is not the murderer then who killed the crown prince? Did you?'

'Yes, I did. I killed him. I killed him with this sword.'

Everyone in the room was shocked by that revelation. Everybody saw the sword in her hand.

'She is lying to save Vandiyathevan. This scoundrel has corrupted her mind.'

Vandiyathevan who was in indescribable grief was surprised. He spoke in a firm voice devoid of all emotions.

'Kandamaran, whatever you say is true. I'm the killer. Your sister is lying only to save me. Princess, I will never forget the brotherly love you have for me. Please listen to your brother.'

Kandamaran was again furious.

'Are you her brother? She respects you more than me. Why? What did you do to corrupt her mind? I will kill you with the sword that is in my sister's hand. I will send you to the lord of death.'

Kandamaran wielded the sword and sprang on Vandiyathevan.

34

Play of Destiny

On hearing the words of his son, Sambuvarayar who had remained frozen until then sprang up and firmly held his hand.

'Idiot! What the hell are you doing? If you kill him then you, I and our entire clan will be annihilated. The whole world will say that we killed the crown prince and his friend, Vandiyathevan who came to save his life. How can you be so stupid?'

'Who will dare to blame us, father?'

'Idiot, idiot. I listened to your words. That's why we are facing this calamity now. It was at your insistance that we had the secret meeting with all the chieftains to decide on the successor to the Chola throne and we invited Aditya Karikalan to our palace now. Malayaman, our old enemy is waiting at our borders with a huge army. Senior Paluvettarayar is also not here now. How are we going to explain the death of the crown prince to Malayaman? How are we going to tackle the situation?'

Sambuvarayar hit his head with his palm several times.

'Father, please don't grieve. Tell me what should be done.'

'First take Manimekalai to the ladies' chambers. Or else put her in a secret room and come here.'

Manimekalai was adamant and refused to leave Vandiyathevan but Kandamaran took her away forcefully.

Now Sambuvarayar ordered his men to bind Vandiyathevan to the cot.

After he was bound, Vandiyathevan spoke to Sambuvarayar in a soft voice.

'Sir, I'm Karikalan's dear friend. What can I gain by murdering my dearest friend? The assassins have escaped through the underground passage. First try to catch them. I will come with you and help you find those people if you release me. I promise I won't try to run away.'

'What were you doing when Karikalan was killed?'

'Nandini and Karikalan were talking. Suddenly the assassins entered the room. I tried to stop them. A Kalamukha with a frightening appearance wrung my neck and I fell down unconscious. When I regained my consciousness, I saw the lifeless body of the crown prince.'

As they were speaking, a big noise was heard from outside the palace.

Sambuvarayar spoke to Vandiyathevan.

'Let me go and find out the cause of the commotion. I'll listen to what you have to say after I come back.'

Sambuvarayar left the room. His men followed him. The room was bolted from the outside and it was plunged into darkness once again. Vandiyathevan was recalling his earlier visit to this palace. How will the emperor bear the death news of his first born who built a golden palace for his father? The entire Chola Empire will mourn. A major civil war will break out. Karikalan's grandfather will surely rout out Sambuvarayar's clan.

Poor Kandamaran was basically a good fellow. But all his love for me turned into hatred because of that devil, Nandini. Her story is also very sad. One cannot shift the entire blame on her. It was all the play of destiny. The cruel hand of destiny did not spare innocent Manimekalai. Why should she love me so much? Why should she take the blame on herself to save me? How am I going to repay that divine love?

Now I will be charged with the heinous crime of killing Aditya Karikalan. I have no evidence to refute the charge. Nandini and her gang must have already fled the scene. No one is making any effort to catch them.

Such thoughts flashed in his mind in quick succession. Suddenly, a screen of fire and smoke enveloped the chambers.

Vandiyathevan saw Aditya Karikalan's lifeless body in that light. All the doors were closed. Who caused the fire? Perhaps the conspirators? Soon the smoke became thicker and thicker emitting heat with uncontrolled fury. Vandiyathevan was staring at the fire without blinking.

All my worries will be burnt down now. My friend Aditya Karikalan and I will be cremated in the same place. But I don't want to leave the world without proving my innocence. Aditya Karikalan was a born warrior and the crown prince of the mighty Chola Kingdom. He richly deserves a grand funeral. His parents, his brother, his sister and thousands of his friends should see his body one last time. I failed in my mission to save his life. Let me at least save his body.

He used all his strength to untie the ropes that bound his hands. It yielded after a long struggle. He even used his teeth to cut the rope. He dragged himself along with the cot towards the entrance of the Hunters' Hall and showed the ropes to the flames. Though painful, the ropes burnt away and set him free.

Tears rolled down his face.

I will give my life to carry the prince's body outside the palace and hand it over to his grandfather Malayaman. I will join him to find the assassins.

He picked up the body of Karikalan on his shoulders and also the mysterious knife with the twisting blade. He reached the terrace through the musical instruments room and walked fast. He crossed many balconies and yards carrying the body of the prince. He was wondering how to climb down the terrace.

Then he looked around and saw a ladder against a wall. But a human figure was standing near the wall.

Who is that? Could be someone waiting for somebody. I have a knife and can handle any situation. Let me use this ladder.

He heard human voices beyond the walls.

Have Malayaman's soldiers started invading the fort? The soldiers are mounting their attack on the main gates of the fort. Several soldiers are jumping the wall from outside. Perhaps Malayaman knows about the death of his grandson. That might have made him order an invasion. Nobody should see me carrying the dead body of the prince. I should find Malayaman and hand over his grandson's body to him.

The man near the ladder quickly went away towards where the noise had come from. Vandiyathevan used this golden opportunity to climb down. The moment his feet touched the ground, unfortunately, that man returned. He mistook Vandiyathevan for one of his men.

'Sir, why are you late?'

Vandiyathevan recognized the voice of the conspirator, Idumban Kari.

Vandiyathevan showed him the knife with the twisted blade as a proof of identity and managed to walk away.

As soon as he was out of Idumban Kari's sight, he started walking towards the main gate of the palace.

35

Malayaman's Grief

Sambuvarayar was in a state of shock and whispered in the ears of his son.

'Kandamaran, we are facing an unprecedented danger. You should get out of this palace right now through the underground passage in my bedroom. That will take you to Tanjore. Meet Senior Paluvettarayar and appraise him of the developments. If he is not there, brief Junior Paluvettarayar and Prince Madurandakan.'

'If they ask me how did Karikalan die, what should I tell them?'

'Tell them that Vandiyathevan killed him. We should spread rumours that Prince Arulmoli sent Vandiyathevan to kill Aditya Karikalan. We should also tell people that Princess Kundavai was an accomplice in this treacherous game. The news of Karikalan's death should reach the Paluvettarayars and Madurandakan before it reaches others. Only then can they plan the future course of action. Go fast.'

'Yes father, I will leave immediately. But I'm a little worried about Manimekalai.'

'Don't worry about her. How strange are the ways of destiny? First, we decided to get her married to Prince Madurandakan. Then we changed our plan and wanted her to marry Karikalan. Now Karikalan is dead. Thank god the silly girl's mind did not go to the crown prince. We can now get her married to Madurandakan as originally planned.'

'But father, Manimekalai loves that crook Vandiyathevan.'

'That's nothing. Go fast my son. Don't delay for even a second.'

Kandamaran heard the sound of Malayaman's approaching army. He left for the secret passage.

After seeing off his son, Sambuvarayar went to the ladies' chambers. The women were crying over Karikalan's death. He ordered them to pack up their essentials and get ready to leave the palace.

Sambuvarayar then came to the front gates of his palace. Malayaman's soldiers were coming in after breaking open the huge gates at the front entrance. Sambuvarayar was shaken to see them followed by Malayaman and Parthiban.

'Sambuvarayar, where is my grandson, the greatest warrior Aditya Karikalan?'

'I want to ask you the same question. Earlier I met you and invited you with reverence. You had agreed to come to my palace tomorrow at an auspicious time. Then why are your soldiers breaking my palace gates now? How do I know the whereabouts of your grandson? Why do you ask me?'

'I warn you Sambuvarayar! Don't play with me. Entrust Aditya Karikalan to me. We will go away. Or else, we will demolish your palace,' roared Malayaman like an offended lion.

Sambuvarayar further irritated Malayaman by his rude and indifferent answers. Parthiban spoke in a conciliatory tone pacifying Sambuvarayar.

'Sir, be cool. There is a reason for the grandfather's fury. Have a look at this palm leaf. Then you will understand.'

He gave a palm leaf to Sambuvarayar.

'Prince Aditya Karikalan's life is in danger. Come at once with a large army.'

Even as he read the message, Sambuvarayar was trembling.

'What is this conspiracy? Who could have sent this message?'

'That is not the question. Bring Aditya Karikalan here right now. Or else take us there.'

'Ok I will take you to Karikalan. I learnt that he has gone to Paluvoor Queen's chambers a little while ago.'

Just then they noticed a raging fire in the palace and a thick black screen of smoke above the flames.

Everyone turned to look in that direction.

'Fire! Fire!' shouts rang out.

Parthiban ran towards Nandini's lodgings.

Malayaman and Sambuvarayar were still accusing each other. At the same time, the womenfolk of Sambuvarayar's palace were coming out to the courtyard. Their facial expressions betrayed their state of mind. But none of them were crying. Manimekalai saw the fire and ran towards the fire screaming.

'Oh my God! There's a fire over there. He is there.'

Sambuvarayar stopped her and slapped her.

Nobody had hit Manimekalai since her birth. She froze and stood staring at her father. The sight melted the father.

When everybody was running chaotically a strange sight caught Sambuvarayar's attention.

'There is no need to run. Look! See who is coming.'

Now all eyes fell on Vandiyathevan as he was dragging himself towards the crowd carrying the lifeless body of Karikalan on his shoulders.

Malayaman lapsed into a pointless stare. A sense of panic gripped his heart. He wanted to ask Vandiyathevan about something. But he could not raise his voice as his mouth felt dry.

Vandiyathevan staggered towards him without taking his eyes off Malayaman's face.

'Here is the matchless warrior Aditya Karkalan. I tried to bring him alive. But I failed. I could only save his body from the fire. Look at your grandson. He was killed by the conspiracy of evil-doers.'

Vandiyathevan laid the body of Karikalan on the yard and collapsed.

The old man was staring at the valiant, handsome face of his grandson. He hit his head and chest with his iron-like hands and started sobbing violently.

'Karikala, my dearest! I have been holding on to my life only to see you as a bridegroom. I never thought in my wildest dreams that I will see you like this.'

He recited Karikalan's acts of valours since childhood and the events starting from the celebrations of the birth of Aditya Karikalan, playing with him as a child, teaching him to handle the sword and also the prince's valourous deeds in the battlefield.

The old man broke down and hit his head several times and sobbed. Suddenly his grief turned into fury. He looked around.

'Sambuvarayar, tell the truth. How did the prince die? How did you trick him to death? Don't try to hide anything from me.'

Sambuvarayar's fury was no less.

'Hey old man, I'm silent because I respect your old age. How could I know about the prince's death? Ask the man who carried the prince's corpse. He might be able to tell you something. What's the point in asking me?'

'The prince died while he was a guest in your palace. And you talk as if you know nothing. Who will believe you?

Soldiers, arrest this Sambuvarayar. Demolish his palace, Come on quick!'

Malayaman thundered.

Parthiban had just returned.

'Sir, we don't have to demolish the palace. The Fire Lord will do that for us. See, he has already started the work in all earnestness.'

Malayaman looked around. The fire which until then appeared to be in the corner of the palace was advancing fast. The fire was quite huge. It consumed the high-rise buildings, the towers and the balconies. Everybody stood there frozen, watching the wild dance of fire.

'The Fire Lord is working for us. Parthiban, let us leave this place immediately. The emperor and my daughter have been wanting to see their firstborn for the last three years. Nothing happened. Let them at least see the lifeless body of their firstborn for one last time. The fire that is destroying this evil man's palace is tainted. Let us not burn our prince's body in that fire. Let's take our prince to Tanjore. Let the father and mother at least cry over the lifeless body of their darling son. Let our emperor decide on the punishment to be given to the killers of our valiant prince.'

36

I Will Save the Empire

Queen Mother Sembiyan Madevi visited the ashram of the great saint, Nambiyandar Nambi in a small village on the banks of the river Kollidam. Alvarkkadiyan Nambi, who was waiting with an important message followed her.

After her interaction with the saint, she left the ashram in her palanquin followed by Alvarkkadiyan Nambi.

After the palanquin had moved a little farther Alvarkkadiyan broke the news of the prince's death to the Queen Mother.

'Nambi, what a terrible news! Oh my God! Which Prince?'

'Please forgive me, mother. The Crown Prince Aditya Karikalan died at the Kadamboor palace. People say that the death was unnatural. We don't know as yet what caused his death. There are several versions. Soon after Karikalan's death, Kadamboor palace was burnt to ashes. The body of the Prince is being carried to Tanjore in a huge procession. Malayaman has arrested Sambuvarayar and his family and is bringing them to Tanjore.'

'Nambi, it's a calamity. A big tragedy. When the comet was seen, people expected a calamity in the royal household. And it has happened now. Oh my God! Should the great warrior's life end so soon? How will the emperor bear this bereavement?'

'Queen Mother, this great tragedy will threaten the security of the Chola Empire. Even our prime minister, the unmatched genius is shaken.'

'Nambi, by the grace of God I will save the empire from that disaster. I came to the saint Nambiyandar Nambi only for this purpose.

There will be a civil war in the country only when Madurandakan and Arulmoli compete for the Chola throne.'

'You alone can save the empire from danger.'

There was silence for a while.

'Nambi, you said that the death was unnatural. Tell me how it happened?'

'Mother, there are several versions being told about his death. Since it happened in Sambuvarayar's palace and his son Kandamaran has also escaped, Malayaman is blaming him.'

'Who on earth would have the heart to kill the emperor's son when he is a guest at their palace? What does Sambuvarayar say about the prince's death?'

'Mother, once a warrior from the Vaanar clan came to Palayarai. Princess Kundavai sent him to Lanka with an important message.'

'Yes. I remember. What about him?'

'He was the one who was by the side of the prince's lifeless body when it was first seen by others. Sambuvarayar says he is the killer.'

'Impossible, Nambi. I clearly remember the innocent face of that young man. He would never do such a heinous crime.'

'But the circumstansial evidence is against Vandiyathevan.'

'Princess Kundavai had placed enormous trust on that young man. She will be shattered when she hears the news.'

Nambi took leave of the Queen Mother.

'Where are you going?'

'The death of Prince Karikalan is shrouded in mystery. I want to unravel it mother, I saw one of the Pandiya conspirators at the banks of Kollidam on my way. I know the place where the conspirators will assemble tonight.'

'Take care. What shall I tell Princess Kundavai? I'm worried about her.'

'Mother, ask her not to worry about it. Tell her that I will find out the real culprit soon.'

'God bless you.' Queen Mother blessed him.

Alvarkkadiyan reached the bank of river Kollidam. The whole area was flooded. He reached the conspirators' meeting place in the Thiruppurambiyam forest near the war memorial. Alvarkkadiyan hid himself behind the dense foliage.

The conspirators were engaged in animated conversation at the war memorial. They were Soman Sambavan, Idumban Kari, boatman Murugaiyyan's wife Rakkammal and others. They were rejoicing over the death of the prince.

Alvarkkadiyan heard the words of Idumban Kari.

'Then let's go to the Pachaimalai Hills.'

Alvarkkadiyan wanted to leave the place before them. He was startled to see a knife dangling very close to his chest. He saw the hand wielding the knife. He relaxed when he saw that it was Poonkulali. They communicated through sign language.

After the conspirators had left, Alvarkkadiyan spoke to Poonkulali.

'Poonkulali, why did you come here?'

'I have come here to avenge my aunt's death. I have been following the assassin for days and finally traced him here. I was surprised to see my sister-in-law Rakkammal along with the conspirators. Meanwhile you too have come. I won't leave without killing the devil who killed my aunt.'

'Your aunt? You mean the mute queen, Mandakini? Why was she killed?'

'They didn't come to kill my aunt. The conspirators sneaked into the palace to kill the emperor. They aimed the spear at the emperor but my aunt became the victim.'

'Is that so? Please tell me the full story.'

'Is this the time for story-telling? We should not lose those traitors. I will tell you what happened on the way.'

'Poonkulali, I know where they are going and also whom they are going to meet there. Let us go to that place.'

After walking three days and three nights, they reached the foothills of Pachamalai Hills. They were disappointed as they could not find the traitors there.

Suddenly they heard the sound of an owl hooting. Alvarkkadiyan signaled to Poonkulali to follow him. They reached a clearing in the forest. There were about eight people there, including Ravidasan, Soman Sambavan and others.

Ravidasan was pointing to a cave and saying something. Noticing this Alvarkkadiyan alerted Poonkulali.

'Poonkulali, the people we are looking for should be in that cave. Let me go into the cave and find out,' said Alvarkkadiyan and headed towards the cave.

Alvarkkadiyan saw a rare sight there, through large holes in the outer wall of the cave. Senior Paluvettarayar was in there, dressed in a tiger's skin like a Kalamukha. He looked very pale and anaemic. A garland of human skulls was also by his side.

He appeared to have just woken up from a bad dream. He looked lost. Queen Nandini was by his side, without any jewels and her hair looking unkempt. Her matchless beauty was shining brighter even then. She was giving him a bowl of food.

But his eyes turned fiery when he saw Nandini.

'Evil woman! Demon! Heartless devil! Is that you?' He threw the vessel away.

37

It's Time to Leave!

Nandini was not upset with Senior Paluvettarayar's anger. She remained calm. All these years she had been making her husband dance to her tune like a puppet. Now the puppet had come back to life and had started thinking for itself. Nandini spoke in a choked voice with folded hands:

'Lord, you always told me that my words were sweeter than the elixir of life. But today my words have become bitter. Please let me speak a few words before I bid farewell to you. The mouth that used to call me "sweet darling" is now calling me an evil woman. Yes, I'm an evil woman. I've been deceiving you for the last three years. You took this orphan from the middle of the forest to your palace and you made me a queen. You loved me so much even when people ridiculed you. You trusted me yet I betrayed you. I lived in your palace only to fulfil my evil mission. I had links with the conspirators and did many things without your knowledge. I unleashed my magical charm on young men like Parthiban and Kandamaran to use them in my game. But I can swear that I was never unfaithful to you.'

'What nonsense are you talking, Nandini? Oh my God! With my own hands... with my own hands... You devil! Evil woman! A ghost in the form of a woman! If only I had known this would happen, I would not have come to your chamber at all. My God! If only the lord of death had taken my life in the floods, I would have been spared of this treachery.'

'My Lord, you have sworn to save the honour and glory of the Chola Empire. So, I didn't want you to swerve from your duty. That is the only reason I sent you away from Kadamboor. But destiny brought you back. Yes, it was destiny which made you doubt my fidelity. If only your motive had been to prevent me from the vengeful act, you would have come right royally through the gates of the Kadamboor palace. You wanted to check whether I was faithful to you or not. That made you choose the secret passage and made you take the guise of a Kalamukha.'

'Stop this nonsense Nandini!'

'My Lord, please forgive me. But I know you won't forgive me. Please listen to me. I want to atone for my sins and I want to compensate you at least in my next birth for what I have failed to do in this birth.'

Senior Paluvettarayar's heart melted.

'Nandini, please leave immediately. If you stay any longer, I may lose my mind and fail in my duty. The miseries you have caused me are more than enough for one lifetime. Go away right now.'

'My Lord, if I had listened to the words of those conspirators of mine, by this time, I would have reached Kongu land. But I had no heart to leave without confessing my sins to you. As soon as you came out of the Kadamboor Palace, you fainted. My men advised me to abandon you. But I was not for it. I made them carry you. We have been walking day and night for the past three days. They told me that we could leave you here. But I insisted that I would wait till you became conscious. I owe you a lot. I can never repay my gratitude during this lifetime. But I was fortunate enough to be able to serve you during the last three days when you were unconscious. This thought will give me solace till I die. Please let me go now.'

'Go away, Nandini. You do not have to take leave of me. The longer you delay the greater is the risk of me losing my mind.'

'Yes, My Lord. You may even kill me and I will consider it as my great fortune. You came in this disguise only to kill me at Kadamboor, right?'

'You explained the reason for my disguise. You told me that I suspected your fidelity and came there to find out the truth. But that is not right. I was afraid that if I had come as your husband and if you had spoken a few nice words to me I would have melted. That was the reason for that terrible guise. I did not want to give room to you to talk. Yes, Nandini, I snatched the knife from Idumban Kari, a staff member of the palace at Kadamboor and I wanted to throw that knife at you. Not only that, Nandini. I didn't want the people to blame me for murdering my young wife out of suspicion. Hence, I came in the guise of a Kalamukha. But as you said just now, destiny willed otherwise. I won't attempt to kill you again. Go away. But tell me this before you go. Had I not come at that time, how would you have accomplished your mission?'

'My Lord, I was about to say that. Your fury has made me lose my mind. I devised a strategy to use Kandamaran, Vandiyathevan and Manimekalai for my work. I had brainwashed Manimekalai that Karikalan and the others were going to kill her beloved Vandiyathevan. And she was willing to do anything to stop it. I created a drama expecting her to kill Karikalan and expecting Vandiyathevan to take the blame on himself to save Manimekalai. That way I thought I could settle a score with Kundavai. But there was no need for all that. The prince killed himself.'

'No, Nandini. Karikalan did not kill himself.'

'My Lord, had you not thrown Idumban Kari's knife, Karikalan would have killed himself with the sword of Veerapandiya.'

'If only I had come a little late, I would not have become a party to that great betrayal. But I would have suspected you. Destiny had its own way. If at all there is a next birth for us, you said that you would like to be my wife. When I die, I will remember those words. But we cannot unite in this life. Nandini, go away.'

'Yes, My Lord. For the love you showed me, I'm eternally indebted to you.'

Now Alvarkkadiyan decided to silently slip away from the cave, as he had already gathered all the information required. It would be dangerous to stay there any longer.

He was thinking about the next course of action and walked out of the cave.

38

Don't Harm My Brother

Alvarkkadiyan and Poonkulali were chatting under a tree at the foot of Pachaimamai hills.

'Poonkulali, the work is over. Can we leave the place now?'

'What about my work? I have to kill my aunt's assassin.'

'Is he not there in that crowd?'

'He is.'

'Then what?'

'Did I come here to have a dharshan of him? I came here to avenge my aunt's death.'

'Who are we to punish the offenders? That's the work of the almighty.'

'Is there a God?'

'Ok, let's leave God. Kings have the responsibility of punishing the criminals.'

'If the king and his officers fail in their duty...'

'Who are we to decide?'

'Nambi, one of the crooks over there threw a spear from the terrace and killed my innocent aunt. She was dumb and noble. She had been unlucky since her birth. I and Junior Paluvettarayar were chasing the killer.

When we went through the underground passage, Junior Paluvettarayar was shocked to see his son-in-law Madurandakan there. But he professed to have come there to check the treasury though it was not the time for checking. Junior Paluvettarayar grabbed his hand and went away to his palace.

Since then, I alone have been following the killer up to this place. Do you want me to go back now without doing anything?'

'Hey girl, given powers you would be an able ruler of a vast country. Look at it this way. Suppose a person wants to kill somebody. Instead, he kills somebody else by accident. Can you charge him with murder?'

'Why not?'

'Take the case of Soman Sambavan whom you have been chasing. He threw the spear to kill the emperor. But the emperor is alive. Your aunt ran between them and got killed. How can you blame Soman Sambavan?'

'Your sense of justice is weird.'

'Not just my sense of justice, but also that of my Lord Narayana.'

'You and your Narayana live with your own peculiar justice system!'

'Poonkulali, I'm not trying to pacify you. There are two people in the mountain cave. One of them killed Aditya Karikalan though it was not his intention to do so. The knife he aimed at somebody else landed on Karikalan and he died. Can we call him a murderer?'

'Who all are there in that cave?'

'The honourable finance secretary, the uncrowned dictator of the Tanjore Palace and the husband of great Queen Nandini.'

Alvarkkadiyan spoke loudly to gain the attention of the conspirators. Ravidasan armed with a small, thick stick came running towards them furiously.

'Hey Nambi! The spy of the prime minister! Caught at last! This time all your escape routes are sealed.'

Alvarkkadiyan spoke in a deliberately loud voice, 'Hey, who is trying to escape from whom? Take refuge in Him for salvation.'

Alvarkkadiyan started singing hymns.

'Stop it. Let your Lord Narayana save you now.'

Ravidasan lifted the stick. Poonkulali took out the knife from her waist to protect Nambi. At the same time, Nandini came running from the mountain cave. Initially, Poonkulali thought it was her aunt.

She was surprised to see Nandini.

By this time Nandini came near Alvarkkadiyan and blocked Ravidasa and firmly held the other end of the stick.

'Ravidasa, don't harm my brother.'

Alvarkkadiyan responded with a smile.

'Thanks for your timely help sister. Look there.'

Alvarkkadiyan pointed towards soldiers armed with spears riding towards them.

Everyone froze on seeing the horses galloping towards them. Ravidasan immediately reacted.

'Queen, I have cautioned many a time about this man. Now this spy has brought these men to capture us. Before they come here, let's climb up the hills.'

Alvarkkadiyan pleaded with Nandini.

'Don't go with these crooks. Let there be no more trails of destruction. It's time to stop all that now.'

Nandini replied politely, 'Nambi, I've been asking you for a long, long time to take me to my mother. Grant me that favour at least now.'

Ravidasan intervened:

'Who is he to take you to your mother? Queen, I will do it for you.'

'Yes, he will surely take you to your mother in heaven after killing you too. One of them killed your mother, Nandini, leave these crooks.'

Ravidasan was furious.

'No, Queen. He's lying.'

Nandini, who was calm until then, suddenly acted as if possessed.

'Is it true, Nambi? Is my mother dead?'

'Nandini, if you don't believe me, ask this girl. Soman Sambavan threw a spear at your mother and killed her. This girl Poonkulali is an eye-witness. She followed him from Tanjore.'

'Yes, I saw with my own eyes. I came here only to avenge my aunt's death!' added Poonkulali.

'Revenge! Did you see how I sought revenge and made a mess of my life?'

She then turned to Ravidasan.

'Traitor! Did you do that?'

'Queen, no, Soman Sambavan aimed the spear at the emperor. That mute woman came in between, took the spear on her body and died. That is her destiny. Tell me what you are going to do. Are you coming with us or not? The horses have come very near.'

Nandini did not hear his words. She sat down. She closed her eyes and broke into a violent sob.

Ravidasan ordered his men: 'Run! Run for your lives. Climb the hill. No point in trusting the queen!'

They all started running. Ravidasan looked menacingly at Alvarkkadiyan and hit him hard with the stick before running up the hill.

They soon reached the cave at the top of the hill. At the same time, the horses reached the foothills. Alvarkkadiyan saw Junior Paluvettarayar, Kandamaran and Chendan Amudan.

'Come, you all have come at the right time.'

Junior Paluvettarayar and Kandamaran jumped down from their horses.

Alvarkkadiyan spoke to Junior Paluvettarayar, 'Senior Paluvettarayar is there in that cave. The conspirators have escaped there. Let us go up quickly.'

Junior ordered his men to go up the hill. Rocks started falling and the soldiers could not proceed.

Alvarkkadiyan also began making his way to the cave followed by Kandamaran and Junior.

A tall, majestic figure staggered out of the cave. It took some time for Junior to recognize his illustrious brother.

Senior's body was full of wounds. He was pale. Junior started sobbing. The voice of Senior was unusually soft:

'Brother, you warned me several times. I ignored them all. And I have lost everything.'

Alvarkkadiyan and Kandamaran tried to enter the cave to follow the conspirators.

Senior Paluvettarayar stopped them.

'Where are you going?'

'We are going after the killers.'

'Which killers?'

'Ravidasan and his men.'

'They are not the killers,' said Paluvettarayar.

'Didn't I say that Vandiyathevan is the murderer?' said Kandamaran.

Senior Paluvettarayar looked down at him.

'How did this foolish man come here?'

'He brought the news of Karikalan's death along with a message from Sambuvarayar to gather all our forces and make Madurandakan the next king,' said Junior.

Senior was not showing any interest in his brother's words.

'Tell me what happened in Tanjore.'

Junior Paluvettarayar started a long narration.

He spoke about the happenings in Tanjore and Kadamboor.

Senior started crying.

'Brother, no one has ever had a brother as devoted as you. Tell me what happened afterwards.'

'I had to leave Tanjore in peculiar circumstances—rumours regarding the emperor's death, capture of the fort by the Kodumbalur Chieftain and the Kaikkola Regiment. I decided that there was no point in staying in the fort any longer. I went to Kadamboor to see you. On the way, Kandamaran told me that you were not in Kadamboor. And later we saw Chendan Amudan who told us his cousin Poonkulali was going in search of the assassins. We followed her and reached here. I have sent a message to all our loyal chieftains to gather a huge army.

Now I have found you here. I need not worry about anything. Let us leave this place at once. By this time a large army should be ready for us to capture the Tanjore Fort.'

His words did not stir Senior. His mind was elsewhere.

'Oh! Is Nandini still here?' asked Senior.

At the same time Poonkulali pointed towards Nandini and said to Amudan,

'Oh! My God, she looks exactly like my dead aunt. From now on I will shower all the love I had for my aunt on Nandini.'

'I will join you in that,' replied Amudan.

Nandini was sitting on a rock and crying. On seeing Senior, she stood and looked around. Alvarkkadiyan was also standing very close to her. He said, 'Nandini! Tell me that you will come with me. Even a nod is enough. Let us go on a pilgrimage chanting hymns. Let us spend the rest of our lives peacefully. I will leave my job and come with you.'

Nandini saw him through a screen of tears.

'Nambi, I let you down. I betrayed you. God will bless you.'

Senior Paluvettarayar came near Nandini.

Nandini prostrated before her husband. As soon as she got up, she turned swiftly to see the horses brought by Junior Paluvettarayar's men. She sprang on a horse and began to gallop away very fast.

Nobody knew what was on Nandini's mind. When the others tried to stop her, Senior thundered,

'Stop!'

Everybody froze. They were all looking at Senior.

Senior Paluvettarayar was staring at Nandini's form which was receding fast from his vision. The horse ran as fast as the wind and vanished soon. The matchless beauty, the woman who was understood little and loved even less, the one and only Nandini vanished once and for all.

39

You Are Not My Son

Karikalan's body was taken in a huge procession to Tanjore. People were moaning the loss of an unparalleled valiant warrior of the Chola clan. Several thousands of people from the remotest villages joined the funeral procession.

When the procession reached Tanjore, it swelled into an ocean of people. The crowd was too big for the fort. The grief-stricken emperor and his family came out to see the dead body of the crown prince. The entire crowd erupted into loud wails that reverberated to the skies.

A stream of people who had never seen the prince earlier came to pay their respects to the dead Prince with teary eyes. But Madurandakan and the Paluvettarayars were missing.

Rumours were rampant that the Paluvettarayars were busy gathering forces. Even after the funeral was over and the royal family had gone back to the palace, people did not disperse; they continued shouting slogans against Madurandakan and the Paluvettarayars.

Initially the volume was low but soon it became louder. A faction of the crowd forcibly opened the gates of the fort and went directly to the Paluvettarayars palace shouting slogans against him.

Knowing that Madurandakan was hiding in the prime minister's house, people surrounded it.

'Where is that coward Madurandakan? Send him out. Right now!' demanded the crowd.

The prime minister was worried it would deteriorate into a law-and-order problem.

Madurandakan was also trembling and he begged the prime minister to save him, 'Help me now. I will make you my prime minister when I ascend the throne.'

'Why should we discuss about succession now, when the emperor is very much alive?'

'The emperor is very weak. I don't think he will survive. Karikalan is dead. Arulmoli is much junior to me. Emperor Sundara Chola wants me to succeed him. I can't see what objection you or my mother can have.'

'Prince, there are other strong reasons. See the reaction of the people. Do you think the emperor's consent is enough?'

The prime minister opened another sensitive topic for discussion.

'When Junior Paluvettarayar ran in pursuit of the killers of the Lankan Queen, you were there in the underground passage. How is that, Prince?'

'Prime Minister, when Ponniyin Selvan entered the fort as a mahout, I didn't like to stay there. I took the underground secret route to leave the fort. There I saw a stranger who claimed to have been sent by Senior Paluvettarayar. He said that Senior was gathering an army to support me. He also mentioned the dreadful mystery surrounding my birth. He said he will come to me after meeting you. I was waiting for him there. What is that dreadful mystery about my birth?'

'Prince, the only person who has the right to tell you is the Queen Mother, Sembiyan Madevi. I know a little, but I can't tell you.'

Now the Queen Mother entered the prime minister's house. The prime minister welcomed her.

'Prime Minister, my husband has gone to his heavenly abode leaving a huge burden on my head.'

The words made Madurandakan furious.

'Why suffer? Why refer my father's name so often? My ascending the Chola throne is almost certain. My only obstacle was Karikalan who is dead now. My other rival, Prince Arulmoli is much junior to me. When I'm alive, they will never crown him. Mother, please help me. If you can't help, at least don't block my way. Can there be a mother who betrays her own son?'

'A mother acting against the wishes of her child is cruel. Yes, I know. But I'm helpless, because it was my late husband's dying wish. I have to honour his words.

Is it not my duty to fulfil his wishes? The throne is coming to you with all its attendant dangers. One obstacle is gone with the death of Karikalan. But didn't you hear the people shouting slogans against you and the Paluvettarayars? They think that both of you are responsible for his death. How will they accept you as their emperor?'

'People will forget all that quite soon. Once I ascend the throne, they will accept me. Do you know who killed Karikalan? Arulmoli's dearest friend, Vandiythevan. They have jailed him and Sambuvarayar. The truth is that Ponniyin Selvan hired Vandiyathevan to kill his own brother to ascend the throne. If people knew that...'

The Queen Mother's eyes emitted fire.

'Crook! How dare you accuse Arulmoli who is an embodiment of love? He is ready to even worship you but you malign him. You will rot in hell. You will be cursed forever.'

Madurandakan was even more furious.

'You bloody witch! You curse your own son and bless my enemy. You can't be my mother.'

'Yes, I'm not your mother. I never wanted to say that to you. But you compelled me to reveal this because of your obstinacy. You are not my son. I'm not your mother.'

Madurandakan's voice was low now.

'Who is my mother?'

The Queen Mother turned to the prime minister.

'Please tell him. I have no strength to talk to him.'

The prime minister spoke to Madurandakan.

'Prince, you have hurt the noble lady who reared you from childhood. Today is the day to reveal the truth to you.'

He began a long narration.

Queen Sembiyan Madevi delivered a child when her husband was away. The prime minister had come to bless the child. Sembiyan Madevi was crying. She was aggrieved because the child lay like a log with no movements.

The prime minister gave a suggestion. Two mute sisters were brought to the palace by Sembiyan Madevi when she came back after a pilgrimage to Kodikarai. One of them had delivered twins, a boy and a girl, at that time. The prime minister approached the mute mother asking for her children to be brought up in the palace. Initially, she refused to part with her children. Later she abandoned the children and ran away.

The mute mother's male child was retained in the palace and Sembiyan Madevi's lifeless child was handed over to the mute mother's sister for burial. The prime minister gave the mute mother's girl child to Alvarkkadiyan with instructions to take the child to the Pandiya Kingdom.

Sembiyan Madevi felt guilty for having exchanged the children. One day she confessed everything to her husband Emperor Kandaraditya. The emperor spoke like a true saint.

He had said, 'That is not an issue, dear. Let him be anybody's child. He too is a gift from God. Bring up the child as if he were ours. But see to it that the child does not at any point of time ascend the Chola throne. That will be the worst act of betrayal to the Chola clan. So, let's bring him up like a saint.'

The prime minister's voice was devoid of any emotions, as he finished his narration.

'Prince, you are not the son of this royal family. You are the son of an orphaned mute woman. This noble woman brought you up showering all her love and affection on you like you were her own child. Listen to her. You will be fine.'

40

Cunning Madurandakan

Madurandakan became speechless for some time.

Suddenly he got up and shouted at the prime minister.

'I know this was all your creation. You love the children of Sundara Chola, particularly Arulmoli. You want him to be crowned. To achieve your goal, you are telling this cock and bull story to corrupt my mother's mind. You are making me somebody else's son to achieve your political aspirations. You cannot be blamed. Princess Kundavai and Prince Arulmoli have instigated you to do this.'

The prime minister remained quiet, unmindful of Madurandakan's outbursts.

'Prince, if I hated you, I would not have rescued you on that rainy day. Never try to malign Prince Arulmoli who is a paragon of virtues.'

'Does Prince Arulmoli know the truth about my birth?'

'No, he doesn't know.'

'Prime Minister, never open your mouth about this to anyone. If you agree, I will gift you the whole of Pandiya Kingdom when I ascend the throne.'

'I don't need anything. Your mother's orders are more than enough.'

Madurandakan looked at his mother. Queen Mother spoke in a voice full of love.

'My dear child, the prime minister is telling the truth. He has known the truth since your birth. He has not told this even to the emperor till now. My dear son, accept my words.'

'Mother, you are the only obstacle to my coronation. I was not born of you. But you brought me up showering all your love on me.

Why do you let me down now saying I am not your child?'

Saying this Madurandakan suddenly fell at the feet of his mother.

'Mother, I don't want the kingdom. I don't want the throne. If you ask me to stay here, I will stay. If you want me to go on a pilgrimage, I will go. But never ever tell anybody that I'm not your son.'

There were tears in Queen Mother's eyes. She hugged Madurandakan and made him sit by her side.

'Madurandakan, honestly I did not want this pain for you. Tell me that you don't want to be the king. If you do that neither I nor the prime minister will need to reveal the truth about your birth.'

Madurandakan was lost in thought for a while. When he spoke, there was nothing but grief in his voice.

'If my birth secret is known, everyone will flee away from me. Yes, I'm the unluckiest person ever born in this world. Mother, I'm confused. Give me a day's time to let you know of my decision.'

The prime minister intervened.

'Prince, you may take two more days to think it over. The cabinet meeting is to be held only after three days.'

'Mother, does anybody other than the prime minister know this secret?'

Madurandakan was suddenly curious. Evil thoughts entered his mind. The Queen Mother was surprised by Madurandakan's excitement.

'The mute sisters know. One of them is your biological mother who was killed in the palace two days ago. The other one is your mother's mute sister who lives in a garden outside the fort. She can't tell anybody. She has a son. The mother and son are serving a nearby temple by giving fresh flowers everyday. I support them by giving some grants.'

'Mother, I know them. Her son, Chendan Amudan helped Vandiyathevan escape. Does he know about this secret?'

'No, my child, he doesn't know. His mother has promised me that she won't tell anybody. Don't worry about it.'

Several evil thoughts flooded Madurandakan's mind. Initially he thought of removing his mother and the prime minister from this world. Then nobody would know. He also suspected that the Queen Mother and the prime minister were deceiving him.

'My dear son, take your time and come to the right decision.'

Something very unexpected happened at that moment.

Prince Arulmoli walked into the room. He prostrated at the feet of Queen Mother.

'Mother, I consider the advice you gave to your son as given to me. I'm ready to renounce my rights to the throne.'

The Queen Mother and the prime minister were taken aback.

'Mother, I had to overhear your conversation much against my wishes. Please forgive me. You said that amongst those who are alive today only you, the prime minister and Chendan Amudan's mother know the secret regarding Madurandakan's birth. That is not correct. My sister Kundavai and I also came to know about it through the Lankan Queen.

We are convinced that my uncle Madurandakan has the exclusive right to the Chola throne. He was born of a noble woman who saved me several times.'

All the three who heard the words of Ponniyin Selvan were stunned.

The prime minister regained his composure and spoke.

'Prince, your words should find a place in the epics and legends of this great country. But we three cannot decide the issue of succession here. We need to consult the emperor and the chieftains of the empire. We also need to think of the possible reaction of the people.'

41

Kundavai Shattered

Princess Kundavai was born and brought up in royal affluence. But today she was immersed in a sea of grief. Her warnings to her brother Aditya Karikalan went unheeded and he had paid the price for that. Losing her brother, who was still young, gave her endless grief.

She expected Prince Arulmoli would realize all the dreams and aspirations of her elder brother Karikalan after ascending the throne. But how many stumbling blocks there were!

The emperor was shattered by the death of his first-born Aditya Karikalan.

Her beloved Vandiythevan, was also imprisoned on the charges of murdering Aditya Karikalan for no fault of his. She could not sleep. She was constantly exploring the ways and means to solve the problem.

They are trying to charge him for the murder of Aditya Karikalan. Parthiban is quite adamant on punishing him. Well, I can talk to my grandfather on behalf of Vandiyathevan. He may listen to me and my beloved may be released. But how can I, a woman, intervene on behalf of a man, accused of murdering my own brother? People may think that I love this wanderer more than my own brother and then that will become a scandal.

Parthiban Pallavan will create such a scandal to malign me and my beloved. He claims that Vandiyathevan was caught red-handed by him and Sambuvarayar at the place where Karikalan's body was found. Poor soul, Vandiyathevan! He must have tried to save him and failed.

Some believe that Arulmoli and I conspired to kill Karikalan so that Arulmoli can ascend the throne. My hands are tied and I'm helpless. Oh my God! I have never had any worries since my birth. Please help me cross this crisis.

She refused to share her grief even with her best friend, Vanathi, who was always by Kundavai's side like her shadow, remaining absolutely silent.

Now Vanathi came to inform her about the arrival of a miserable woman in tears. Kundavai was surprised.

'Who is she? Why has she come here?'

'She is Manimekalai, daughter of Sambuvarayar. Sambuvarayar's family has been imprisoned in the palace of Junior Paluvettarayar. This girl has managed to come here. I asked her what the matter was. She said that she will tell only to you. Sister, if you see her once, you will melt.'

'Are you implying that I have a heart of stone?'

'Why do I need to imply? I'm sure of it. Your heart is made of stone. Otherwise, you would not let Vandiyathevan suffer in the underground prison.'

'We'll discuss that later. Bring the girl in.'

Vanathi ran out to bring Manimekalai.

Manimekalai entered Kundavai's chambers like a mad woman, her eyes swollen. Kundavai did not pity her as her brother's heinous murder had taken place in her father's palace.

Suddenly she remembered that Manimekalai's brother and Vandiyathevan were close friends. Kundavai became curious.

Why has she come here? To plead for her father and her brother?

'Hey girl, why are you crying? Your brother is still alive. It was my brother who was brutally killed at your palace. I should be the one crying. Are you upset because the tragedy took place when he was a guest at your palace? What can you do, dear? There were several elders present at the time in your house. It is their responsibility, not yours.'

'No, Princess. The responsibility is entirely mine. That is why I'm unable to control my grief. When I realized that I killed him with my own hands, I was unable to bear the grief.'

Kundavai was shocked.

'What are you saying? Are you mad?'

'No, Princess. I'm not mad. But I will go mad soon. I came here to confess my crime and get the punishment I deserve.'

'Do you want me to believe you? Tell me, who has tutored you to make this false confession?'

'No one, Princess. Nobody believes me. Even my father and my brother don't believe my words.'

'Why are you spinning this yarn? Are you saying this out of your imagination to save your father and brother?'

'Princess, why should I save them? They tried to get me married against my wishes. First, they wanted me to marry Madurandakan. Then they asked me to marry Aditya Karikalan so that I could become the empress, much against my wishes. They want to sacrifice me at the altar of greed. Why should I put the blame on my head for their sake?'

'Many princesses had been waiting for the good fortune of marrying my brother. Why did you decline to marry him?'

'I consider you as my own sister and I will confide everything in you.'

'You say you killed my brother. Then how dare you call me your sister?'

Kundavai was furious.

'Princess, I have the right. Karikalan considered me as his sister. I'm here to seek retribution for my heinous sin.'

Now Kundavai was calm.

'Poor girl! What has happened, has happened. It is all destiny. Now you can say whatever you want to.'

'Princess, as a woman you understand another woman's feelings. Imagine a situation like this. A woman loses her heart to a good man. Her man is alone, unarmed. Suppose another man draws his sword and runs up to kill him. If the woman truly loves the man, what will she do? Will she be a mere spectator?'

'How can she be a spectator?'

'It was a bad time for me. I had no one to guide me. I listened to that evil Nandini and killed the man who loved me as his sister. My brother Kandamaran had been telling me about his friend for quite some time. I fell in love with him at first sight when he came to our palace a few months ago.'

Now Kundavai's voice became feeble.

'Who is that lucky man who stole your heart?'

'Princess, you call him lucky? Do you think a prisoner in the underground dungeons of Tanjore is lucky? Is it possible to see him?'

'You have not yet told me who your lover is.'

'The Prince of Vallam, Vandiyathevan.'

Vanathi intervened.

'Why are you bothered about him? How are you connected to him?'

Manimekalai was stung.

'Who are you to ask that?'

But then, Manimekalai regained her composure.

'Sorry. Please don't mistake me. I didn't mean it. Aren't you the Kodumbalur Princess, Vanathi? Please grant me a boon. Your uncle is now in charge of the Tanjore Fort. Please ask your uncle to release Vandiyathevan from the underground prison. Let me be imprisoned in his place as I was the one who killed Prince Karikalan.'

She turned towards Kundavai.

'Princess, I also beg of you. If Kodumbalur Chieftain does not render justice, you have to help me. I want to plead directly to the emperor.'

Kundavai was confused.

Is she speaking the truth? Or was she induced by Nandini to do that heinous act of killing Karikalan. Or is she is lying only to save Vandiyathevan?

'Manimekalai, I appreciate your determination and your love for Vandiyathevan. You are ready to make a confession to save your lover.

I may believe you but others won't.

Your father and brother say that Vandiyathevan was found near the dead body of Karikalan. Tell me, will the people believe you or them? There is another reason I can't believe you. It was I who sent Vandiyathevan to my brother Karikalan with strict instructions not to leave him even for a moment. He was seen with the prince at the time of his death. He should have given his life to save the life of Karikalan. He did not do that. He has clearly failed in his duty. And he ought to be punished for that.'

'Princess, he never swerved from his duty.'

'Is there any evidence of that?'

Manimekalai, then, took out a palm leaf. She gave it to Kundavai who received the leaf with surprise. She read the letter written by Karikalan in his own hand. The letter was addressed to Kundavai.

'Dear sister, I have not slept well for several years. Today I saw the comet falling from the sky. Let this bad omen have all its ill-effects only on me. May God keep our father and Prince Arulmoli safe. I had a lot of dreams about our Chola Empire. I could not realize all my dreams. I'm sure our brother Arulmoli will do it. He is born to rule this world. He will be ably supported by the valiant Prince of Vallam, Vandiythevan. Sister, if anything happens to me here, it is only due to my destiny. Vandiyathevan is not to be blamed. He tried his best to stop me from going to Kadamboor. He failed because of my obstinacy. He was following me like a shadow. He became close to Sambuvarayar's daughter, Manimekalai to accomplish his mission. With her help, he would find out my itinerary and would go there even before I went. He strived hard to save me from danger.

Kandamaran and Parthiban are fully caught in the seductive net of Nandini. Vandiyathevan is the only man who did not fall for her seductive charms. I consider Sambuvarayar's daughter Manimekalai like my own sister. I'm giving this palm leaf only to that girl. Thank God, she can't read. You are the most intelligent person in our family. I did not listen to your advice. And I'm going to pay for it, at least let our brother Arulmoli take your advice and bring glory to our great Chola Empire.'

Kundavai burst into tears after reading the letter.

'How did you get this leaf?'

'The prince himself gave it to me. Nandini had told me several bad things about Prince Karikalan. I made my friend Chandramathi read it for me. Prince Karikalan considered me as his own sister. To think that I have killed that noble soul with my own hands... my heart bursts out. Let no mercy be shown to me.'

'Manimekalai, do you still insist that you killed Karikalan?'

'Yes, Princess.'

'You told me that you had your friend read this letter. Why should you kill a man who loved you like his own sister?'

'If only I had read the leaf earlier, I would not have committed this crime. Princess, I killed him without knowing what was in his mind. I thought he had given me a love letter. That devil, Nandini, had corrupted my mind.'

'How?'

'During the final moments, Karikalan was in a state of frenzy. "Where is Vandiyathevan? I shall kill him right now," he had said several times. I thought it was true and I used my knife.'

'Let's not talk about that any more. I may believe that a timid girl killed the most valiant Karikalan. But the world won't.'

Manimekalai broke down. Amidst sobs she pleaded with Kundavai: 'Princess, you must save him. You alone can do it.'

42

The Barrier to Freedom

Princess Kundavai was worried about Manimekalai. She wanted to console her but could not.

Prince Arulmoli entered the chambers just then.

Vanathi and Manimeklai left the place.

'Brother, what is happening? I heard that the people are rallying behind you, shouting slogans.'

'Sister, I'm helpless. When we are all mourning the death of our brother Karikalan, these people are shouting slogans demanding that I should ascend the throne. I can't bear this. I even think of running away from the country. But that may lead to some serious complications.

Sister, you talk to our grandfather Malayaman and the Kodumbalur Chieftain not to instigate the people to raise slogans demanding me to accept the throne. They don't listen to me. Perhaps they may listen to you.'

'Brother, I have tried my best. They are very stubborn. Let us think of some other strategy.'

'Sister, your friend Vanathi has taken a terrible vow not to sit with me on the Chola throne. If we break this news to him, the Kodumbalur Chieftain will refrain from making me the king.'

'I have already informed him. Do you know what his response was? "We can't ruin the empire because of a silly girl! If not Vanathi there are hundreds of princesses waiting for the prince to ascend the throne". He said that and cast a furious glance at his niece.'

Arulmoli smiled.

'Sister, let us take the case to the emperor. The two old men will only listen to him.'

'That is not as easy as you think. There is another stumbling block. If the Queen Mother insists that Madurandakan should not be crowned, then the emperor will have no other option.'

'Sister, then let us first meet the Queen Mother and change her mind. The reason she does not want Madurandakan to be crowned is what we guessed. I met her a little while ago. She revealed the truth to Madurandakan only today. Our uncle's face became the face of a devil. Thank God, I went there at the right time.

I pleaded to our grandmother with folded hands. "So what if Madurandakan was not born of you. The child brought up by you is your child. He should be crowned".'

'Brother! Didn't you tell her that even though Madurandakan is not Queen Mother's son he has the right to the throne? Didn't you tell her that he is our father's own son and that he is your elder brother?'

'No, sister. I didn't.'

'Why not? Were you afraid that it would malign our father's name? Or did you want to say so at a later time?'

'Sister, Madurandakan and Nandini are not born of our father as we believe. They were born two years after our father returned from Lanka. So, they are not our blood brother and sister.'

Kundavai thought for some time.

'Brother, do you still wish to give up the throne for Madurandakan? Even after knowing about his birth?'

'Yes sister, Madurandakan is the son of Mandakini, brought up by Queen Mother. This makes him eligible. And I have no desire for the throne.'

'Perhaps the astrologer's words may come true. Even if you don't want the crown, the throne will come to you, your stars are like that.'

'What is this, sister? You have also joined sides with our grandfather, Malayaman? Have you changed your mind?'

'Grandfather's advice did not change my heart, brother. But

brother Karikalan's letter changed it. He expects you to fulfil all his dreams...'

Kundavai broke down and gave the palm leaf to him.

Ponniyin Selvan was also upset after reading Karikalan's letter.

Kundavai spoke with firmness in her voice.

'My mind is clear now. After learning Madurandakan and Nandini do not belong to our clan, I can't bear to see Madurandakan as the emperor. A person not born to our clan cannot become the Chola Emperor.'

'Sister! What are you saying? I vowed before the Queen Mother that I don't want to ascend the throne. I told the same to thousands of people. How can I go back on my word?'

Kundavai was confused and bemoaned her fate.

'Sister, who gave this palm leaf to you? Why didn't you tell me about this leaf earlier?'

'I saw this only a few minutes ago. Sambuvarayar's daughter, Manimekalai brought it here.'

'How did she get this palm leaf?'

'She is here. You can ask her.'

Kundavai called Vanathi and Manimekalai.

Manimekalai came in crying. Arulmoli spoke to her politely.

'Sister, we are indebted to you forever for bringing this letter to us.'

Manimekalai broke down and fell at Arulmoli's feet.

'Prince, I killed your brother. Throw me in the underground prison. Please release him.'

'Sister, what is she saying? Is she sane? Who is in the underground prison?'

'Brother, have you forgotten the warrior of the Vaanar clan through whom I sent a message to you?'

'Oh my God!'

Prince Arulmoli's mind had been preoccupied with many grave events which had followed one after another. He had totally forgotten about Vandiyathevan.

'Oh my god! Is my dear friend Vandhiyathevan in jail?'

Ponniyin Selvan heard the whole story and was shattered.

'I know just how devoted he was to our brother Karikalan. Who dared to make him responsible for Karikalan's death? Let me go to the underground prison and free Vandiyathevan. I will bring him here. Meanwhile, you console Manimekalai.'

When Prince Arulmoli reached the door, Thirukovilur Malayaman and the Kodumbalur Chieftain stopped him. Ponniyin Selvan was shocked. 'Commander, are you going to imprison me?'

'Prince, we forbid you to go to the underground prison.'

'What authority do you have to block me?'

'I'm now the commander of Tanjore Fort. You are the emperor's son. Even then, you don't have the authority to release a murderer. Only the emperor has that authority now. Or the person who is going to succeed him will have that authority. You have been telling everyone that you are not going to ascend the throne.'

Malayaman was softer.

'My child, what he says is true. As Junior Paluvettarayar has run away, the emperor has made Kodumbalur Chieftain the commander of this fort. So, you don't have the authority to release anybody from the underground prison.'

Ponniyin Selvan did not know how to respond. The room was silent but for the sobs of Manimekalai.

43

Truth May Be Out

After listening to the discussion between Arulmoli and the two chieftains, Princess Kundavai invited them to come inside the palace.

'Please come inside. Prince Arulmoli won't go against you.'

Malayaman and the Kodumbalur Chieftain came in. The Kodumbalur Chieftain spoke to Kundavai.

'Princess, if only Prince Arulmoli agrees to become the king, there will be no issue. We will give up our lives to execute his orders.'

'Uncle, I'm also making the same request to the prince. Now this girl Manimekalai, Sambuvarayar's daughter has come with a plea and the prince wants to go to the prison to release Vandiyathevan.'

'Perhaps, she is distressed because her father is in jail. The emperor has issued orders to release Sambuvarayar.'

'Grandpa! She is worried about Vandiyathevan and not about her father. She says, "I killed the Prince; not he".'

'Oh! If she is so adamant, let's throw her also in jail. We can't release him,' said the Kodumbalur Chieftain.

Manimekalai continued sobbing, 'That is precisely what I pray of you. Please jail me along with him.'

Kodumbalur Chieftain hit his head with his hand and spoke.

'This girl has lost her mind.'

Now Vanathi spoke, 'She has not lost her mind. Vandiyathevan is the best friend of Ponniyin Selvan and the slain prince Karikalan. Those who have imprisoned him alone have lost their minds.'

Kodumbalur Chieftain retorted, 'When did this girl become a

chatter box? Vanathi, you should not open your mouth when the elders are speaking.'

Malayaman came to Vanathi's rescue.

'Commander, why are you angry with her? After all she is saying what's in the minds of the people.'

'If Arulmoli agrees to become the king, there is no problem. On the day of coronation, all the prisoners will be released.'

Now the prince came forward.

'I will go meet the emperor right now and get his orders for the release of Vandiyathevan.'

When Prince Arulmoli was about to leave the room, the Kodumbalur Chieftain intervened.

'Prince, please don't meet the emperor with that plea. That will lead to complications.'

Kundavai questioned then, 'What complications will arise if Arulmoli pleads for Vandiyathevan's release?'

'Miscreants have floated terrible rumours.

Ponniyin Selvan, out of his greed for the throne, hired Vandiyathevan to kill Karikalan.'

The Prince was shocked.

'Oh my god! How cruel!'

'You know how our soldiers treated those two rumour-mongers? They were torturing them by ducking them into the river again and again.'

'Nobody will believe this cruel rumour,' said Ponniyin Selvan.

'Prince. You don't know our people. The same rumour will spring up again after some time. And people may believe it.'

'General, simply because of such false rumours, should I let my dear friend suffer in prison now?'

Kundavai's fair face became pale.

'General, who has spread such an evil rumour?'

'Kandamaran.'

Manimekalai came forward.

'I'm ashamed of my brother. He was a good man. Later he became evil in the company of Nandini. I was the one who killed Aditya Karikalan. Put me in jail. Release Vandiyathevan.'

Manimekalai was sobbing.

Princess Kundavai comforted her.

'Be calm, Manimekalai. Nobody will believe you. Your version will only lead to more rumours. Let us find out a way to resolve this issue.'

She then turned to the Kodumbalur Chieftain.

'Uncle, my brother and I accept your advice. Releasing Vandiyathevan now will complicate things. We will have to find out the murderer first. Let us wait for Alvarkkadiyan's fact finding report. The truth will come out if Senior Paluvettarayar returns. Let me also ascertain from Manimekalai.'

Vanathi spoke after a long pause.

'Let us all go to the underground prison and meet Vandiyathevan.'

Everyone agreed to Vanathi's suggestion

Kundavai spoke to the Kodumbalur Chieftain.

'Vandiyathevan was with Karikalan on that fateful night during his last moments. We can ask him to describe the events of that day. The truth may come out.'

They all went to the underground prison. The mint was silent as they had stopped minting gold coins after Junior Paluvettarayar had left the fort.

There were only a few guards. They reached the cell where Vandiyathevan was being held. But Vandiyathevan was not there. In his cell they saw the doctor's son, Pinakapani. He was bound by chains which were fastened to the iron rings on the wall.

When he saw the visitors, he screamed.

'Please free me. I'm not guilty.'

44

Escape from the Prison

During the grueling journey from Kadamboor to Tanjore as part of the crown prince's funeral procession, Vandiyathevan remained mostly unconscious. He was bound to a cart and carried along.

Vandiyathevan slowly regained consciousness. The wailing sound coming from people resembled a mighty ocean in turbulence. He knew that the funeral procession of Aditya Karikalan had reached Tanjore.

Vandiyathevan had tried to save the crown prince but had failed. And to add insult to injury, he had been accused of murder.

'This one is Sambuvarayar. And that is Vandiyathevan, the one who killed the crown prince.'

The people commented as he and Sambuvarayar were led to the underground prison.

Will Ponniyin Selvan and Princess Kundavai save me? Will they believe I'm innocent? Will there be an enquiry? No, Senior Paluvettarayar will stop it as Nandini will get exposed.

When the guards locked him in the prison, Vandiyathevan lost all hopes.

He heard somebody singing the song of Lord Shiva in the adjacent cell.

'Lord Shiva, whose body is of the golden hue.'

Vandiyathevan was immediately reminded of Chendan Amudan but it was not Chendan Amudan's sweet voice.

'Who's that?' shouted Vandiyathevan.

'It's me, the madman.'

'You don 't sound like a madman. Who taught you this song?'

'Some time back there was a man in your cell. He stayed here for a few days. He used to sing this song all the time. I learnt it by heart.'

Vandiyathevan immediately knew that the person being referred to was Chendan Amudan.

'Do you know him?' asked Vandiyathevan.

'Of course. His name is Chendan Amudan. He is the son of a dumb woman. If only the world knew his real identity...'

'What would happen?

'The world would turn upside down.'

'If it did, will we be released from this cell?'

'Definitely.'

'Then please tell me who he is.'

'No, I won't. How can I so easily part with such crucial information?'

'You know such important information. Then why do you call yourself a madman?'

'I know the place where the Pandiya's ancestral crown and opal necklace are hidden in Lanka. I have been telling everyone that if I'm freed, I will show the place. They call me a madman. Do you believe me?'

'But what is the use of my believing your words? I'm also a prisoner like you. I can't help you in any way.'

'Don't lose hopes. You are in a lucky cell. Nobody stays in it for more than a few days. Some queen or princess will come to release you.'

'No such luck for me, my friend.'

'Never mind, I will release you.'

'Now you are talking like a madman.'

'No. Trust me.'

'I have no other choice but to trust you.'

'Then wait patiently till the guards come and give us dinner.'

The guards completed their last routine rounds for the day. Pin drop silence prevailed in the cell.

He noticed a hole in the wall. After a few minutes, the hole became bigger and the mad man entered Vandiyathevan's cell.

'This is the fruit of six months of my labour.'

'What is the use of making a hole in this wall? You should have made it on the outer wall.'

'There is no outer wall in this underground prison. We have to go only through the room where the tigers are kept. The guards are new. They don't let the tigers out from the cage in the night. We can attack the guards together, tie them up and escape.'

'When can we leave?'

'Patience brother, patience. Let us wait for the right time.'

The madman was talking to Vandiyathevan for a long time. When he learnt about the death of the crown prince, he was excited.

'Then it is even more necessary that I should get out immediately.'

'Why?'

'Somebody has to be made a crown prince in his place.'

'Some chieftains prefer Madurandakan. Others prefer Ponniyin Selvan.'

'What is on the emperor's mind?'

'He wants to avoid an internal conflict at any cost. He wants to crown Madurandakan.'

'Then it is extremely important that we should get away immediately.'

Vandiyathevan was curious to know the truth about the successor to the Chola throne from the madman.

'I won't tell that now. If we both survive our escape attempt, I will share the secret with you. If not, let the secret die with me.'

The doctor's son, Pinakapani, cherished an ambition to hold a high post in the government. The prime minister had given him the crucial assignment of bringing the mute queen from Kodikkarai. But he could not accomplish the mission fully and he had been bedridden for some time.

When he was healed, he sought the audience of the prime minister. Meanwhile, so many things had happened. The Lankan Queen had sacrificed her life to save the emperor. Crown Prince Aditya Karikalan was killed.

Therefore, the prime minister's mind was flooded in a sea of worries. When Pinakapani mentioned a crazy man in the underground prison, the prime minister got excited as the crazy prisoner knew of the secret hiding place of the ancestral crown of Pandiyas in Lanka and the mystery shrouding Prince Madurandakan's birth.

The prime minister used the doctor's son for the job of gathering more information from the crazy prisoner. Pinakapani met the mad man in prison to discern the secrets from him. He realized that the prisoner was not crazy.

'First get my release order. I will tell you everything after that.'

The prime minister also agreed to release the mad prisoner and orders were served for his release.

Pinakapani wanted to know the secret information before they met with the prime minister. But the prisoner was smart. He and Vandiyathevan overpowered him and bound him with heavy chains. Vandiyathevan took away Pinakapani's headgear and wore it himself. He also secured the official signet ring from him. He quickly left the cell along with the mad prisoner.

Vandiyathevan produced the official signet ring. The guard mistook Vandiyathevan to be Pinakapani.

'You may go. The prime minister's men are waiting for you at the gates.'

They now reached the prison's exit gate and the prime minister's men received them to take them inside the palace. Ponniyin Selvan was coming along just then, with Princess Kundavai and the Kodumbalur Chieftain. Little did Vandiyathevan know that they were on their way to the prison to see him.

The guards accompanying them got distracted by the procession. Vandiyathevan and the mad prisoner made use of the opportunity and escaped. Their escape became easier as the bylanes of the fort were deserted. They hid behind dense bushes near Senior Paluvettarayar's palace.

Vandiyathevan sat on a log. He made the mad prisoner sit by his side.

'We can resume our journey when it becomes dark. Till then, I want to listen to your story.'

He started a long narration. It seemed like the work of a creative writer with many unexpected twists and turns.

45

Secret Unravelled

Karia Thirumal also known as Karuthiruman or Thiru belonged to a place called Thopputhurai near Kodikkarai. He earned his livelihood by ferrying passengers.

About twenty-five years ago, while returning to his place from Lanka, he saw a woman floating in the sea water. She was unconscious. He rescued her and took her in his boat to the shore.

At that time a few men came riding on horses. The leader of the horsemen told Thiru that the woman was mute and requested him to leave her somewhere on the Lankan shores. He gave Thiru loads of gold for that service.

Thiru took the woman in his boat to Lanka. On the way he saw a man clinging to a log on the high seas. He was totally exhausted. Thiru rescued him as well and took him also in his boat to Lanka. He dropped them at Ghost island near Lanka. An old man on that island told him the mute girl was his daughter and her name was Mandakini. She had lost her mind and could not recognize her own father.

The man rescued by Thiru gave a palm leaf to be delivered to the King of Lanka. Thiru came to know that the man rescued by him was the Pandiya King. On delivering the palm leaf, the Lankan King sent his men to bring home the Pandyia King. The two kings visited the hilly region of Rohana at the southern tip of Lanka. Thiru accompanied them.

The Lankan King showed them a cave. Inside it, there were mounds and mounds of gold coins, priceless gems and diamonds and a golden box containing a shining crown and an opal necklace.

The Panidya King said that one day he would destroy the entire Chola clan and would be crowned as the emperor in Madurai and will wear the shining crown and the opal necklace publicly at the coronation function. The Panidya King gave Thiru loads of gold to take care of that dumb woman Mandakini. Then he could join him in the Pandiya Kingdom.

When Thiru went back to Ghost Island, Mandakini and her father were missing. He went to Kodikkarai in search of them. He saw Mandakini there. Her father was no more. She was under the care of her brother, the caretaker of the lighthouse. She was pregnant. He also met Vani, sister of Mandakini. She too was mute like her sister. He took pity on Vani and wanted to marry her.

Meanwhile, Mandakini and Vani were taken away to Palayarai palace by Queen Sembiyan Madevi during her visit to Kodikkarai temple. The queen was also pregnant.

Thiru went to the Pandiya Kingdom and met the Pandiya King in the battlefield. The Pandiya King requested him to bring the mute woman, Mandakini, to him.

Thiru went to Palayarai mainly to meet Mandakini and if possible, marry Vani. On the way to Palayarai, he happened to see Vani digging a pit in a garden to bury a small cloth bundle lying by her side. When he heard a child's cry coming from the cloth bundle, he was horrified.

'Brother, imagine my plight, how I would have felt at that time. I will tell the rest of the story only to somebody from the King's family. If only I had not been to Palayarai at that time, I would have been saved from a lot of troubles.'

Vandiyathevan smiled.

'Let us start now. Tell this story to somebody in the royal family to solve the mystery.'

The sun had set by now. They approached the river through the secret underground passage in Senior Paluvettarayar's palace.

They were delighted to see a boat caught in the tangled roots of a tree on the bank. They could easily reach Kodikkarai using that boat.

Vandiyathevan was excited to see the boat. Vandiyathevan and his companion got into the boat. No sooner had the boat moved when four men sprang into the boat. Two of them sprang on Vandiyathevan, pushed him to the floor of the boat and bound him to the planks. The other two, blocked Thiru and all his escape routes.

The stout guard was none other than Alvarkkadiyan. The prime minister had sent him as a back-up in case Pinakapani failed in his mission. Vandiyathevan and Thiru were bound to the boat and the guards started rowing. The flood waters were turbulent. The guards were unable to row upstream. They wanted Thiru, who was an expert boatman to row them to safety. Thiru and Vandiyathevan made use of this opportunity and overpowered the guards and pushed them into the water except Alvarkkadiyan. Now the boat was in their control.

Vandiyathevan thought for a while and spoke to Alvarkkadiyan.

'You have saved my life many times. I don't know your real motives. Whatever they may be, I don't want to kill you but you have to help me.'

'I was born in this world only to help others. Tell me what you want. Release me from this binding.'

'We want two horses for our onward journey. If you tell us where we can find them, we'll leave you here in this boat and get down at the bank. The boat will safely take you to a destination.'

'Do you know Vani's house? There are two horses there.'

'Vani who?'

'Chendan Amudan's mother.'

Thiru got excited.

'I know the house. It's in the garden.'

'There are two good horses at that place.'

'How are you so sure about it?'

'One is mine and the other belongs to Amudan. Chendan Amudan is down with fever.'

Vandiyathevan was concerned.

'Who is there to take care of Amudan?'

'His mother and Poonkulali are with him.'

Thiru entered the conversation suddenly.

'Which mother?'

Alvarkkadiyan and Vandiyathevan were surprised.

'What did you say?'

'Does Queen Sembiyan Madevi know about Amudan's illness?'

'Probably. She has bestowed some endowments to support the family. When everybody in the palace is grieving for Karikalan's death, who will care for Amudan?'

Vandiyathevan looked at Thiru.

'Can we visit Chendan Amudan and his mother before we leave?'

Thiru nodded his head.

They proceeded to Amudan's house.

46

We Are Poles Apart

Vani and Poonkulali were nursing Chendan Amudan in his garden house. Poonkulali was very sad.

'What is bothering you, Amudan? The doctor says that your recovery is delayed because of your worries.'

'My only worry is that I will recover soon.'

'Amudan, are you in your senses?'

'If I'm cured you will leave me. I'm worried about that, Poonkulali.'

'I don't have the heart to leave you. Nor can I be with you.'

'Yes, Poonkulali. The sea beckons you. Take me with you. I will be alright.'

'Amudan, my vow blocks the way.'

'What is your vow?'

'I will marry only a king or else I will remain a spinster.'

'I know, Poonkulali. Ponniyin Selvan is in your heart. But do you think it is possible?'

'Amudan, you are wrong. Everyone loves Ponniyin Selvan. I too love him.'

'Are you sure?'

'Amudan, my aunt fell in love with a king. Her life was full of miseries. Whatever she failed to achieve, I will achieve in my life through my marriage.'

'It is my ill-luck that such a desire has sprouted in your mind.'

'Don't lose your heart, Amudan. Is there any rule that only those born of a king should become king? People like you born in ordinary families have established kingdoms by their acts of valour. You too take a vow to establish a kingdom of your own. I will serve you as long as I live.'

'Poonkulali, I was not born to rule. I'm not enamoured of the crown. I'm not suited to you. We are poles apart. My desire for you is like the desire of a lame man pining for honey on the mound.'

All of a sudden, drastic changes took place in Poonkulali.

'Amudan, I have abandoned my desire for royal life. Your love is a million times more precious than royal pleasures. As you refuse to change for me, I've decided to change for you. Yes, I will marry you.'

Chendan Amudan became excited.

'Poonkulali, is this all a dream?'

'My aunt Mandakini's death has taught me new lessons. I've learnt the trials and tribulations of palace life. Palace life can never be equal to the carefree life in the sea. Let us marry soon and sail in the seas. There, you are the king and I'm the queen with no one to rival us.'

'I'm already cured.'

Amudan sprang up from his bed. They heard a knock on the door.

Poonkulali opened the door to see the Queen Mother, Sembiyan Madevi and Madurandakan. There were guards holding torches behind them. Amudan and Poonkulali received them with reverence. Queen Mother entered the hut. Madurandakan stood outside. Madurandakan was burning with fiery jealousy and impotent anger.

'Mother, you could not have come at a better time. We have happy news to share with you and get your blessings. I have not yet shared the news even with my mother. At last, this girl Poonkulali has consented to marry me. Mother, you should conduct our wedding ceremony and bless us. After the marriage, we plan to move to Kodikarai.'

Was the Queen Mother happy? Or was she sad? There was a smile on her lips and tears in her eyes. Nobody could guess whether the Queen Mother was happy or sad.

The young ones prostrated before her to get her blessings. Queen Mother's voice was choked.

'My dear children, may you be blessed with a happy married life.'

Amudan's mother, Vani entered the hut at that time. Queen

Mother communicated to her in sign language that she had come to enquire about Amudan's health. And she was happy to hear the wedding news. There was a strange expression on Vani's face. After some time, the Queen Mother took leave of them and walked towards the palanquin.

After ensuring that no one was around, Queen Mother spoke to Madurandakan in a soft voice.

'Did you see him? Yes, Chendan Amudan is my son. I bore him in my womb for ten months. I knew this when he was five years old. When he was eight days old, there was no movement in his body. I thought he was dead. As I badly wanted a child, I adopted you as my son. I even ordered that my child should be buried. Vani took him. She did not return. I came to know the truth when I saw her and this boy after five years. But I didn't abandon you. I didn't invite him to the palace for the only reason that he was born of me. I thought of the whole thing as God's play. My love for you never dimmed. Now I seek a boon from you. Promise me you won't aspire for the Chola throne. I won't object to your desire to become king but I'm worried about the possibility of your descendants being dumb.'

Madurandakan was shocked as if possessed. He had married the daughter of Junior Paluvettarayar. The couple had a two-year-old baby who could not speak. Unable to bear the shock, Madurandakan leaned on a tree nearby.

Queen Mother spoke very softly:

'My dear child, come let's go. Reflect on what I have told you.'

Madurandakan spoke in a dull voice.

'Mother, what is there to reflect on? You go ahead. Let me talk to the person who should have been in my place in the palace. I will come a little later.'

'Take care. When you return make sure the screens of your palanquin are pulled in to cover you. If the Kodumbalur soldiers see you, they may raise slogans against you.'

Queen Mother walked towards her palanquin. In the dark night, she did not notice the fire on Madurandakan's face.

47

Who Are You!

After Queen Mother had left, Madurandakan waited outside Amudan's hut deliberating whether to go into the hut or leave.

Pinakapani was furious when Vandiyathevan and the mad prisoner escaped after binding him in the cell. Later he met the prime minister and the Kodumbalur Chieftain demanding the capture of Vandiyathevan. As nobody was keen, he decided to follow Vandiyathevan and take revenge. He landed up at Amudan's house.

After instructing the palanquin bearers and the guards to wait, Madurandakan walked towards Amudan's hut.

Suddenly Thiru emerged from behind the tree. Madurandakan took out his knife. Thiru stopped him.

'Please don't do that. I'm not your enemy.'

'If you are not my enemy, then who are you?'

'A friend.'

'Good. When the whole world is slipping away from me at least I've got you.'

'You are right. I will do something which no one in this world could do.'

'What is that? I have to go to the palace, you know.'

'You want to go back to the palace where you have no right to stay?'

Madurandakan was shocked.

'What the hell are you saying?'

He flashed the knife once again.

'Please don't use the knife on me. I overheard the conversation between you and your mother.'

'So, you know the truth.'

'I knew the secret long back. I know much more. She might have told you that she is not your mother and Emperor Kandaraditya is not your father. She might have told you who your mother is. But she could not have told you who your father is.'

'Do you know that?'

'Yes.'

Madurandakan was scared and his voice was full of anger. 'Who are you?'

'I'm your father's servant.'

Madurandakan was relieved.

Thiru came near him.

'Your father is...'

He revealed a name. As soon as Madurandakan heard it, he felt dizzy and he was about to fall down. Thiru prevented him from keeling over.

'Is that true? Do I really belong to a royal clan?'

'Yes, I was looking for a chance to talk to you in private but Junior Paluvettarayar threw me into the underground jail.'

'When did you come out? How?'

'I came out only today. A young man named Vandiyathevan helped me to escape.'

'I heard that. Was he not charged with the offence of murdering Karikalan?'

'Yes. But he is innocent.'

'Why should we worry about it? Let him be the murderer. Who cares? Where is he now?'

'He is there hiding behind the fence. He is waiting for me. He has horses for both of us. He will be angry if I spend time talking to you. But I'm not bothered. I'm happy that I met you here.'

'It's all right. What are you going to do now?'

'Whatever you want me to do. Are you going back to the palace even after knowing about your birth? Bear this in mind. The prime minister and his spy Alvarkkadiyan know that you do not belong to the Chola clan… Someday or the other…'

'You are right. I don't want to go back to the palace. What do you suggest?'

'There are two horses here. You make a show of going into the hut and coming back. Meanwhile, I will engage Vandiyathevan in a conversation and distract him. You throw the knife at him and kill him. We shall take the horses and go to Kodikarai and from there to Lanka. The Lankan King is an enemy of the Chola clan and friend of the Pandiya King. I know the Lankan King. I know where he has kept the Pandiya crown and the opal necklace. What do you say?'

'Should I kill him?'

'If you can't, give that knife to me. I will do it for you.'

'No. I have another job for this knife. I know Vandiyathevan. He is a warrior. We will take him with us.'

'You go engage Vandiyathevan, meanwhile, let me meet the resident of this hut.'

Thiru walked towards Vandiyathevan.

But Vandiyathevan was not there.

Vandiyathevan walked to the hut to ensure Amudan's health and peered through a makeshift window. He was delighted to see him happily talking to Poonkulali. He wanted to interrupt their conversation to take leave of Amudan.

Suddenly Vandiyathevan saw a figure holding a short spear in his hand. The figure peered into hut through another window and was about to throw the spear at someone inside the hut.

Vandiyathevan started running towards the figure. The shadowy figure which was about to throw the spear on somebody inside the hut was distracted by the sound of Vandiyathevan running.

He threw the spear at Vandiyathevan. The spear pierced his body near the costal bone. Vandiyathevan fell. The shadowy figure did not wait to see what had happened. It was Pinakapani running away.

Pinakapani had come to Amudan's house expecting to find Vandiyathevan. But when he saw Poonkulali talking intimately with

Amudan, he could not contain his jealousy. After all, Pookulali had snubbed him when he had proposed his love for her in Kodikarai. He was aiming the spear at Amudan through the window. When he saw Vandiyathevan running towards him, he threw the spear at him and started running.

48

Tell the Truth

The prime minister and Alvarkkadiyan were keen on letting Vandiyathevan and Thiru escape as Vandiyathevan was not guilty. Moreover, if the two prisoners were in Tanjore, there had to be an enquiry on so many sensitive old issues. Even a perfunctory enquiry against him might ruffle some feathers and embarrass top brasses. Under these circumstances, the only way out was to let him escape from prison.

Alvarkkadiyan was waiting in the boat for Vandiyathevan and Thiru to pass his way on their horses along the river bank. He wanted to extract some truth from Thiru.

Soon the horses came near.

'Who is that? Please stop! Please help me...'

The horses which had crossed him stopped at a distance. He was frozen to see the rider on the second horse. The first horseman came back and Thiru jumped down and came near Alvarkkadiyan's boat.

Alvarkkadiyan sprang on him and pushed him down. Thiru did not expect this sudden attack.

'Please leave me. Let me go. Your friend Vandiyathevan is waiting for you there. If he knows that you have played a cheap trick on me, what will he think of you?'

'You are the worst liar I have ever seen. Tell me who is there on the other horse. I will kill you if you trick me.'

'Yes, I lied. Vandiyathevan is not on the other horse. It is Prince Madurandakan. Leave me. I will get you a good reward from him.'

'The rewards can wait. Where is Vandiyathevan?'

'He is at Chendan Amudan's house.'

'Where are you guys going?'

'Lanka.'

'Why is Madurandakan coming to Lanka with you?'

'How do I know? Better you ask him.'

Alvarkkadiyan increased the pressure on Thiru's chest.

'Tell me. Whose son is Madurandakan?'

'Dumb question. No, no. Please don't press my chest. I will die. Madurandakan is Mandakini's son.'

'Who is Madurandakan's father? Tell the truth or consider yourself dead.'

Thiru told the truth.

'Good. You are saved. One last question. Whose son is Chendan Amudan?'

'Why do you ask me? You already know.'

'Isn't he the son of Emperor Kandaraditya and Sembiyan Madevi?'

'Yes. But for me, he would have died long back. Vani, who is both deaf and dumb was trying to bury the child alive thinking it was dead. I was there by sheer coincidence. I heard the child crying. I saved the child. Leave me alive at least for having done that good deed.'

'I'm letting you go precisely for that good deed.'

Alvarkkadiyan got up from his place.

Thiru ran towards his horse. He sprang on the beast. The two horses ran along the bank of the river in the shadowy darkness of the rainy season.

49

Day Dreaming by Madurandakan

Alvarkkadiyan was returning to the fort. Suddenly a man came running as if possessed.

'Oh, the doctor's son! Why are you running like a mad man?'

'Oh, Nambi! Did you see two men on horses go by?'

'Yes, I did. Why do you ask?'

'Oh my God! That was Vandiyathevan escaping!'

'What nonsense are you talking? Vandiyathevan is in the underground prison.'

'No, he has escaped along with the mad prisoner. Come with me. We can capture them alive.'

'Let them enjoy their hard-earned freedom. Why should we bother about that?'

'I'm surprised how the prime minister employs such dull-heads like you. Don't you know that Vandiyathevan killed Aditya Karikalan? Added to that he attacked somebody with his spear before running away on a horse.'

'Oh my God! Who was the victim?'

'I didn't see who it was. Don't block me. Let me follow and catch them.'

'Doctor's son, I have seen many fools in this world. But you are the greatest. They are two. You are one. And you are on foot. They are on horses. They run for their lives. Do you think you can catch up to them let alone capture them? It's not my problem any way. Go away.'

'You are right. That's why I asked you to come with me. But you refuse...'

'What can I do? I tried to stop them. One of them hit me with a stick. It still hurts. If I were in your place, I would go back, tell the right people, get five or six men on horses and go in search of them. I would also go riding on a horse armed with a sword and a spear.'

The doctor's son thought for a while. He had attacked somebody with a spear in Chendan Amudan's house. That could probably be Prince Madurandakan. If so, he should shift that blame also on Vandiyathevan. A person who killed a prince would not hesitate to kill another. The punishment was going to be the same.

'Nambi, you should tell the right person to help me with men and horses. I told this to the Prime Minister and the Kodumbalur Chieftain. They called me a fool. I want to prove myself. That's why I started on this mission alone. Those rogues will have to stop at Kodikarai. I have enough people there to help me.'

'Then what are you waiting for? Go. Best of luck.'

'Even then it would be better if I go on a horse. And take a few men with me. Will you help me?'

By this time, they had come near the gates of the fort. The prime minister along with the other important persons of the empire were waiting at the gates to receive the Paluvettarayars and their allies.

'Parthiban and Kandamaran are there. Why don't we tell them? They will evince interest in capturing Vandiyathevan, dead or alive,' said Alvarkkadiyan.

The procession came near them. Junior Paluvettarayar saw Alvarkkadiyan and the doctor's son.

He stopped the horse.

'Nambi, any important message?'

'Vandiyathevan has escaped from the underground prison.'

'How could he have done that? Is he a magician? Something is fishy here. Somebody in power must have helped him.'

'It must be the work of that Kodumbalur Chieftain,' said Kandamaran.

'Nambi tell me the truth. Did you go around to the fort to stop their escape or to aid it?'

Parthiban never had a good opinion of Alvarkkadiyan.

'If it was any other time, I would have given a fitting retort. This is not the time for personal fighting. This man, the doctor's son, has brought some strange news. He tells me two people were going fast on their horses along the river. He says one of them is Vandiyathevan and the other one is the mad prisoner. I too saw two men riding fast on horses.'

'Pinakapani, is that true?' asked Junior Paluvettarayar.

'I promise, it's true. Please help me with four horsemen, I will bring back those rogues.'

Parthiban intervened.

'Let us help him. The emperor has asked me to bring you back to the palace. Otherwise, I will go with him. We must immediately capture Vandiyathevan.'

Kandamaran jumped in.

'Leave that to me. I will go with him and capture Vandiyathevan; even if he has entered the gates of the house of death, I will bring him back.'

Junior Paluvettarayar agreed. Immediately Kandamaran, Pinakapani and four armed soldiers mounted their horses.

Madurandakan was not used to horse-riding whereas Thiru was an expert rider. They saw a make-shift bridge across the river made of bamboo poles. Before crossing the river, they wanted to relax for some time.

Madurandakan was restless. Thiru tried to comfort him. Soon there would be a war among the chieftains of the Chola Empire. When the entire Chola Kingdom will be in chaos, the Lankan King would come with a huge army to invade and capture the Pandiya Kingdom from the Cholas and crown Madurandakan in Madurai. Madurandakan was excited and he had never been so enthusiastic.

He even heard the war drums in his mind and the music played during the coronation ceremony. Thousands of people were raising slogans.

'Hail the Pandiya Emperor!'

While Madurandakan was building castles in the air, the sound of horse hoofs shattered his dreams. He could see torches at a distance. Thiru never thought the search party would catch up with them so soon.

Madurandakan and Thiru cut the bamboo bridge and laid it as a hidden obstacle in the path. Thiru asked Madurandakan to cross the river and go to the other bank. He climbed a tree and waited for the search party.

The obstacle in the path tripped the horses that came in search of them. Pinakapani and Kandamaran fell down from the horses. Thiru laughed weirdly from atop the tree. Pinakapani was terrorized and screamed. 'Ghost! Ghost!'

Kandamaran sprang up with a spear, aiming at the man on the horse crossing the river. He thought it was Vandiyathevan but it was not he. It was Madurandakan. The spear hit Madurandakan and he fell into the water. This sudden development shocked Thiru. He hadn't expected the fallen horsemen to get up so fast and react.

He jumped down from the tree screaming. He hit Kandamaran with demonic force and stabbed the doctor's son Pinakapani to death. He then ran across the bamboo bridge and cut it after reaching the other side so that nobody could follow him.

The mad prisoner Thiru escaped before Kandamaran's men could reach. Kandamaran went along the river bank looking for Vandiyathevan's body. But he couldn't find it. He saw a waterfall. It may take several days for Vandiyathevan's body to be washed ashore. So, he abandoned the search and went back to Tanjore.

Meanwhile, Alvarkkadiyan and his men walked towards Amudan's house. He ordered his men to search the garden thoroughly and they found Madurandakan's crown, clothes and jewels.

Alvarkkadiyan heard someone moaning in pain inside Amudan's

house. He knocked the door but Poonkulali refused to open the door. Alvarkkadiyan convinced her and she finally opened the door. After chatting with him for some time Poonkulali said:

'Nambi, I have abandoned my dream of marrying a prince and becoming a queen, I know being a king and ruling a country makes our life miserable. I want to share some happy news with you. I have decided to marry my cousin, Chendan Amudan. I told this to the Queen Mother who came here a little while ago. We have got her blessings too. As soon as Amudan recovers, we will leave for Kodikarai to start a new life.'

'Good decision, Poonkulali. You have abandoned the palace life for the sea life. But who are we to decide that? If it is your husband's destiny to bear a crown and rule the world that is bound to happen. You cannot prevent it. I want to bless you both with a long life. But if you have helped escaped prisoners, my blessings will go to waste.'

'What is this? We never helped anybody to escape from prison.'

Now a moan was heard from under Chendan Amudan's cot.

50

Prince for a Day

As soon as Alvarkkadiyan heard the moaning sound from below Amudan's cot, he shouted:

'Now I know. You are lying.'

Poonkulali took the knife from her waist and flashed it against Alvarkkadiyan's face.

Amudan got up from his cot.

'No, Poonkulali. Never do that. Lying and cheating can never do us good. Let us tell him the truth and ask for his help. After all, he is Vandiyathevan's friend.'

Alvarkkadiyan told Amudan,

'Good of you.'

Poonkulali and Amudan lifted Vandiyathevan from below the cot and placed him on bed. Amudan's mother Vani gave him herbal treatment.

Vandiyathevan opened his eyes to see Alvarkkadiyan.

'Nambi, you sent me here and also sent someone to kill me.'

After uttering these words, he fainted again.

'Nambi, did you send Vandiyathevan here?' asked Poonkulali.

'Yes, I did. But I did not send anybody to kill him.'

'Why did you send him here?'

'I wanted him to escape. I had even kept two horses for him and his friend.'

'Nambi, Vandiyathevan came here at the right time and saved me from becoming a widow even before my marriage.'

Alvarkkadiyan and Chendan Amudan were shocked.

'What are you saying?'

Poonkulali turned towards Amudan.

'I did not even tell you. There was someone outside waiting to throw a spear at you. Vandiyathevan blocked him and took the spear on himself.'

There were tears in Amudan's eyes.

'Oh my God! Was my dear friend hurt because of me?'

'But who could have the heart to hurt this innocent young man? Poonkulali, did you see the culprit?' asked Nambi

'Yes, I did. I recognized him. He is that devil Pinakapani, the doctor's son. If we keep him here soldiers will come in search of Vandiyathevan. Please save him.'

'Soldiers are out in all four directions in search of him. I don't know what excuses to give them.'

Poonkulali pleaded.

'Nambi, even the prime minister listens to your advice. Please show us a way to save Vandiyathevan.'

'Princess, that is not very easy.'

'Till yesterday you called me a boatgirl. Now you call me princess. There is a change in your tone.'

'Yes, Princess. There is only one way to save the valiant Vandiyathevan. This lucky man who is going to marry you should act as a prince just for a day.'

Amudan intervened.

'Nambi, why are you making fun of me?'

'Prince, let me share a secret. First look at this.'

Alvarkkadiyan displayed Madurandakan's crown, jewels and clothes.

'Madurandakan has left these jewels before running away with the mad prisoner.'

'Why should Madurandakan abandon his crown and run away?'

'I don't know. I will talk to the prime minister and send men in search of him. But before that, I'm afraid, many disasters will happen.'

'What disasters?'

'The emperor wants to have peaceful smooth succession. But before the peace talk commences, the first question the Paluvettarayars would ask is "Where is Madurandakan?" If he is not found, they will suspect the Kodumbalur Chieftain. They will say Madurandakan was killed to enable Ponniyin Selvan to ascend the throne. That will lead to a civil war in the country.'

'Then what do you suggest?'

'Let Amudan wear this crown and these jewels. Let Amudan get onto the elephant and proceed to the palace. I will place Vandiyathevan in Madurandakan's palanquin and draw the screens. I will make my men shout "Hail Prince Madurandakan" and walk with the elephant. Madurandakan's palanquin is also here. You walk by the side of the palanquin. I will take care of the rest.'

'An outrageous suggestion,' said Amudan.

'Simply because he has a crown on do you think that people won't find him out?'

'Princess, it's night time. He is going to be on an elephant. Again, people will look deeply only when they suspect something. I will also come with you and take you all to the prime minister's house. There is no other way to save Vandiyathevan.'

Finally, Chendan Amudan and Poonkulali consented.

51

Amudan as Prince

The armies of the Paluvettarayars and their allies assembled at the gates of the fort. It appeared like a meeting of the great oceans. All the chieftains were welcomed by the prime minister.

'Oh, great kings, each one of you has contributed to the growth of the Chola Empire for generations. Your support and cooperation is needed in the future as well. That is why our emperor has invited you all to decide on the issue of succession setting aside his grief over the loss of his beloved son.'

Junior Paluvettarayar responded, 'We are anxious to meet our emperor and honour his wishes.'

'Our emperor will meet you all tomorrow. He wants all of you to rest peacefully tonight in your respective places in the fort.'

Junior Paluvettarayar intervened again.

'When the emperor is meeting us tomorrow, why should we enter the fort tonight?'

Kodumbalur Chieftain added fuel to the fire.

'Perhaps Junior Paluvettarayar fears staying inside the fort.'

'Fear? What does that look like? Black or red or will it have horns or wings? Perhaps the Kodumbalur Chieftain who ran away from the Lankan battlefield may know better.'

The prime minister was embarrassed.

Senior pacified him, 'Brother, the Kodumbalur clan is known for its integrity. For them a word given, is a word given. The Kodumbalur provides security for us, we might as well stay inside the fort.'

'We don't need anybody's protection. I have been the commander of this fort. I will step in only after regaining my position,' said Junior.

Kodumbalur Chieftain spoke to Senior,

'I will give back the fort any time if the emperor orders me to do so.'

'Did he capture the fort with the emperor's orders?' asked Junior Paluvettarayar.

'No, with the power of my sword,' said the Kodumbalur Chieftain.

'Then I will regain it with the power of my sword,' retorted Junior.

Senior tried to convince his brother.

'Brother, this is not the time for the sword.'

'Brother, what is the guarantee that we won't be arrested inside the fort?'

Senior provided sane counsel to his brother.

'You have even left our families and Madurandakan inside the fort in his care. Why should we mistrust him now?'

'Yes, that was my blunder. Madurandakan and his mother left the fort but only his mother has returned. What happened to Madurandakan?'

Now their conversation was interrupted by a sudden buzz of activities at the gates of the fort.

'Hail Prince Madurandakan!'

Everybody turned towards the direction of the sound. Now the prime minister spoke.

'Commander, Madurandakan's re-entry into the fort was delayed. Vani's son Amudan was injured. Sembiyan Madevi ordered that Amudan be brought to the fort in a palanquin. Madurandakan carries out his orders and he is riding on an elephant and Amudan comes in his palanquin.'

52

He Failed in His Duty

Usually, Madurandakan travelled in a palanquin. Therefore, Junior Paluvettarayar was surprised to see him entering the fort on an elephant with so much fanfare. The prime minister convinced him that it was a rehearsal...

'Anyhow, he has to get over his shyness some day before his coronation.'

'It is blissful to see Madurandakan riding on an elephant with Kodumbalar soldiers guarding him.'

Junior walked a few steps towards the elephant. Then he changed his mind and came back.

Finally, he asked his brother.

'You may all go inside the fort but I won't. You meet the emperor and let me know what is on his mind. Kandamaran has gone after Vandiyathevan. Let me find out how Vandiyathevan escaped from the underground prison and who helped him.'

Kodumbalur Chieftain wanted to say something. Senior Paluvettarayar intervened.

'General, my brother has lost his mind. Come, let's go.'

But the emperor insisted on the presence of Junior Paluvettarayar during the deliberations.

Senior spoke reverentially.

'Your Majesty, please forgive me. My brother will accept whatever decisions we take here.'

'Minister, your dearest brother was present in all the cabinet meetings in the past. No decision was ever taken without him. Why should that intelligent warrior refuse to join us now?'

'Your Majesty, let me tell you the real reason for him not coming in. This fort was under his command for several years. Now the command has shifted to new hands. That is why my impudent brother refuses to come here.'

'Let us render justice. The unimpeachable reputation of the Chola clan is founded on the principles of justice. One of my ancestors killed his own son because he had inadvertently crushed a calf under his chariot wheel. That was the kind of justice system that prevailed in the Chola Empire. Why should I deviate from the ancient tradition? Kodumbalur Chieftain should not have taken over the command of this fort by sword. As I was grieved on the death of my beloved son, I overlooked the injustice meted out to Junior Paluvettarayar. I now request the general to give back the charge of this fort to Junior Paluvettarayar.'

Kodumbalur Chieftain's face fell. Malayaman defended him.

'Your Majesty, when Junior Paluvettarayar was in charge of this fort, he did not discharge his responsibilities properly. A conspirator sneaked into the fort and threw a spear at you. A mute woman had to intervene to save your life. What is the point in holding hundreds of swords and spears? What is the big deal in employing so many soldiers and the warriors? Junior Paluvettarayar miserably failed in his duty. What is wrong in Kodumbalur Chieftain capturing the fort?'

The emperor now spoke softly to his father-in-law, Malayaman.

'Who can be blamed for destiny's fault? In spite of your best efforts, you could not save your dear grandson.'

'Emperor let us hold an enquiry to find the truth about Karikalan's death as well,' said Malayaman.

'We were waiting for the arrival of Senior Paluvettarayar. We can hold the enquiry soon as he reaches,' said the Kodumbalur Chieftain.

'Vandiyathevan has escaped from the high security underground prison. Who is responsible for that security lapse?' questioned Parthiban.

Now the prime minister spoke

'Your Majesty, I take full responsibility for that. Vandiyathevan escaped because of my mistake. I will take the responsibility of bringing him back here.'

'Kandamaran has gone in search of Vandiyathevan,' said Parthiban.

Prime minister replied to Parthiban.

'Pallava Prince, your friend Kandamaran is undoubtedly smart. But we can't trust him with a task like this. He could not save the life of Karikalan when he was staying in Kandamaran's own palace. How can he capture Vandiyathevan? I don't think he can.'

Now the emperor spoke.

'The prime minister has taken up the responsibility of bringing Vandiyathevan back. Kodumbalur Chieftain should now give back the charge of the fort to Junior Paluvettarayar.'

'If that's the royal decree, I obey it right now,' said Kodumbalur Chieftain with irritation.

The emperor now pacified Kodumbalur Chieftain.

'You are senior to me both in age and experience. I love you as I love my own father. Who am I to order you? I just voiced my opinion. Let us also know what the others think on this subject.'

'I'm not for it, Your Majesty. Junior Paluvettarayar has failed in his duty. Let us not entrust the fort to him again,' replied Malayaman.

'What does the prime minister think?' asked the emperor.

'What has happened has happened. Your Highness has invited us all to settle the issue of succession. Let that be our first priority,' suggested the prime minister.

'We can't decide without Junior Paluvettarayar,' said the emperor.

'I endorse the views of Malayaman. My brother has failed in his duty. No need to entrust the fort to him again,' Senior voiced his opinion.

Everyone in the assembly was surprised by his words and even more surprised, shocked even, by what the emperor said next.

'Junior Paluvettarayar did not fail in his duty. I neglected his advice. Junior Paluvettarayar often cautioned me about the former bodyguards of Pandiya Kingdom and their connections inside the fort. He wanted to seal the secret passage connecting Senior's palace and mine. You know that Junior Paluvettarayar worships his brother. In spite of that he complained against his own brother. He told me that his brother was being deceived by people. He even suggested that the palace of Senior Paluvettarayar be shifted to some other place. The underground treasury should also be moved to a safer place. I didn't listen.'

Senior Paluvettarayar now spoke, devoid of all emotions.

'Your Majesty, you did not question me about certain things out of your love for me. I was caught in the seductive net of Nandini. My brother warned me against that witch several times. I did not heed his words. Even then I would say that he failed in his duty. When he knew for sure he ought to have killed my wife and those conspirators. If I tried to save them, he should have killed me as well. He did not do that. Hence he failed in his duty.'

The whole assembly was stunned.

The emperor now pacified Senior Paluvettarayar.

'I also know that your brother is capable of killing anybody who stands in the way of his duty. But I prevented him from doing his duty. I warned him not to complain about you or your wife.'

Tears rolled down the cheeks of Senior.

'Your Majesty, I too ignored all his warnings. Junior Paluvettarayar is blameless. He brought to my notice Vandiyathevan's connections with Nandini. That treacherous man deceived Princess Kundavai and the prime minister too. They sent very important messages through Vandiyathevan.'

The prime minister now spoke.

'Emperor, I might have been deceived but not the princess. She did send message through Vandiyathevan but she also requested me to keep an eye on him. I sent my disciple Alvarkkadiyan to Lanka to spy on him.'

Now the emperor said in a majestic voice,

'Vandiyathevan and another person have escaped from the underground prison. Had the fort been under the control of Junior Paluvettarayar, this would not have happened. General, entrust the fort to Junior Paluvettarayar.'

'As you please, Your Majesty. So can we take leave of you now?' said the Kodumbalur Chieftain.

He had calmed down now. The emperor's compassion melted his heart.

'Yes, we can meet after Junior Paluvettarayar joins us. I too need some time to discuss the issue of succession with the Queen Mother,' Concluded the emperor.

That very day, the command of the fort was given back to Junior Paluvettarayar.

Though the top brasses had reconciled, there were a few minor altercations between the men of various factions.

53

I Will Save the Empire

Queen Mother came to see the emperor. She was surprised to see the emperor standing at the gates to receive her.

'Queen Mother, thanks to the divine lady Mandakini I have regained my capacity to walk. Though my health has improved now, I don't want to live anymore especially after the sudden demise of the greatest warrior of this empire, my dearest first-born Aditya Karikalan. In fact, I should have died before him.'

'Emperor, people like your fair and just rule and you have to live long.'

'Queen Mother, Aditya Karikalan was isolated and was lured into a trap and killed by those cowards. People cast aspersions on Senior Paluvettarayar alleging his hand in Karikalan's murder.'

'Why don't you ask him?'

'He is like my father. Unless he himself comes forward to tell me what actually happened on that day, I cannot ask him. How can I forget the contributions he and his clan have made for this mighty empire? He was solely responsible for the victory of the battle at Thakkolam which we almost lost. After his valiant fighting in all the battlefields, we have now ordered him not to risk his life anymore. Now we have made him the finance minister. Let us wait and see.'

'Emperor, is there no other way to know the truth?'

'Mother, they say that Vandiyathevan was near the body of Karikalan. We thought we could know the truth from him. But now he has escaped from jail. Queen Mother, you should guide me in this hour of crisis. And also save this empire from destruction.'

Upon hearing this, the Queen Mother broke into a sob.

The emperor continued.

'The kings of this empire sacrificed their lives to make it strong and powerful. I have also sacrificed my personal preferences for the welfare of this great empire. For some reason or the other, the Paluvettarayars and some chieftains did not like Aditya Karikalan. They prefer your son Madurandakan for the throne. There is nothing wrong in it. In fact, I should not have become the king myself. At that time the elders forced me to wear the crown. I didn't have the heart to go against their wishes. I'm reaping the consequences of that act now. I have suffered enough for one life. I don't want to see this large empire destroyed by a civil war. Queen Mother, you must help me.'

Queen Mother wiped her tears.

'How can we make my son the king? Even if I agree, the world won't. Everyone wants Prince Arulmoli to wear the crown.'

'Mother, how can I agree to their proposal when it is against the principles of justice? Please grant me the permission to crown Madurandakan. I can convince Kodumbalur Chieftain and Malayaman.'

'Emperor, how can I can go against the word of my husband? Let us call Madurandakan and ask his views.'

'Yes, let us ask Madurandakan's views to proceed further in this matter. Where is Madurandakan?'

Sembiyan Madevi spoke in a choked voice.

'I've been asking the same question for the past three days. No one answers me. Where is my son?'

'Mother, Junior Paluvettarayar also keeps asking the same question. He says that you and the prime minister have joined hands to make him disappear. Let me summon them to discuss on this issue.'

Junior Paluvettarayar and the prime minister came in.

'Commander, Queen Mother is asking the same question which you asked, where is Madurandakan?'

'Your Majesty, the whole world worships Queen Mother. I too adore her. But I have a duty to share my doubts. Three days ago, Queen

Mother and Madurandakan went out to the hut of Chendan Amudan to enquire about his health. But Queen Mother alone returned to the fort. A little later an elephant and a palanquin entered the fort. The men were shouting slogans:

"Hail Prince Madurandakan!"

Prince Madurandakan who normally stays in my palace, has not come to my palace till today. We could not find him anywhere. I saw him entering the fort. How did he vanish without a trace? Queen Mother and the prime minister must have conspired to get rid of Madurandakan.'

Queen Mother spoke in a choked voice.

'Commander, whatever you just said is baseless. There is no conspiracy here. On that evening Madurandakan and I went to Chendan Amudan's hut. When I left the place, Madurandakan said that he would come a little later. I've not seen him since then. I'm also searching for him.'

'I accept the words of Queen Mother. Now I appeal to the prime minister to unravel the mystery.'

'What mystery?'

'The mystery of the missing son.'

'Commander, you said that you have searched everywhere. Is that true?'

'Except your palace.'

'Why not?'

'Because you are the prime minister.'

'Commander, then you have not done your duty, the Queen Mother and I are not involved in any conspiracy. But let me tell you something. The person born of this divine lady's blessed womb was in my palace for the last three days. Now he is waiting outside the room to see his mother and the emperor. If you permit me, I will bring him in.'

Everyone in the room gasped. The Emperor was the first to speak.

'Prime Minister, what is this game? Come on. Bring him in.'

The prime minister clapped his hands. The next second Chendan Amudan entered the room followed by Alvarkkadiyan.

Junior was furious.

'Are there no limits to your games?'

But the Queen Mother extended her arms, 'My son, my dearest!'

The commander was confused. Amudan was not perturbed.

'Mother, at least now you called me your son.'

With tears streaming from his eyes, he approached Queen Mother. The divine woman, out of whose womb was born Madurandaka Uthama Chola, celebrated as one of the greatest kings of Chola dynasty by history, hugged her son and shed tears of joy.

54

No Crown for Me

When Amudan was five years old, Queen Mother saw Amudan and his foster mother Vani for the first time after several years. She thought that the five-year-old boy was Vani's own child. He was intelligent and well-mannered.

Queen Mother had a soft corner for the mother and son. She bestowed endowments on them for their livelihood. One day something struck her mind like lightning, leading to a doubt. The doubt gave her pain and pleasure with a vague fear. She tried to dismiss her doubts but could not. She was constantly thinking of her child which she had thought was dead. She was restless.

Finally, she summoned Vani to her palace to clear her doubts. She told Vani that she wanted to see the place where the child was buried to build a memorial. Vani who hesitated initially, finally revealed the truth. She said that the child was not really dead. When she was about to bury the child alive, a man called Thiru stopped her and took her with him to his village. After five years, Vani returned to Palayarai with the child.

The Queen Mother's joy knew no bounds to learn that Chendan Amudan was her own son. Tears of joy streamed from her eyes. She wanted to proclaim Amudan as her son and hug him in public. But she restrained herself realizing the complications.

What if my child grows in a hut or a palace? All are children of God.

However, Queen Mother was sure that the child growing up as Madurandakan in her palace should not ascend the throne at any cost as he was not from the Chola clan. She had already confessed everything to her husband and had got his pardon. She recalled her husband, Emperor Kandaradityaʼs words, ‘Everybody born in this world is Godʼs child. But ensure that he does not ascend the throne ever. And in the worst scenario, proclaim the truth.’

She was firm about fulfilling the words of her late husband who had died without knowing that his own son was growing up in Vaniʼs hut. Finally, Queen Mother made a tough decision.

The words of the prime minister describing Amudan as the one born of the womb of this divine mother served as a trigger that made her love burst out in a flow.

Queen Mother became speechless. Amudanʼs words hit her like a gale.

‘Mother, at least now you have the heart to call me your son.’

The import of these words was clear. It only meant one thing—that Amudan already knew that she was his real mother (Amudan had come to know of it through the mad prisoner Thiru while in prison). Yet he didnʼt ever reveal his identity. Why didnʼt he tell the world that he was the son of the empress? It took some time for Queen Mother to steady herself. She then hardened her heart and asked him.

‘Son, did you know that I was the ill-fated mother who bore you? Were you angry with me?’

Words charged with emotions flowed out of Amudanʼs mouth.

‘Mother, I knew you were my mother. My only prayer was that one day you should call me your son. I was waiting for the issue of succession to be resolved as I didnʼt want the throne. I want something even more precious. The greatest privilege of calling you mother. Yes, that is my birthright. Three days ago, there was an attempt on my life, soon after your visit to our hut. I would have died without cherishing this moment but for my friend.

Iʼm the luckiest person in the world. I want nothing else from you. Let this secret be known only to those who are here. Let it not lead to complications. Poonkulali and I are leaving for Kodikarai to start our new life. Please bless us, Mother.’

There are no words in any language to describe the effect of these words on Queen Mother.

In a choked voice punctuated by sobs, the Queen Mother said,

'My son, my child! You are the best of the best. You are divine. You have inherited your father's greatness.'

The emperor, Junior Paluvettarayar and Princess Kundavai could not come out of the shock of this sudden revelation.

Kundavai was the first to regain her power of speech.

'Father, now I know why Queen Mother did not want Madurandakan to be crowned.' Then the emperor emerged from the shock.

'You are right, dear. But that has changed now. She cannot object to her own son, being crowned as the next Chola Emperor.'

Queen Mother was disturbed.

'Emperor, did you not hear my son's words? "Let this secret not be known to anybody else." My son is not staking his claim for the crown.'

'Yes, Your Majesty. There are enough problems in the empire now. Please let me go.'

Chendan Amudan and Poonkulali fell at the feet of Queen Mother and the emperor.

Queen Mother spoke for her son.

'Emperor, let them go. Whenever I feel like seeing them, I'll visit them.'

The emperor was adamant.

'Impossible. I won't allow them. Mother, you have found your son after several years. I won't let him go away from you so soon.'

55

Who Killed My Brother?

The issue of succession was getting complicated with mob violence everywhere. Prince Arumoli went around the kingdom to convince the people that he had no interest in the crown. But his campaign had the opposite effect. He was embarrassed to see that even his opponents wanted him to become the king. He was already upset about the missing Prince Madurandakan. He even doubted the Kodumbalur Chieftain.

Perhaps Madurandakan was kept as hostage by him till the succession issue is resolved.

He was worried that the blame might fall on him also.

Today people adore me. But will their mind remain the same? People are generally fickle-minded. They often change sides. They will even say that I killed my own uncle Madurandakan to become the king. Oh my God, I'd rather die than hear such baseless charges. I want to pour out my mind to somebody and seek their advice.

He lost hopes even with his dear sister, Princess Kundavai as she was involved in a secret mission. Even his beloved Vanathi was hiding something from him. She was secretly going somewhere and he closely followed her to find out the secret.

When Vanathi was about to enter a room, Prince Arulmoli blocked her way.

'Tell me, what are you hiding from me?' he demanded.

Vanathi smiled.

'Why don't you step in and find out for your self.'

Prince Arulmoli expected to see Madurandakan there. But when he saw his friend Vandiyathevan, he was both happy and pleasantly surprised.

Vandiyathevan sat up on his bed and welcomed the prince.

'Prince, I was expecting you. Please release me from the prison of these women.'

'What is this friend? How did you come here? You escaped from the underground prison. Then how were you imprisoned by these women? I thought you would be in Lanka by now. I had even planned to join you there after the succession issue was resolved.'

'Yes, Prince. I should have been in Lanka by now to go after the ancestral crown of the Pandiyas. I tried to save Chendan Amudan from the spear of the doctor's son, Pinakapani. In the process, I bore the spear and became unconscious. I don't know how I landed here. Please help me escape from this prison.'

Vanathi spoke, 'If he escapes, the blame on him will be confirmed. He should be here till the truth is out. Of course, no one should know that he is here.'

'My friend, I think Vanathi speaks sense. If you try to run away, people can easily blame you and me too. People may even say that I engaged you to kill my own brother. So better to prove to the world what really happened. First tell me what happened on that day in Kadamboor.'

Vandiyathevan started a long narration. Prince Arulmoli raptly listened but at the end of it, he could not conclude the cause of the death of the Crown Prince Aditya Karikalan.

56

I Will Be the King

Vandiyathevan concluded his narration: 'Prince, Senior Paluvettarayar is the only person who can save me. But I don't know if he will come out with the truth. Hence, please let me go away. I will go to Lanka in search of the Pandiya crown and bring it for you.'

Suddenly something flashed in the mind of Prince Arulmoli.

'I have decided to be crowned as the Emperor of Chola Kingdom. Only to save my innocent friend. I can't see you suffer.'

Vandiyathevan spoke in a choked voice.

'Prince, if you become the king for my sake, it is the good fortune of this great kingdom. Prince Madurandakan is a coward and is unfit to rule the country as he keeps getting involved in one conspiracy or the other to get the throne. No wonder people love you and hate him.'

'I will abandon all efforts to find him and will instead, become the king.'

Princess Kundavai heard these words just as she was stepping into the room.

'Brother, I don't think you can become the king now. Our uncle has finally come out of his hiding. Even if he refuses the crown, you will have to force it on him.'

Kundavai's words surprised everyone. Ponniyin Selvan spoke.

'Sister, where was he all this time?'

'He has been with us all the time but we could not recognize him. Brother, he is born of Queen Mother's womb. That makes him more qualified to become the emperor than you. The throne belongs to him. A miracle happened in his life.

Four days ago, there was an attempt on his life. But for this warrior lying on the bed, he wouldn't be alive now. Another untimely death would have happened in the Chola clan. The Chola clan is indebted to him.'

'Sister, who are you talking about? Where is our uncle now?'

'Ponniyin Selvan, he will be here in a few seconds. You can hear the story directly from the horse's mouth.'

The prime minister, Alvarkkadiyan, Chendan Amudan and Poonkulali, entered the room. A princely crown adorned Amudan's head.

'Brother, he is the one born of Queen Mother,' the Princess said.

'It was an intricate game played by God that made him live in a hut till now with all the innate qualities of the Chola clan.

Once he helped this warrior of the Vaanar clan to escape from the fort. And he and Poonkulali were the ones who brought you safely to Nagapattinam. Can we ever forget that, brother?

We should celebrate this grand re-union. But we cannot celebrate it now and this news should not leak out of the palace.'

Ponniyin Selvan hugged his uncle.

'Uncle, I loved you earlier even without knowing your true identity.'

Kundavai spoke to her brother.

'Brother, our dear Queen Mother was objecting to Madurandakan's succession only for this reason. We were also not happy with Madurandakan being crowned. He had none of the royal qualities found in the valiant Chola clan. Queen Mother tried her best to plant the seed of nobility in his heart but in vain. Now we are all happy.'

The prime minister responded, 'Princess, before the coronation let us find out from Senior Paluvettarayar what happened at the Kadamboor Palace. We should also know what happened to Madurandakan.'

Chendan Amudan now addressed Prince Arulmoli.

'Prince, you called me uncle. These people call me prince. But I can't call you "my son". I have been living in a hut for so many years. I can't suddenly think of myself as a prince. I helped Vandiyathevan to escape from the fort and was thrown into the underground jail. I learnt about my birth secret from a mad prisoner in the adjacent cell. He told me that the son of the dumb woman is growing up as a prince in the palace, whereas the son of the empress is growing in the dumb mother's hut. Then I realized the truth. I also understood why Queen Mother loved me so much. My only dream was to hear her words "my son". That dream has come true today. I want nothing else.'

The prime minister interrupted him

'Prince, what matters is not what you like, but what is just and fair.'

'Prime Minister, I have already thought a lot and come to a clear decision. I love Poonkulali dearly. But she had an ambition to marry a prince and ascend a throne. She even rejected me because I was not a prince. Even then I never revealed the truth by saying, "I'm a prince and if I wish this Chola Empire will be mine" to win her love. I was even ready to sacrifice my love for Poonkulali. But thank God, at last she gave up her ambition to become the empress.'

'Uncle, even after knowing about your birth, your act of sacrificing your right for the crown shows your large heartedness. We all want you to be our king. Why refuse?'

'Princess, you want me to be the king. But what will the people say? All the people want Prince Arulmoli to ascend the throne. How can I go against their wishes?'

Nobody knew how to respond to that outburst. Prince Arulmoli spoke in a majestic voice.

'Let's stop the discussion at this point. When you entered the room, I was telling Vandiyathevan that I want to be crowned. I said that mainly to save Vandiyathevan. No more discussions on this.'

57

Durbar Hall

Emperor Sundara Chola was seated on the ceremonial seat in the durbar. On either side of him were seated the most important women of the royal household, ministers, generals and princes.

The emperor glanced around.

'Why is the Kadamboor Chieftain missing?'

'Kandamaran just arrived. Father and son will join us soon,' said the prime minister

'Has Kandamaran brought back those who escaped from jail?'

'No, Your Majesty. He claims to have killed Vandiyathevan but he could not catch the madman prisoner,' replied Parthiban.

'Any information about the prince's death?' asked Malayaman. 'It will be better if we know the truth before proceeding further.'

'Yes. We can't discuss the succession issue without knowing the truth behind the prince's death,' said the Kodumbalur Chieftain.

'Celebrated warriors! Whatever has happened has happened. Our emperor is already upset about the death of his beloved son. He feels that there is no point in digging up the past,' said the prime minister.

'That won't be just or proper. Chola's system of justice is world renowned. Even if an orphan dies suspiciously, it is enquired into and justice rendered. How can we just brush aside the murder of the crown prince without even a preliminary enquiry?' asked the Kodumbalur Chieftain.

The emperor let out a long sigh.

'Please listen, Kodumbalur Uncle. Can anybody else grieve more than I for the death of my dear son? I don't want an enquiry. Do you know why? No one is responsible for the death of my son. I lost my son as a punishment for my past sins. Tell me if there is any way in which I can atone for my sins.'

Junior Paluvettarayar spoke now.

'Your Majesty, if you take a stand like this, people will think that you are trying to save the guilty. The people have already started building stories about the death of our prince. It is better to investigate the case and find out the truth.'

Parthiban responded,

'Well said, Commander. That is the right thing to do. If we don't hold an enquiry into such a grave crime, then people will lose faith in the system of justice.'

Kandamaran who had entered the hall spoke for the first time.

'Respected elders, why should we debate on a settled issue? The guilty has been punished. I killed Vandiyathevan with my own hands.'

Prime minister now questioned Kandamaran.

'Kandamaran, is it true that you killed Vandiyathevan? You went after him in the dark. Were you able to see him?'

'Prime Minister, I know you won't believe me. Do you think I can't recognize him even at night?'

Kodumbalur Chieftain asked Kandamaran.

'Brother, why are you so keen on punishing Vandiyathevan?'

'Should I have to give the reason? The tragedy happened in our palace. And if the culprit is not caught, won't you suspect me and my father?'

The emperor came to his defence.

'Kandamaran, even if the whole world suspects you, I won't. I know Sambuvarayar's loyalty to me. Where is your father?'

'Your Majesty, it is my misfortune that I have to recount the tragic story of my family at this august assembly. When I told my father that I had killed Vandiyathevan, my sister Manimekalai, overheard me and came to kill me with a knife. My father is trying his best to pacify her. He will be here soon.'

Malayaman said: 'Brother, your sister has been saying, "I killed the Prince."'

'Yes, she took the blame on herself only to shield Vandiyathevan. At that time, she was only half-mad. Now she has completely lost her mind. Our clan is afflicted with a grave misfortune.'

The prime minister's voice was majestic,

'Kandamaran, are you sure that it was Vandiyathevan who killed Prince Karikalan? Did you see him killing the Prince? Or did you hear that from an eye-witness?'

'Honourable Minister, Vandiyathevan was the only person found where the prince was killed. Just by seeing his face, one could identify the culprit. The place was the bed chamber of Junior Queen of Paluvoor. What was Vandiyathevan doing there? If he is not guilty, why should he escape from the prison?'

Parthiban came in defense of Kandamaran.

'Our prime minister owns the responsibility of producing him. I just want to remind him about it.'

'Parthiban, it is true that I assumed the responsibility. I never expected that this man, Kandamaran, would take upon himself the role of a judge to punish the accused. Vandiyathevan hails from an ancient warrior clan that once ruled over a large empire. The Chola Kings have married the women from Vaanar clan in the past. Therefore, it is fair and proper that the emperor himself should sit in judgment in this case.'

Retorted Parthiban: 'If somebody has run away from the prison, he can be brought alive or dead. That also is a convention.'

'But Kandamaran has neither brought him alive nor dead,' said the prime minister.

Sambuvarayar entered the assembly hall. All eyes turned towards him. They saw the enormous grief on his face.

Kandamaran went near his father and whispered: 'How is Manimekalai?'

'No improvement. I have asked your mother to be with her.'

The emperor now addressed Sambuvarayar.

'If you want to be with your daughter, you may please go. We can have this discussion tomorrow.'

'No, Your Majesty. I can't do anything by staying near my daughter. If that warrior of the Vaanar Clan, Vandiyathevan, who was killed by my son comes back alive, then it may help my daughter.'

Silence prevailed for a while in that assembly.

Prime minister spoke to Sambuvarayar.

'The members of assembly want to know the circumstances surrounding the unnatural death of our prince. Do you have anything to say about that? Your son, Kandamaran, says that Vandiyathevan was solely responsible for the death of our prince. What do you say?'

Sambuvarayar looked around and said,

'Yes, yes. I invited Prince Karikalan only on my son's suggestion. That led to all these disastrous consequences. That has caused a blot on me and on my clan.'

Malayaman melted.

'Calm down Sambuvarayar, calm down. What has happened, has happened. Nobody here wants to blame you for Karikalan's murder. We just want to know what happened.'

'How can I help you? My son says something. My daughter's version is entirely different. I couldn't believe either. I don't know what happened. I was totally blind when the event took place. Senior Paluvettarayar can help. Ask him. He was the root cause of everything. He was the one who brought Madurandakan secretly to Kadamboor seeking my daughter's hand for him. Our bad time started from then onwards. I now learn that Prince Madurandakan is missing. Then Senior Paluvettarayar came with his wife, the junior queen. Then he invited the crown prince and made them stay in my palace and went away. Ask him where he had gone. Ask him where his Junior Queen Nandini is now.'

Sambuvarayar was gasping for breath.

The emperor interrupted.

'Enough. Stop. It was precisely for this reason that I didn't want an enquiry on the matter. You didn't listen. You are already fighting amongst yourselves. My son's death should not add to your feuds. Sambuvarayar, you are not responsible for my son's death. That was why I ordered your immediate release from the underground prison. Nobody needs to talk on this matter.'

Senior Paluvettarayar cleared his throat like the roar of a lion.

'Oh, Great King, I have a duty to tell you the truth as I know it. Otherwise, there will be unnecessary doubts and rumours; many innocent people may be blamed.'

The emperor tried to stop him but Senior Paluvettarayar was adamant.

'No, Your Majesty, have mercy on me and hear me out.'

Senior Paluvettarayar started a long narration.

He told the assembly how he met Nandini and fell a prey to her stunning beauty. He neglected the sane counsel of his brother, Junior Paluvettarayar. It was only at the insistence of Nandini that he conspired against the emperor along with the other chieftains.

He started doubting Nandini only when Vandiyathevan came into the scene. But even at that time, his vision was blocked by his lust for Nandini. It was only after he was caught in the floods at the Kollidam River and overheard the conversation between the conspirators that he came to know the true colours of Nandini. He also came to know of the conspirators' plan to kill the crown prince and rushed to Kadamboor to avert the disaster.

On the way he disguised himself as a Kalamukha and took the help of Idumban Kari, the conspirator who worked at Kadamboor palace and entered through the secret passage. There he hid himself in the room where musical instruments were stored and overheard the conversation between Nandini and Karikalan. When his attention was focused on their conversation, suddenly the prince fell dead. He rushed in to bear the prince but the lights went out. He was attacked by many people and became unconscious. He gained his senses only at the Kolli Hills cave.

'I harboured the conspirators from the Pandiya Kingdom in my own palace, of course, without knowing it. I let them steal gold from our treasury. The conspirators planned to kill you and your two sons on the same day. You were saved by a mute woman who sacrificed her life. Ponniyin Selvan was saved by an elephant. I tried to save Aditya Karikalan but failed. Your Majesty, I'm therefore fully responsible for the untimely death of the crown prince. Now that I have failed in my duty I will fulfil my vow by killing myself.'

Suddenly, Senior Paluvettarayar took the sword in his hands. Everybody was shocked. Ponniyin Selvan slowly came near him and grabbed the sword from his hand.

'Please wait. It has been an established tradition that Paluvettarayars should place the crown on the emperor at the time of coronation. When I'm crowned, I want you to do that honour to me with your blessed hands.'

58

The River Changed Its Course

Everybody thought that Madurandakan was the son of the Queen Mother. The prime minister knew the truth, but not the whole of it. He thought Madurandakan was the son born of Sundara Chola and Mandakini. That's why he did not object to Madurandakan being crowned as the next emperor. But when he came to know the whole truth, the prime minister hesitated.

When Ponniyin Selvan himself volunteered to become the king, everyone was happy. The prime minister was relieved.

Ponniyin Selvan saved Senior Paluvettarayar at the nick of time. The words and actions of the prince melted him. He spoke with tears streaming from his eyes.

'Ponniyin Selva, the gem of the Chola clan! My joy knows no bounds to hear the news of your becoming the king. That is my prayer also. Your great grandfather had willed that only your father's children should ascend the throne. I treacherously conspired to crown Madurandakan against the wish of that saintly emperor. Having done that Ponniyin Selva, therefore, I'm unfit to adorn you with the Chola crown on your coronation day. The only holy duty I now have is to kill myself as a punishment for my sins.'

'No, don't do that.'

Several voices rose in favour of Senior.

Emperor Sundara Chola spoke in a choked voice:

'Uncle, what are you talking? Instead of my sons, you wanted my cousin Madurandakan to be crowned. How could it be a betrayal?'

Before the emperor could finish what he was saying, the prime minister intervened.

'My Majesty, the whole country wants Prince Arulmoli to be the King. The blessed son of Emperor Kandaraditya, the new Prince Chendan Amudan, who is the rightful heir also wishes the same.'

Chendan Amudan, the new found prince endorsed.

'Even if you think differently, I won't accept it.'

'I second my son. There is no need for further deliberations,' said the Queen Mother.

The emperor relented.

'If that is God's wish, let it happen. But Paluvettarayar is needlessly blaming himself.'

Senior Paluvettarayar cleared his throat.

'Please listen to me, Your Majesty. If only I had succeeded in my treacherous mission, there could not have been a greater disaster to the Chola Empire. Madurandakan whom I originally thought as Emperor Kandarditya's son, is actually the son of our enemy King Veerapandiya.'

'Oh, my God!'

'It can't be!'

Many voices rose in the assembly.

'The woman whom I lusted for, the woman for whose beautiful face I became a slave, the woman whom I made a despot of my palace is the daughter of the slain king Veerapandiya. I heard her telling this to Aditya Karikalan.

She came to Paluvoor palace only to avenge her father's death. She was biding her time to kill Karikalan. She and her fellow conspirators had planned to kill Karikalan and place Veerapandiya's son, Madurandakan on the Chola throne. By God's grace, that calamity has been averted.

God sent Vandiyathevan to open my eyes which were blinded by lust. It was only through him that I learnt several other terrible secrets. I wanted to hear so many things from him. But this idiot Kandamaran killed him and tossed his body in the river. Idiot, fool.'

The assembly was shocked by this sudden outburst. Kandamaran spoke in a weak voice:

'Anyhow Vandiyathevan belonged to that conspirators' gang. What's wrong in my having killed him?'

Senior Paluvettarayar cast an angry glance at him. Prime minister spoke to him.

'He claims to have killed Vandiyathevan. But we can't be sure about it. He could have killed somebody else.'

Parthiban was sarcastic.

'If only the river changed its course, ran west and brought back the body of the deceased, we'll know the truth!'

'Who knows, the river might change its course,' claimed the prime minister.

As if to make his words almost literally true, Vandiyathevan entered the assembly with a frightened look and clumsy appearance, water dripping from his wet clothes. Everyone in the assembly thought that a corpse caused by some magic spell was walking into the hall.

'Aha! The river has changed its course. It has brought back the dead to life,' claimed the prime minister.

After consenting to accept the throne, Ponniyin Selvan, Kundavai and others had left Vandiyathevan alone to rest. But he was restless; looking out of the window of his chambers on the first floor overlooking the river flowing below his balcony with several thoughts bothering him.

Who was the other man who escaped with the mad prisoner? Could it be the missing Prince Madurandakan? If so, the mad prisoner will take him to the Lankan King and get him the crown which rightfully belonged to him and invade the Chola Kingdom. I have to stop it.

Down below in the garden, he saw a girl running towards the river. It was Manimekalai who plunged into the river with a knife in her hands.

Vandiyathevan was shocked. He ran up to the terrace and then jumped into the river.

Manimekalai was floating towards him. Was she alive? Or dead?

Would he suffer the misfortune of carrying the corpse of Manimekalai who loved him, this woman who loved him very intensely? He sprang into water and bore Manimekalai on his hands.

Oh God, please save this innocent girl.

With the prayer in his heart, Vandiyathevan brought Manimekalai to the steps and placed her there. She was still breathing. He did not have the energy to resuscitate her. He decided to seek the help of a woman to revive Manimekalai.

He ran blindly into every door in the palace shouting,

'Anybody here? I urgently need somebody to save the life of a woman.'

He pushed open one huge door to see the emperor and all other nobles in the Durbar Hall. When he recognised Poonkulali, he shouted at her:

'Ocean Princess! Manimekalai has fallen into the river. Please come with me and help her...'

Vandiyathevan screamed.

59

The Mighty Mountain Fell Down

Vandiyathevan entered the Royal Court through the gate meant for the royal women. Poonkulali was the first to turn around to hear his voice. Poonkulali, Kundavai and Vanathi rushed out of the court hall to save Manimekalai.

The entire court was shocked to see Vandiyathevan alive. Parthiban was quick to come out of the shock and sprang on Vandiyathevan. Firmly holding his shoulder, he said,

'Your Majesty, he is a murderer. He is the one who killed the crown prince.'

Parthiban and Kandamaran firmly held Vandiyathevan's other shoulder and they both dragged Vandiyathevan and brought him before the emperor.

The emperor looked at the face of Vandiyathevan.

'This man has the innocent face of a child. He is my son's messenger. And you say he killed my son. I won't believe it.'

Junior Paluvettarayar charged Vandiyathevan with a series of offences. Kandamaran added to the charges.

'He stabbed me on my back and ran away like a coward.'

Though upset, Prince Arulmoli walked up majestically and stood near Vandiyathevan. He addressed his father, the emperor.

'Father, this is the Prince of Vallam and my best friend. He is the one who saved my life when I was in Lanka and when I had delirious fever in mid-sea. I'm happy that he is alive. Accusing him of murdering my brother is equivalent to accusing me.'

The majesty in his voice silenced the assembly.

Prime minister spoke.

'Ponniyin Selva, I request you to reconsider your views. This man is said to have been killed by Kandamaran. But he is alive. They are accusing him of murder. Should we not enquire to ascertain the truth?'

Kandamaran added fuel to the fire.

'There is a rumour that Prince Arulmoli engaged Vandiyathevan to kill his own brother to become the king. We should not give room to such rumours.'

The assembly was stunned into silence. Sambuvarayar came up to his son and slapped him on his face.

'Idiot! You are going to destroy our ancient clan once and for all. If there is ever a competition of saying utterly stupid things at the most inappropriate occasion, you will be the winner.'

Kandamaran was trembling.

Senior Pauvettarayar ran up to them and held Sambuvarayar and spoke.

'Sambuvarayar, your son has compensated all his foolish deeds. He has done a great service to the Chola clan. Soon you are going to be proud of him. Please be patient. Control yourself.'

He pulled Sambuvarayar away from his son. Then he talked to Kandamaran.

'You said that you threw a spear on this Vandiyathevan and killed him. Do you know for sure that he was the one who crossed the river on horseback?'

The prime minister intervened.

'Please allow my disciple to have a word on this issue.'

Avarkkadiyan came forward.

'Your Majesty, Vandiyathevan did not escape on a horse. He saved the life of Chendan Amudan, the rightful heir, new prince and in the process, he was grievously injured. I brought Vandiyathevan in a closed palanquin inside the fort the same night. He has been here in this palace for the last four days. So Kandamaran could not have thrown the spear on this man.'

Senior Paluvettarayar added.

'Prime Minister, I too guessed that. Sambuvarayar, forgive your son. He has done a tremendous service to the Chola clan. The person he killed must be the son of Veerapandiya who grew up here in the Queen Mother's palace as Madurandakan. We have not seen him since that evening. God has saved this empire from great disaster through your son.'

Before the assembly could recover from the shock of his revelations, Senior continued to reveal more shocking information.

'Your Majesty, please listen to my last words. If I could name one person who saved our empire from catastrophe, I would name this valiant young man, the Prince of Vallam, Vandiyathevan. He opened my eyes which had been blinded by lust for my young wife. When my brother told me that Vandiyathevan met my wife Nandini outside the fort and talked to her, I started doubting them. When I decided to punish her after knowing the truth through the Pandiya conspirators, Princess Kundavai told me that Nandini was her sister and got a promise from me that I should not harm her.

Nandini planted in me the seeds of desire to become the next Chola Emperor. I should crown Madurandakan for name's sake, drive him away after some time and usurp the throne for myself.

On that fateful day, I heard the truth about Nandini's birth in her own words. I also learnt that Prince Aditya Karikalan's character was spotless.

Your Majesty, please make Ponniyin Selvan the king. The empire is going to attain greater glory under his rule.'

Prime Minister spoke to him in a pacifying tone.

'Your wish will be honoured. But you have not told us how Karikalan died. Unless we know who killed the prince, we cannot clear the name of this young man, Vandiyathevan.'

'Oh my God! Who blames this young man?'

'Kandamaran and Parthiban.'

'Idiots! Fools! Kandamaran! Parthiban! Why blame this young

man? How do you say that he killed Karikalan? What weapon did he use?'

'This knife with a twisted blade which still has a blood stain on it.'

Parthiban showed the knife to Senior Paluvettarayar.

When Vandiyathevan had carried the body of Karikalan from the flaming palace and had placed it on the yard of Kadamboor Palace before he fainted, Parthiban had retrieved the knife from him and had been saving that weapon for an opportunity like this.

'Give me that knife. Let me have a look.'

Senior took the knife from Parthiban.

He examined it intently.

'Yes, this is Idumban Kari's knife.'

Then he shouted.

'Kandamaran, Parthiban, you should go around Vandiyathevan three times and then fall at his feet. You two were caught in the seductive net of Nandini in the same way I was. Vandiyathevan was the only man who could not be lured by that devil. He never threw this knife. Nor did he kill Karikalan.'

'How are you so sure?' asked the prime minister.

'I'm sure. I know who threw this knife and killed Karikalan.'

'Who? Who?'

'Finally, the time has come to tell the truth. This young man, Vandiyathevan, was hiding in the musical instruments room. I too came through that room. I did not want him to scream on seeing me. I held his neck from behind and tried to wring it. He became unconscious and fell down. He could not have even known who killed Aditya Karikalan.'

'Then who killed the prince?'

'I got this knife from Idumban Kari. I was the one who threw this knife. Yes, this right hand of mine threw the killer weapon. The knife was aimed at that devil Nandini who lured me into the path of treachery and betrayal. But somehow the knife missed its mark and landed on the heart of Karikalan.'

'No, No!'

'Oh! My God!'

Several voices were heard in the assembly.

'I have brought shame to the Paluvoor clan which has been serving the Chola clan for more than a hundred years. I don't know how I can remove that stain.'

'Brother, I will remove the shame and disgrace.'

Junior Paluvettarayar roared, unsheathed his sword and came near his brother.

'Brother, you and I have vowed that we shall kill any one who betrays the Chola clan. I will fulfil the vow on your behalf. I will kill you this very moment and remove the stain of shame and disgrace fallen on us because of you.'

Junior Paluvettarayar lifted the sword.

The emperor shouted: 'Commander. No bloodshed here.'

Arulmoli sprang and firmly held the hands of Junior Paluvettarayar.

Senior Pauvettarayar spoke in a voice drained of all emotions:

'My dear brother, I won't entrust that work of removing the stain of shame and disgrace to you. If you kill me, the world will accuse you of killing your own brother. I don't want you to be blamed on my account. I will fulfil the vow I took before our family deity.'

Senior lifted the small knife with twisted blade and aimed it at his own heart.

Before Arulmoli could run to his side, Senior Paluvettarayar had stabbed himself and fallen down. The fall was like a mountain falling.

On the night when Senior Paluvettarayar was struggling for life, the emperor, prime minister, Prince Arulmoli and Princess Kundavai were with him for a long time. They praised the glorious service rendered by the Senior Paluvettarayar to the Chola clan.

Alvarkkadiyan brought a message from Nandini to the dying Senior.

Alvarkkadiyan initiated the conversation.

'I've brought a message from my sister Nandini. She wanted me to thank you for taking the blame of killing Karikalan on yourself to save her. She has told me that she will remember your love in all her births.'

'Let her be happy. She has betrayed me and destroyed me, yet I cannot forget her. Nambi, let me confide a secret with you now. The knife I threw did not land on the prince. Even before that he had fallen dead. I lied, not to save Nandini but to save your friend Vandiyathevan. None could blame this noble Prince. Also ask Princess Kundavai to forgive me for working against her on the insistence of Nandini.'

The god of death was glaring at the old warrior. He was gasping for breath. Even the hard hearted Alvarkkadiyan melted. Kundavai was sobbing silently.

'Nambi, please convey this to the prime minister. Somehow, we have to bring the Pandiya crown and the opal necklace from Lanka and make it Chola property or else the conspirators from the Pandiya clan will always stake a claim for their crown and kingdom. The Lankan King will also cause trouble on this account. The only person who can do that great deed is Vandiyathevan. You can go with him on this great mission and bring back the crown and have the coronation of Ponniyin Selvan once again in Madurai.'

Senior Paluvettarayar's voice suddenly stopped. The light of life was gone and his soul departed from his body.

60

The Parting of Friends

The four warriors—Parthiban, Kandamaran, Vandiyathevan and Ponniyin Selvan were riding towards the river Kollidam. The first two were to get into a boat and cross the river. The other two had come to see them off. As soon as the horses reached the boat jetty, the warriors dismounted. Ponniyin Selvan spoke in a lighter vein:

'Kandamaran, I'm sure all your hostility towards your old friend is gone now.'

'Yes Prince, I'm angry with myself. Vandiyathevan has forgotten all my misdeeds and was kind enough to accept me as his friend again. Nothing could match his magnanimity. He saved my sister from drowning in the river. I should have married my sister to him as originally planned. If only I had done that, she would not have lost her mind.'

'Don't say she has lost her mind. She is a little disoriented, that's all. She will be fine soon.'

'Prince, I don't think that it is an ordinary disorientation. She remembers everybody else and everything else. But she cannot recognize me and Vandiyathevan. When I think of the love she had for me once! Oh my God! My heart will burst. Her scream is still ringing in my ears: "I killed my dear brother with my own hands".'

'Why should she scream like that? You are after all alive, aren't you?'

'I am, Prince. It would have been better if I had died. She thinks that I killed Vandiyathevan and she killed me in revenge. At times she cries for me and my friend. She wails,

"Will the warrior of the Vaanar clan come back?"'

'Oh my God!'

Ponniyin Selvan turned to see tears trickling down from Vandiyathevan's eyes.

'How sad! If only she knew that Vandhiyathevan is no longer the Prince of Vallam, but the King of Vallam, how happy she would be!'

Kandamaran looked at Prince Arulmoli with a look of surprise.

'Yes. The emperor has decided to give back the kingdom to Vandiyathevan and make him the King of Vallam. He has also decided to gift the area near Vallam to you, Kandamaran. You two will be neighbours, hereafter. Your friendship should continue as before.'

Kandamaran became emotional. Arulmoli continued,

'Your old palace has been completely burnt down. If you go there, you will be disturbed by old memories. Build a new palace and as soon as your sister is cured, she will join you there.'

'Prince, Manimekalai won't come back to us. Queen Mother has plans to take her along on her pilgrimage. Manimekalai likes the Queen Mother very much. Even today Queen Mother has taken my sister to Thiruvaiyaaru.'

'Yes, they have gone with my uncle Chendan Amudan and his bride Poonkulali.'

Parthiban added, 'Your uncle's marriage was a very simple ceremony.'

'My coronation ceremony will be simpler still,' said Ponniyin Selvan.

'Prince, do you want us to miss the grand occasion? Why are you sending us up north at this time? Vandiyathevan will be here to celebrate your coronation. He is a lucky chap,' said Parthiban.

'No. I'm sending Vandiyathevan to Lanka. One thing is for sure. My coronation won't happen without you all. You are going to be the pillars of my reign to make it as glorious as my great grandfather Paranthaka's. Parthiban, I have appointed you as the commander of our northern forces succeeding my illustrious brother Aditya Karikalan. His untimely death has planted many desires in the hearts of our enemies. Kandamaran, you are the commander of north Pennai. First you go to Kancheepuram and renovate the golden palace built by my brother. The emperor wants to leave for Kanchi the moment he places the crown on my head.

And I'm making Vandiyathevan, the commander of our forces in Lanka. I'm confident that you will do well in your new assignments.'

'Thanks a lot, Prince. As soon as the day is fixed send word through a horseman. We will be here well in time,' said Kandamaran.

Before getting into the boat Kandamaran went up to Vandiyathevan.

'My dear friend, have you forgiven me for my wrong-doings?'

Vandiyathevan did not reply. Instead, he stretched out his arms and held Kandamaran in a tight hug.

The friends remained silent for some time, shedding tears.

Then Parthiban and Kandamaran got into the boat that was waiting for them.

Ponniyin Selvan and Vandiyathevan watched the boat till it crossed half the distance. Then they turned back, mounted their horses and galloped towards Tanjore.

61

Bless Us

There was jubilation all around the kingdom to witness the coronation ceremony of Prince Arulmoli.

After seeing off Kandamaran and Parthiban, Ponniyin Selvan and Vandiyathevan were returning to Tanjore. They enjoyed the lush green scenery all around. It was a sight to see the paddy fields, ripe for harvest, laden with the full-grown grain. The scenery appeared to be like a painting by a master artist.

'Can there be a country as beautiful and fertile as our Chola Kingdom? What good fortune to be the emperor of this great country!' remarked Ponniyin Selvan.

'Prince, now I've a doubt. I don't know whether you are sending me to Lanka with a higher responsibility or to keep me away from this beautiful Chola Kingdom!'

'My friend, I want an intelligent man like you as my prime minister and would like to keep you close to me all my life. But Prime Minister Aniruddha Brahmarayar won't give up his post for your sake.'

'If that is the only issue, then I can talk to the prime minister.'

Prince Arulmoli laughed.

'My dear friend, don't you want to go to Lanka?'

'Prince, I'm ready to go to countries even beyond Lanka if you order me. The sooner the order comes, the happier I will be.'

'Do you feel happy about getting away from me?'

'Prince, it is always safe to be away from emperors to always be friends with them.'

'Soon, I will join you in Lanka. I'm planning to take you with me in my expeditions to all those fantasy lands and islands beyond the high seas.'

When they were nearing Tanjore, they saw a palanquin on the royal highway surrounded by guards and the usual retinue.

Princess Kundavai and Princess Vanathi were in the palanquin. Their faces blossomed to see Prince Arulmoli and Vandiyathevan. They were on their way to Thiruvaiyaru to join in the temple celebrations with the Queen Mother, Prince Chendan Amudan and Poonkulali who were already there.

As soon as the palanquin moved on, Prince Arulmoli said to Vandiyathevan, 'Friend, I don't think that the princesses are going to Thiruvaiyaru for the temple celebrations. I learnt that the famous Kumbakonam astrologer is now in Thiruvaiyaru. They are probably going to consult him.'

The prince said this with much mischief in his eyes. Vandiyathevan understood the message and both of them directed their horses towards Thiruvaiyaru.

Ponniyin Selvan was right. Princess Kundavai went to the astrologer's house for a consultation. Just as they were leaving the astrologer's house, two Chinese merchants came there. Chinese merchants would frequent the Chola Kingdom for trade purposes.

The royal ladies were witnessing the temple celebrations from the balcony of their palace in Thiruvaiyaru. The Chinese merchants were there, mingling with the crowd. They visited the Chola Palace to sell some silk sarees.

After much reluctance, those merchants were let in on the recommendation of Poonkulali.

Kundavai was irritated with the impertinent merchants.

'I don't know why you are in such a hurry. You could have come tomorrow. Why did you choose this night?'

One of the merchants spoke.

'Princess, it has been several days since we came to Tanjore. We tried our best to see you but we could not. That's why we have come here now. A ship is leaving Nagapattinam tomorrow. We have to be on that ship at any cost. We don't know when the next ship will leave. Ship-travel is no longer regular and reliable as it used to be.'

He spoke Tamil like a native with a strange intonation. Kundavai asked him, 'Why is ship travel not regular?'

'Sea voyage is no longer safe because of pirates in the high seas. They not only loot our ware but also kill our men. They fight like fanatics. These days merchant ships don't sail alone. We go in a convoy of ten or fifteen ships. Have mercy on us and see our ware.'

The merchants started to unpack the goods.

Kundavai stopped them.

'We can't assess the quality in darkness.'

One merchant stood up with folded hands

'Princess! We have brought it as coronation gifts.'

'Then you have come to the wrong place. None of us are going to be crowned. The person to be crowned is Prince Arulmoli.'

'Princess, we have come to the right place. People say that if you want to get favours from the prince, we should first please Princess Kundavai. That is the easy way of winning favours from the prince.'

'Who told you that?'

'All in the Chola Kingdom say that the prince will never go against the words of his sister.'

The other merchant who was silent until now, said,

'If it is Arulmoli's coronation, it is as good as Princess Kundavai's.'

Everyone laughed.

'I want to submit a petition to Ponniyin Selvan.'

'What petition?'

'During the times of Emperor Paranthaka, sea voyages were safe. The only dangers were storms. There were no pirates then. The ships used to navigate as though they were passing through the royal high road touching many countries like Lemuria, Kadaram (Cambodia), etc., before reaching China. Similarly, our Chinese ships came freely.

This has become a dream now.'

Kundavai's large, beautiful eyes became even larger in surprise.

'Do you think Ponniyin Selvan can do that?'

'All the merchants strongly believe in Ponniyin Selvan. Even the Kumbakonam astrologer endorsed our views.'

'What did the astrologer say?'

'Ponniyin Selvan will mobilise a huge army and destroy all the pirates and make sea voyages safer. The Chola Kingdom will recapture its glory.'

Meanwhile Prince Amudan had finished his prayers and had returned. He quickly identified the merchants as imposters and in a quick motion, he pulled one of the merchant's headgear along with the false beard. It was Vandiyathevan.

'Prince, you should save me.'

Vandiyathevan hugged the other merchant. His turban and beard also fell off. It was Ponniyin Selvan with his mesmerizing smile. All the women had a hearty laugh.

Prince Amudan smiled.

'Can't I recognize my friends?'

Kundavai told Vanathi, 'At last, you and I were made fools.'

'Sister, why should they fool us in guise?'

'Vanathi, my brother is innocent. He never tells lies. But now he is under the influence of bad company.'

'Sister, don't blame Vandiyathevan. This was purely my idea,' Ponniyin Selvan defended his friend.

'Soon after my friend and I are leaving for Lanka and other far lands on high seas. Bless us.'

Queen Mother also joined them and blessed them.

'My dear children, always be on the side of good. Destroy the pirates and save our merchants. If you let the pirates have their way, they will soon infiltrate into our borders and disturb our peace and stability. One more wish from me. The Chola clan should be preserved for ever. Persons born in the royal family should be ready to face death at any time. But they should also do everything to preserve their clan. Your brother Karikalan died without getting married. As of now you are the only member of the Chola clan. So, before you go on a ship to cross the high seas, you should have the wedding ceremony along with the coronation.'

'Mother, your wishes are granted.' Ponniyin Selvan smiled.

62

Vanathi's Day Dreaming

Queen Mother, Prince Amudan and Poonkulali left for Tanjore the next morning.

(Ponniyin Selvan had promised to show the Grand Anaicut to Vandiyathevan.) He took leave of his sister Kundavai and visited the backyard of the palace to see Vanathi.

He saw Vanathi sitting on the steps of the river bank with a plate full of flowers by her side. Ponniyin Selvan walked without making any noise and stopped near her. Her intuition revealed her beloved's presence. She appeared like a statue of a woman throwing flowers into the river one by one. She did not turn around. She stopped throwing flowers and remained frozen in her place.

Prince Arulmoli broke the silence.

'Vanathi, were you daydreaming?'

'Yes, Your Highness. I'm daydreaming.'

'Vanathi, I too think of you always. You are tormenting me day in and day out. The stars in the sky remind me of the glow in your eyes and the rustling of leaves remind me of the sound of your anklets. You disturb me so much I'm afraid that you may not let me achieve what I want to.'

'Prince, I will never hinder your work.'

'No, you won't. For that matter, no one can. Nobody can stop me, Vanathi.'

'I want a gift from you before you go on the high seas. I have made a garland of the flowers gathered from the palace garden. Please place the garland around my neck and make me your eternal slave before you leave for your voyage.'

'I too have brought a necklace of priceless gems as my coronation gift for you. I got it from those Chinese merchants. Promise me one thing. Whenever I return from my voyage, you should welcome me with a victory garland.'

'Not one, My Lord. I will be eagerly waiting for your return with hundreds of victory garlands.'

63

The Coronation

As the coronation ceremony was nearing, the entire Chola Empire was reveling in a series of festivities. The city of Tanjore was wearing a festive look like the celestial city. Guests were pouring into all houses. Finally, the day of coronation dawned with bright sunshine all around. People assembled several hours ahead of the appointed time.

All the royal family members, kings, chieftains, high ranking officials, members of the governing council, priests of temples, monks, poets, artists and other elite guests also arrived.

When Ponniyin Selvan entered the coronation hall along with Vandiyathevan, the sea of people surged like the ocean on a full moon day.

Once the coronation rituals were completed, the ancestral crown, the pearl necklace, the sword and the sceptre kept on a large painted plate, were taken around the coronation hall to get the visitors' blessings.

The court poet sang songs praising the glory of the Chola clan and its kings. Junior Paluvettarayar was chosen to place the crown on the head of Ponniyin Selvan. Junior Paluvettarayar cut short the words of felicitation to end the ceremony quickly. He was startled by a man who came near him. It was Alvarkkadiyan in disguise.

Alvarkkadiyan whispered in the ears of Paluvettarayar and they immediately left to an isolated place.

Ponniyin Selvan who was watching this addressed the poets.

'Beloved poets, what have I done to deserve the ancient Chola throne? I'm making a beginning only today. You sang the glory of all my ancestors. I'm born in this ancient clan and hence the words of praise apply to me. But, beloved poets, they apply more to my uncle, Prince Amudan also.'

All eyes were on Prince Amudan. The sudden focus of attention on Amudan embarrassed him.

Meanwhile Alvararkkadiyan shared some disturbing news with Junior Paluvettarayar. Rakkammal, the boatman, Murugaiyyan's wife, who was a member of the Pandiya conspirators' gang had been seen in the crowd. She disappeared into the crowd near the palace of Junior Paluvettarayar.

She suddenly reappeared with Junior Paluvettarayar's daughter who was carrying her child. They got into a closed palanquin a little way away from the gates of the fort.

Junior Paluvettarayar was worried about his daughter who was married to Madurandakan. He rushed to his palace requesting Alvarkkadiyan to explain his absence to the emperor.

'Emperor, Junior Paluvettarayar has gone out to attend to an emergency. But let not the coronation ceremony wait for him. There are many distinguished men in the audience. Any one of them can place the crown on the head of the future king.'

Then Ponniyin Selvan addressed the gathering.

'I'm a descendant of great kings known for their fairness and justice. Can I usurp something belonging to somebody else? We are surrounded by enemies burning in jealousy over the prosperity of the Chola Kingdom. Pirates are robbing the merchant ships in the high seas.

We have to build a strong navy. We should train our men in the fine art of sailing. I seek the permission of the emperor, elders, veterans, warriors and scholars and the people in this august assembly to go on a voyage on the high seas.'

'My dear son, will I stand in the way of your work?' responded the emperor.

The assembly gave a sign of approval.

'Father, I need a clear conscience that I've not usurped something that rightfully belongs to somebody else to succeed in this ambitious mission.'

Prince Amudan looked at Prince Ponniyin Selvan who was holding the ancient crown of the Chola clan.

'Junior Paluvettarayar has not come back. So what? Let me conduct the coronation ceremony. There is one person who deserves this crown more than me. I'm placing this Chola crown on the blessed head of Queen Mother's son, my uncle, the great Prince Chendan Amudan.'

Ponniyin Selvan walked up to Chendan Amudan and placed the crown on his head.

Amudan melted.

As soon as the crown was placed, Ponniyin Selvan hailed.

'Hail Chendan Amudan! Hail Emperor Madurandaka Uthama Chola.'

Vandiyathevan joined in.

Sundara Chola was immensely excited and blessed the new Emperor Chendan Amudan by showering flowers on him.

Amudan walked up to Queen Mother to get her blessings.

'My dear son, neither you, nor I, for that matter, nobody can go against the wishes of the almighty.'

In a few minutes, the news of Amudan being crowned spread like wildfire.

A little later, Amudan rode on the royal elephant. Ponniyin Selvan became the mahout for the coronation procession.

When the procession culminated at the gates of the palace, darkness set in. A shower of flowers poured on the new emperor and Ponniyin Selvan from the terrace.

'Oh mahout!'

A sweet feminine voice came from the terrace. Ponniyin Selvan looked up to see the smiling face of Princess Vanathi.

Ponniyin Selvan shouted to her.

'Hey girl, the reign of the new emperor has begun. In his rule, the country will scale greater heights.'

64

My Country Is Great

A month and a half went by since the coronation of the new emperor—Uthama Chola. Winter was bidding farewell, giving way to spring. Mother earth swelled in ecstasy at the onset of spring. All flowers—lotus, lilies, roses, jasmine and parijatha flowers were in full blossom to welcome the maiden spring. The joy of the Chola citizens perfectly reflected the uplifting mood of the season.

Political instability was gone. People were gearing up to celebrate the Spring Festival. Vandiyathevan was mesmerized by the scenery around as he rode towards Palayarai. For the first time, he was entering the city without a disguise and reached the palace of Princess Kundavai.

Kundavai warmly received him and her joy was beyond description. They were head over heels in love with each other. But their love had not translated into action. They conversed with each other as if they were colleagues working together.

'I learn that your mission was not fully successful.'

'Princess, you are right. I have never had full success in any of my missions,' sighed Vandiyathevan.

'Not like that. You brought my brother back from Lanka at the most crucial time to save the country from disaster.'

'Who can match the large heart of Ponniyin Selvan? When I was accused of murdering Prince Aditya Karikalan, he changed his mind and expressed his willingness to become the emperor only to save me from punishment. Thank God, at the last moment Senior Paluvettarayar took the blame on himself and saved me from disgrace.'

'Without him the entire kingdom looks empty to me. His place can never be filled.'

'It is really sad that Junior Paluvettarayar also has passed away.'

'Oh My God, is he dead? Are you sure?'

'When I took leave of him, he was alive. But how could a man who had had a fall from a great height survive?'

Vandiyathevan started a long narration.

Junior Paluvettarayar's daughter went away with Rakkammal, when the coronation was going on. Junior Paluvettarayar took a few trusted soldiers with him and went in search of her. He could not bear the thought of his daughter joining hands with the Pandiya conspirators. He rather preferred killing his own daughter than being branded as a traitor. He galloped fast.

On the same night soon after the coronation was over, Alvarkkadiyan apprised Prince Arulmoli of the developments.

Junior Paluvettarayar was ready to kill his own brother when he confessed that he had killed Karikalan. Arulmoli suspected that Junior Paluvettarayar would not think twice before killing his own daughter.

So, it was decided that Vandiyathevan and Alvarkkadiyan should go as a team to save Junior Paluvettarayar and bring him back. They were also given the task of finding the whereabouts of Ravidasan and his gang and their future plans and also the fate of Madurandakan, whether he was really dead as claimed by Kandamaran.

They followed the trail of Junior Paluvettarayar. They reached a hilly region on the border of the Chola Kingdom. The mountain before them was almost perpendicular. When they looked around for a path to climb, they saw a strange sight. Two men were seen fighting with each other at the peak of the hill. They were now dangerously close to the edge. One of them was Junior Paluvettarayar and the other was his son-in-law, Madurandakan.

The tragedy happened before their eyes; they were quite helpless. Junior Paluvettarayar slipped and fell into the deep valley. Madurandakan walked up to the edge to see him falling down and then disappeared.

The two friends ran up to the valley. They waited for some time. The body of Junior Paluvettarayar floated to the surface of the pool. They pulled him out of the water. Seeing signs of life, they resuscitated him.

Finally Junior Paluvettarayar opened his eyes to make a dying statement.

'I came here and saw my daughter with about a hundred conspirators headed by Ravidasan. I was invited to join the gang as my son-in-law was to be crowned as the Pandiya King soon. The Lankan King and Cheras had come forward to help my son-in-law recapture the Pandiya kingdom. I did not interrupt him because I wanted to know what was on their minds. Then I shouted, branding them as conspirators and asked them to send my daughter back with me.

Madurandakan said, "If your daughter is willing to come with you, you can take her".

I looked at my daughter. She refused to come with me. I shouted and sheathed my sword.

"I would rather kill you with my own hands than leave you with these crooks," I told her.

"Who the hell are you to kill my wife?" My son-in-law Madurandakan appeared from nowhere and started a sword fight with me.

My end is near. Leave me here and go away. Invade the hostile kingdoms and Lanka. If you don't, the Pandiya Kingdom will go away from our folds. Go fast. Don't bother about me.'

The friends did not want to let him die like an orphan in that godforsaken place. So, they decided that one of them should stay with him while the other should ride fast to Tanjore to carry the disturbing news. Of the two, Vandiyathevan was a good horse rider. So, he left for Tanjore immediately while Alvarkkadiyan stayed with Junior Paluvettarayar in that forest.

65

Lost in Love

Vandiyathevan ended his long narration of the series of incidents leading to the near death of Junior Paluvettarayar. Kundavai could not believe all this.

'Your wavering eyes confirm my doubts.'

'Princess, when I talk to you, my eyes rest on yours. I don't know what you have in those big, black and beautiful eyes. I lose myself.'

Kundavai's rosy lips blossomed into a beautiful smile.

'There is no magic in my eyes. Maybe you saw your own image which I hold gently in my eyes. You have some secret magical powers. Even the tough-hearted Nandini, who came to destroy the Chola clan, had a soft corner for you.'

'Why mention that poisonous snake at this beautiful moment?'

'Prince, don't speak ill of her. She is the daughter of Mandakini, who saved my brother several times and sacrificed her life for my father.'

'But Princess, she is behind the conspirator who threw the spear at the emperor and also caused the death of the crown prince.'

'Why did she do that? Only to avenge the death of her father Veerapandiya. She is a valiant lady.'

'Veerapandiya's daughter growing up in a Chola palace has given rise to more complications.'

'But are you sure Nandini is Veerapandiya's daughter?'

'Nandini herself said so.'

'She might have lied to avenge the death of Veerapandiya. When she wanted to save Veerapandiya from Karikalan, she had told him that the Pandiya King was her lover. Will any woman born in this land call her own father as her lover?'

'When Karikalan killed Veerapandiya, he was in a state of murderous frenzy. We can never know what she told him and how Karikalan understood her. How do we know that Nandini called Veerapandiya her lover?'

'We don't know the truth. You and my brother crowned Amudan Uthama Chola. It is not easy to bear the burden of governing this vast empire.'

'The one who is going to bear the burden of governance is your brother Prince Arulmoli.'

'That is true. But the two great pillars of the Chola Empire, the Paluvettarayars have gone. Sambuvarayar has lost the enthusiasm to live. Malayaman is already very old. Kodumbalur Chieftain feels that he has been let down. Arulmoli needs good friends.'

'Thank God we have Parthiban on our side.'

'Prince, I'm not sure about that. Arulmoli considers you as his best friend. Parthiban hates this.'

'Princess, I can apologize to him and try to win over his support for Arulmoli.'

'That will only add fuel to fire.'

'Is there no way to convince him?'

'He suggested something...'

'The emperor would have readily agreed.'

'But that does not depend on the emperor. It depends on his daughter. Parthiban wants to marry the daughter of the emperor.'

Vandiyathevan's face fell.

Kundavai was silent.

Vandiyathevan spoke after some time.

'What was the emperor's response?'

'He asked his daughter.'

'What did the blessed daughter say?'

'She refused.'

'Why?'

'She will reveal that only to those who are sincerely interested.'

'Princess, I ask you now with boundless sincerity.'

'You will have to ask the emperor.'

'Princess, Prince Arulmoli and I have great dreams for our Chola Kingdom. After we realize at least a part of our dream, I will return with victory garlands. I will then approach the emperor and seek his permission to adorn his daughter with those garlands. Wherever I go, whatever I do, the sweet elixir of your love will always protect me. Princess, will you wait for me?'

Vandiyathevan was very close to the Princess, he felt her warmth and her fragrance.

Princess Kundavai was looking deep into his eyes. Both of them were lost in love.

The long silence that prevailed was broken by the voice of Vanathi.

They both turned around.

Vanathi came running to them,

'Sister, he has got an urgent message from Manimekalai's brother Kandamaran.'

Vanathi gave a palm leaf to him.

66

Divine Love

Vandiyathevan took the palm leaf from Vanathi and read the message. Lines of grief suddenly clouded his handsome face.

'Anything serious?' asked Kundavai.

Vandiyathevan handed the leaf to Kundavai. She read the leaf.

'To my dear friend Vandiyathevan, greetings from your friend Kandamaran. Please forgive me for whatever I did to you. Please come to see my sister Manimekalai for one last time.'

'Looks like, Manimekalai has been found at last,' exclaimed Kundavai.

'What do you mean? Where had she gone?' enquired Vandiyathevan.

'Manimekalai was here with the Queen Mother. But Sambuvarayar persisted on taking her back with him. On the way they camped near the Veeranam Lake. When he woke up the next morning, Manimekalai was not to be seen. He sent some men to Palayarai in search of her. We don't know what happened to her after that. Now after reading Kandamaran's letter, it's clear that she has been found.'

Vandiyathevan took just a day to travel from Palayarai to Veeranarayanapuram. But unlike the earlier occasions, one day appeared like a hundred years to him. His mind was full of earlier memories and experiences.

He was thinking of all those who had helped him. But Manimekalai stood a class apart. Why should she love him so much? All because of that idiot Kandamaran. In the beginning, Kandamaran spoke very highly of Vandiyathevan to Manimekalai. The silly girl lost her mind to him.

Kandamaran asked Manimekalai to forget Vandiyathevan as they were planning to get her married to a king. But Manimekalai never changed her mind. She publicly proclaimed her love for Vandiyathevan. She was as pure and innocent as a child.

Vandiyathevan's horse was as fast as his mind. Kandamaran's men were waiting for him near Veeranam lake.

'Where is Kandamaran?' asked Vandiyathevan.

'At the lake. In a boat.'

Vandiyathevan reached the banks of the lake.

He saw a boat standing near the bank with Kandamaran.

Vandiyathevan got into the boat. As the boat moved, Kandamaran looked at Vandiyathevan and became emotional.

'Dear friend, you have come in time. Or else you could not have seen Manimekalai alive.'

Vandiyathevan's eyes were filled with tears.

'What are you saying Kandamaran? Is her life in danger? I know that she had lost her mind.'

Vandiyathevan broke down.

'Dear friend, Manimekalai has got her sanity back. But nobody can tell how long she will live. I have been praying to every god that she should at least stay alive till she sees you.'

Kandamaran told him what happened.

Kandamaran had been renovating the golden palace at Kancheepuram for the emperor's stay. Soon the news reached him that Manimekalai has been lost near the Veeranam lake. He immediately rushed to the spot. Men were sent in all directions in search of her.

After four days of futile search around the lake, Kandamaran suddenly remembered the resthouse on one of the islands in the lake. He remembered that Karikalan, Vandiyathevan, Manimekalai and Nandini had once spent some time there.

As soon as he reached the spot, old memories haunted him. At first, the resthouse appeared deserted and he sighed. When he heard the sound of somebody else sighing in the vicinity he ran towards the source of the sound. Manimekalai was lying on the steps on the other side of the resthouse.

She had shrunk and looked pale with scratch marks all over her body.

At first Kandamaran thought she was dead. Kandamaran felt as if he had been pierced by a thousand spears simultaneously.

He lifted his sister, placed her on his lap and wailed. He had a faint hope that she might be alive. He sprinkled water on her face. He also poured some water into her mouth. A few minutes later Manimekalai opened her eyes.

'Is that you, brother? I knew I would see you and him in heaven. Where is he?'

Kandamaran had to struggle to muffle his sob.

'He is here. He will surely come to see you.'

He sent a message to Vandiyathevan asking him to come there immediately.

'Friend, I have no words to thank you for coming here in response to my message. Manimekalai may not live long. The one force keeping her alive is her desire to see you.'

The boat had reached the island. They heard a song.

Manimekalai was singing.

'Yes, Kandamaran. She is singing.'

They got down from the boat. It was the same song which she had sung when they were in the same place earlier.

Is that all a dream, my friend
The time we spent together
On the mountains
Beside the waterfalls
Beneath the fruit trees
Hand in hand lost in joy
....
....
Defying all security

Like a thief you came in stealth
With limitless love hugged me tight
Smothered me with kisses

Vandiyathevan waited on the steps till the song ended. Then quickly reached the resthouse.

When Manimekalai saw him, her face blossomed and she tried to stand up but she couldn't. She was about to fall down. Vandiyathevan rushed to her and held her in his arms and then gently placed her on his lap.

Manimekalai looked at his face again and again.

'My brother did not deceive me. Love is divine.'

'You are right, Manimekalai. It's all real. It is true that I have come to see you. It's not a lie.'

In spite of his best efforts, tears rolled down from his eyes.

Manimekalai's face glowed with divine grace.

Her lips which resembled a pomegranate bud tried to speak something. Vandiyathevan listened with rapt attention. But he could not understand a word of what she spoke.

Why should he understand? What she spoke were not mere words. It was the elixir of love which flowed out of her heart.

A few minutes later Manimekalai's pearly lips converged. Her eyelids closed. The divine glow on her face faded. It was replaced by peace that was beyond all human understanding. Some of the red flowers from the tree fell on her. The flower of life in Manimekalai withered. Manimekalai was gone.

Where did she go? Did she merge with the wind or with the waves in the lake? Or did she merge with the heart of Vandiyathevan who had frozen like a statue with tears continuously streaming out of his eyes?

But one thing was certain. We are never going to see the playful, mischievous and naughty Vandiyathevan any more. We will only see a mature and intelligent Vandiyathevan seasoned by experience and made divine by the love of Manimekalai. The goddess Manimekalai was now living in the temple called Vandiyathevan's heart. That goddess would accompany him wherever he went and would protect him in all his endevours.

Oh, valiant young man!
The Prince of Vallam!
Beloved Vandiyatheva!
We bid you farewell
But your glory will be eternal.
Oh, beloved Prince Arulmoli!
May you live long!
May both your names
Find a place of pride
In the history of mankind.

WHAT HAPPENED TO THE HISTORICAL CHARACTERS AFTER THE STORY?

- Kundavai and Vandiyathevan get married after many hurdles and difficulties.
- Junior Paluvettarayar comes back alive and serves the Chola nation again in several ways.
- Alvarkkadiyan continues to be a spy. He finds out the activities of Nandini and the Pandiya conspirators and reports them to the emperor.
- Ponniyin Selvan along with Vandiyathevan establishes a mighty naval force and leaves on an expedition to the far-off lands and counters the atrocities of the sea pirates.
- With the help of the Pandiya conspirators, Lankan and Chera kings, old Madurandakan tries to capture the Pandiya kingdom but gets killed in the battle by Ponniyin Selvan.
- The little boy who was crowned in the Thiruppurambiyam war memorial also claims his right to the Pandiya throne but gets defeated by Rajendra Chola—Ponniyin Selvan's son.
- Later, Nandini kills herself. But before that, she meets Ponniyin Selvan and reveals the secret about her birth and the murder of the Crown Prince Aditya Karikalan.
- Ponniyin Selvan marries Vanathi and the son born to them rises to be one of the most powerful Chola kings—Rajendra Chola—who captured several parts of the world through his naval power.
- Ponniyin Selvan orders an enquiry into the murder of Aditya Karikalan after the death of Nandini, and the conspirators Ravidasan and his accomplices are punished.
- The Emperor Sundara Chola lives in the Golden Palace in Kanchi as per the wish of his slain eldest son and passes away there after three years.
- Parthibendra Pallavan tries to revive his Pallava Kingdom but fails in his attempt and dies in the battle with Cholas.